❧ ❧

"Author Jill K. Sayre does a great job of fleshing out the main character, Claire, so that she feels multi-dimensional, with believable worries and problems. It's a sweet story about one girl's struggle to believe.

This is also a great story if you love learning interesting historical facts or new vocabulary. I love a book that makes me a little bit smarter just by reading it."

—Miranda, Fairy Fictionfor Young Fans
www.fairyfiction.com

❧ ❧

"Jill K. Sayre has a real talent for bringing her characters to life, each one vibrant and immediately endearing."

—Danni, Goodreads

❧ ❧

"I really enjoyed the story, watching Claire become more aware of the magical world around her and find a connection to her grandmother was endearing."

—Cubicle Blindness Book Reviews

❧ ❧

"Mysterious, enlightening and inspired, *The Fairies of Turtle Creek* will not only have you wondering if fairies really do exist, but will leave you with a warm feeling of something shared and passed on from the old to the young."

—Bill Howard, Readers' Favorite

❧ ❧

The Fairies of Turtle Creek

5/8/20

To: Lilly

Pixie dust wishes~

Jill K. Sayre

So glad you are enjoying the peddleboat!

Jill K. Sayre

The Fairies of Turtle Creek

Cover and interior design by Ted Ruybal.

Manufactured in the United States of America.

For more information, please contact:

Wisdom House Books
www.wisdomhousebooks.com

Hardback
ISBN 13: 978-0-9885066-4-0
ISBN 10: 0-9895066-4-5

Paperback:
ISBN 13: 978-0-9885066-6-4
ISBN 10: 0-9885066-6-1

LCCN: 2012922921

Juvenile/Folklore/General
Fantasy & Magic

Second Edition
2 3 4 5 6 7 8 9 10

Contents

Dedication

To those wonderful grandmothers in our lives~
Goga, and in memory of
Granny Goose, Grandma, Nonie, Nanny,
and Nana.

Always remember, "Nana loves you!"

Hearing Voices

"Exceptions are not always the proof of the old rule;
they can also be the harbinger of a new one."
— Marie von Ebner-Eschenbach

acey and I walked along the creek bed on our way home every Friday, but on that particular day, strange things began happening. As we hopped from rock to rock, our balance was thrown off by the heavy backpacks we carried, and our feet slipped into the water now and again. *Splash!* Splotches of sunlight broke through the greenery overhead, flashing across our faces. The warm air whispered reminders that summer vacation was just around the corner.

"I can't wait 'til we can do this all day long!" With my arms straight out, I spun around, my feet sloshing in an ankle-deep pool. I slid on the slimy creek bottom and almost fell, teetering over far to the right. But, finding my balance, I landed and struck a superhero pose. "Ta-da!"

"Easy there, Claire," Lacey laughed. "Ya nearly wiped out!"

"Are you saying that wet school books wouldn't be a very good thing?"

Lacey raised an eyebrow and tilted her head, a smile bursting on her lips. "No, it wouldn't." Standing there, her black hair gleaming in the sun, she looked so pretty and confident. It was no wonder that she had so many friends. I caught my own reflection in the water and sighed.

"I'll try to be more careful, Lacey, but hurry up. We're almost to the stone bridge."

We continued along the wet, rocky creek, edged with trees that quietly cheered us on with their waving leaves.

"There it is." I pointed at the great grey arch made of giant stones just as we came around the bend. As we got closer, the cement plaque in the middle got clearer: "1913."

"Let's sit on the bank and soak up a few rays," I suggested, scrambling up the vine-covered slope to sit atop a boulder.

Lacey climbed up the bank and sat on the rock next to me.

"All of this here goopy moss is getting on my new water shoes." She frowned and began picking the green muck off of the toes of her pink spandex with a long stick. "And it smells so musty in these parts."

"I *told* you to bring an old pair of tennis shoes for creek hiking."

"Sorry, Claire, but the shoes you're wearing are far from fashionable," Lacey replied, bobbing her head from side to side.

"Who cares about fashion when you're in this mini-ecosystem? Down in this creek bed, creatures, plants, and lots of *algae* grow as if they're in a cool forest. We are in a *microclimate*. They don't realize they're really in a hot, dry city." I spotted a smooth stone on the ground next to me and stretched my arm down to pick it up. I studied it—all grey with a nature-made hole in the middle. Cool.

"I love how the hustle and bustle of the world passes overhead while we are down here in a calm, organic place. We're in what they call a *chasm*." I held up the stone and stuck my finger through the hole to illustrate.

"*Chasm*—really, Claire? You're always using such big ol' words." Lacey examined the rubber soles of her shoes. They were caked with green mud. A gush of air came from her lips. "I give up," she said, tossing her stick to the ground.

"Shh! Did you just hear someone say something?" I looked around for another person, slipping the holey stone into my pocket.

"Hear what? I was just saying that I give-"

"Just listen a sec."

We sat there quietly. At first we heard only birds chirping and water trickling, but then it happened again.

She's coming! She's coming!

"Did you hear it that time, Lacey?"

"I did. Someone's whispering."

"Who's here?" I called out, jumping to my feet, searching the banks.

"I think it came from under the bridge," said Lacey.

"Come look with me."

Lacey stayed seated on her rock, wide-eyed.

"Lacey, I need you for moral support. You wouldn't want anything bad to happen to me, would you?" I gave her my best sad puppy look.

She rolled her eyes. "All right, but I'm bringing a weapon."

Lacey got off her rock, picked up the stick she'd been using to clean her shoes, and hurried over to me.

I saw how tightly her hand was clenched around the stick. "Are you scared?"

"Maybe a little. The voice didn't really sound human. It sounded strange."

"It'll be okay. I'm sure there's a logical explanation for what we heard." I grabbed her other hand. "I'll show you."

Wading through the water, with backpacks on, our shadows looked like two Ninja Turtles. Just when we'd reached the inside edge of the bridge bottom, we heard the hiss of *She's coming! She's coming!* again, but this time it was mixed with squeals of *Soon! Soon!*

"Goodness gracious!" Lacey quickly wrapped her arms around me, still clutching her stick. "There are *many* voices!"

We froze, standing just inside the arching blackness.

"Hello?" I called. "Who's there?"

We waited, but there was no answer. "Let's go in a little further."

Lacey gulped really loudly and I could feel her body trembling. Huddled together, we cautiously took a few more steps into the dark.

"No worries, Lacey. There has got to be a reasonable-"

Whiz, whiz! Buzz, buzz! The sound of a hundred beating insect wings whooshed around our heads, and in their vibrations we heard: *She's coming! Soon! She's coming! Soon!*

"I don't like this!" Lacey yelled as the buzzing got louder and faster.

My heartbeat started to match the frantic pace of the strange sounds.

"Run!" I shouted.

We let go of each other, screaming as we dashed through to the other side into daylight.

"What in the world was that?" Lacey panted, the stick held high above her head.

"I don't know, but you can put your bludgeon down."

"Oh, yeah." Lacey lowered her arm.

I threw my backpack on a dry part of the bank and walked back toward the bridge.

"Claire Collins. What in the world are you doin'?" Lacey glared at me, her hands on her hips.

"I'm taking another look."

She shook her head. "Feel free, but *I'm* not going anywhere near that bridge, not even with a flashlight."

"Oh, flashlight!" I ran back to my backpack, took my penlight key ring out of the zipper pocket, and ran back beneath the bridge. "Thanks for reminding me that I had this."

"Be careful!" Lacey yelled after me. "Want my stick?"

"No, thanks. I'll be okay," I replied, just before stepping back into the deep shade of the stone curvature. Once darkness surrounded me, I listened for the voices. Nothing. I clicked the small black button on the end of my light and shined the narrow beam over the bridge bottom. Some yellowing vines, a Styrofoam cup, dirt, rocks—but nothing else.

"Hello?" My voice resonated.

Lacey called, "Everything okay in there?"

"Nothing's here," I yelled back.

"Well then, let's go."

"Just a minute while I try something." I stood right in the center of the bridge bottom and clicked my light off.

I heard Lacey ask, "What are you doing?" just before the whizzing and buzzing of the mysterious insects returned. This time, their rapidly moving wings murmured a crazy mixture of *She's coming soon!* and *We've missed her!* and *Go home!* These words repeated over and over, spinning around my head, and in the whirlpool of chaos, a strong wind picked up, growing faster and faster, until my long hair clung to my face.

"Ahh!" I yelled, struggling to find the button on the penlight in my hand. The wind whirred even more vigorously, and the wings buzzed frantically until—*click!* My light flashed on and everything stopped. It was calm again.

I rapidly shined the beam of light everywhere around me, but there was nothing to see. No insects, no people, not even movement from a gust of wind—the Styrofoam cup hadn't even moved.

"You've gotta be kidding me!" I scratched my head, searching my mind for some explanation of what had just happened.

I heard Lacey's feet splashing as she ran to my side. "Are you okay? I heard those voices, and then you screamed, so I followed the light . . ." She was breathing hard.

"Brace yourself for something really weird."

"I don't like weird. Let's just go . . ."

"Stand here beside me and get ready."

"Ready for what?"

"Shh!" I tuned off the light, and we stood in the dark.

"I don't like this," Lacey moaned, pressing against me.

"They're not gonna hurt you."

"They? *Hurt?*"

"Just give it a minute," I whispered.

We stood there for a bit, the only audible sounds were the echoes of dripping water and the airiness of our breathing.

Finally, Lacey quietly said, "Nothin's happenin.'"

"One more minute, please." I put my arm around her shoulder and we waited.

After a few more minutes passed, she announced, "I just counted to 60 three times in my head. Can we go now?"

"Okay, I guess so," I said, hunching my shoulders. "I really wanted you to experience what I just did."

We walked quickly to the outside edge of the bridge, Lacey leading the way. "Heard more voices, huh?"

"Yes, and they not only said, 'She's coming soon,' but also 'We missed her,' and 'Go home.' And there was even more flapping of insect wings—and strong winds!" I shined my light toward the bridge bottom one last time. "But now, nothing. I wish I knew how that all happened."

Lacey shrugged. "Beats me."

"Gusts of wind and insect swarms are both parts of nature, but we heard talking. So weird. And it only happened in the dark, under the bridge." I grabbed my backpack off the brown earth. "How could moving wings make word sounds?" I was itching to look on the Internet to see if this sort of thing could happen.

"Maybe hanging out in this old creek is causing mold to grow on our brains." Lacey pointed both index fingers at her head and grinned.

I put my penlight away, a smile involuntarily taking over my mouth. "Yeah, maybe we're suffering from creek-algae-itis!" I chuckled as I put on my backpack.

"Maybe! And ya know the cure for anything that ails us, right?" Lacey began climbing up the side of the dirt-covered creek bank, using protruding roots as stairs.

"Fro-yo!" I said, pointing to the sky, leading the charge.

"Frozen yogurt to the rescue!" laughed Lacey, copying my gesture.

I ran to catch up and we high-fived before sloshing our way to the yogurt store in our wet, green-mucked shoes. Still, a funny feeling had taken hold of me and it wouldn't let go.

2

Winds of Change

"Hand in hand, with fairy grace,
will we sing and bless this place."
— *William Shakespeare, A Midsummer Night's Dream*

I came home with a frozen yogurt headache after gobbling down a big cup of strawberry fro-yo topped with Gummi bears. To stop the brain freeze I pressed on the roof of my mouth with my thumb, like my science teacher had told us to do, but it didn't help. Maybe hanging out in the late afternoon sun would.

On my way out to the front porch, I heard Mom and Aunt Azalea visiting in the kitchen like they do every week. Aunt Az is exactly 20 years older than Mom, and I am 30 years younger than Mom, so my aunt is 50 years older than I am—she's 50 years my *senior*. But Aunt Az doesn't look or act 63; in fact, she frequently likes to quote Mark Twain: "Age is an issue of mind over matter. If you don't mind, it doesn't matter." She's definitely a spunky, loud Texan, and is somewhat well known in town. After marrying into the Sterret family, which opened the S&S Tea Room in 1931, she now owns the establishment. It's located in the fancy shopping area of Highland Park Village.

Mom and Aunt Az were just pulling the Texas Longhorn Apple Muffins out of the oven. The "longhorn" part refers to the pair of apple slivers stuck in each cup of batter just before they were baked, arranged to look like bull's horns; the Texas part, well, that's where we live. The sweet scent of cinnamon wafting from the kitchen used to make me happy, but these days I knew better. The last time Mom made these muffins was the day my brother Val announced he was joining the army. Something was going on, and I didn't want to know what. I tiptoed over to grab the book I was reading off the dining room table, but it slipped from between my fingers and landed on the ground with a *smack!*

"Claire-Bear, you home?" Mom called.

"Yep!" Darn. So much for a clean getaway.

"Come in here a minute, please."

"Coming!" I bent down, picked up the book, and tucked it under my arm. I took a deep breath before stepping around the corner.

Aunt Az smiled at me from her seat at the kitchen table. Her short, grey hair was quite stylish; it showed off her high cheekbones, the part of her body she was most proud of, often claiming they rivaled those of actress Meryl Streep. She wore a shiny blouse in her favorite color, cobalt blue, which brought out her eyes. My aunt is definitely the most stylish person in the family.

"Hey, Claire-Girl," Aunt Az greeted. "Ready for the school year to be over?"

"Counting the days, Aunt Az," I replied, boosting myself onto the shiny white tile countertop. "Only four more."

The bright yellow walls were cheery, like my mom always seemed to be—she was even wearing a yellow checkered dress to match. She looked at the book under my arm. "Reading again? Is it a good one?"

It's so irritating that Mom asked questions about the obvious. She'd seen me looking at the words on the page yesterday, hadn't she? That should tell her I'm reading it, right? And according to the bookmark, I'm more than three quarters through, so I must like it.

I just nodded.

"Why don't you read outside? It's such a glorious day." Mom smiled hopefully, however, she knows that as long as weather permits, I always read on the front porch. Another instance of stating the obvious.

"Need help with the dishes, I see," I said, trying to show by example. What's clear should be merely a statement. It's easy to do.

"No, no, I didn't call you in for that." Mom's chipper tone sounded a bit forced now. "I wanted to let you know about a special someone who will be staying with us for a while."

"Someone very dear to us," Aunt Az added.

"Is Val coming home early?" I said with excitement. "I thought he had six months of duty to go before we get to see him."

"No, honey. I wish your brother was on his way home, but he's not. It's your Grandma Faye." She said the name like it was as familiar as her own, but it wasn't familiar to me at all.

"Who?" I knew my reply sounded snippy, but it wasn't as if we'd ever really discussed her before. At least not recently. Sure, I knew she lived in England, which was far away, but my grandmother hadn't ever visited. I had always wondered why. It was her fault we'd become so distant. No, unfamiliar. No . . . I needed to find just the right word, and often it was the bigger, more exotic ones that best expressed what I wanted to say. We are . . . ah, yes! *Estranged.*

"*Grandma* Faye. Your grandmother, our mother," Aunt Az chimed in.

"Well, your mother . . . ah, Grandma . . ." I mumbled. Referring to this woman with such familiarity felt dishonest. ". . . she's pretty *old*, isn't she?"

"Eighty-seven years," Mom said.

I had to know. "How long is she staying?"

"She says she's coming to *live* here."

Coming to live here? This was when a sickeningly ticklish feeling started in me.

"Live here?" Aunt Az sounded as shocked as I was.

"But at Golden Oaks, or some place like that, right?" I pointed out. "If she's that old, she probably needs a lot of help getting around and stuff."

All I could think about were the terrible things I'd seen the nurses doing at Golden Oaks, the convalescent hospital where my mom worked, like dabbing food off craggy lips and sponge-bathing wrinkled skin. And I couldn't help but worry that Mom may make me help take care of my grandmother. My studies were important, and when I had free time, I cherished my moments spent sketching by the creek. I didn't want to sound like a brat, but the truth was, a high-maintenance grandmother would really cramp my style.

"Her doctors tell me she's still pretty fit and energetic." Mom flashed me a disapproving smile. "Besides, I deal with elderly people just like her every day, Claire. She will be perfectly fine in my care, here at home. If she wants to come and stay, I welcome it."

Suddenly Mom turned her head toward the kitchen window, but not before I caught a glimpse of the tears that filled her eyes. "And it all really comes down to one thing: *she's my mother*. Your grandmother, Claire. She's family."

I sat there, silent and unable to move. Was all this for real? Mom and my aunt began to talk as if I weren't even there.

"This is the first time in nearly a decade that she has ever visited us, and she only let us visit her in England once," Mom complained. "Didn't she want to see her children? Her grandchildren?"

"She said we wouldn't understand her life there. Now, the Brits may be a bit snooty, but I can handle 'em." Aunt Az put both hands on her hips and gave a dramatic nod before she continued. "Some of the customers I have to deal with are nothin' but ornery, let me tell you! Their tea is either too hot or too cold, and I ask 'em, 'Who do y'all think I am, Goldie Locks?'"

Mom laughed, but I was still busy wrapping my mind around the news.

"I do feel guilty for leavin' her alone all of these years in that old drafty house." Aunt Az sighed. "But that's what she wanted."

"I wonder why she's willing to get on a plane and see us *now*." Mom shifted in her chair. "Why the change of heart all of a sudden?"

"She's always been a bit . . . eccentric, leaving her family and home behind in Texas to illustrate gardens in the middle of the dreary English countryside. That's plain ol' nuts, if ya ask me." Aunt Az lowered her voice, "I swear, Amy, she may be goin' a little daft. Talkin' nonsense about seeing *fairies* and all."

Fairies? That's ridiculous. What kind of kooky adult would believe in fairies?

"Az, cut her some slack. Mother's eighty-seven years old. She's been sharp as a tack all these years. It's completely normal for her mind to slip now and then. I see it happen to my patients all the time."

Oh, my gosh. My grandmother is cuckoo.

I'd only seen the woman once and all I remembered was her bright pink lipstick. I had just met her, but those puckered pink lips closed in on me and planted a big sloppy kiss on my cheek—my skin had a pink stain for several days. Oh, and those wacky lips were always whispering strange things in my ear, like: "One day, I'll tell you something very special" and "You'll be the heir of amazing knowledge." Even now, remembering the eerie way she said it gave me shivers.

"I suppose you're right. Her mind could just be gettin' weaker with age." I had to really listen now since Mom, the neat freak, had switched on the dishwasher. "But Amy, she's goin' on as though they're *real* now. The last time I called, the caregiver said she'd caught Mama sneaking into the kitchen in the middle of the night to get butter and sugar, explainin' that it would attract *fairies* to the house."

"Well," Mom's voice grew quiet as she wiped down the kitchen sink with a giant pink sponge. "I still think it's difficult to understand what's going on with her when she's so far away."

"So, when is she coming?" I managed to say.

"She's actually flying here Monday night." My mom paused for a minute, as if making a silent wish.

In three days? I wobbled, nearly falling off the counter.

Mom sat down in a chair, silently sipping her coffee.

"Okay, Amy, I know that look. There's somethin' wrong." Aunt Az crossed her arms. "Out with it."

"Well . . . she has convinced herself that she only has a few more months to live. There's no medical reason for it. She just says that 'those who know better than doctors have told her she won't live past September." Mom set her coffee cup down with a loud *clunk!*

"Oh, boy. Are you sure she's mentally okay? No Alzheimer's or anything?" Aunt Az said with concern in her voice.

"Her doctors say she's pretty healthy, especially considering her age. I guess we'll see when she gets here."

"Well, she can stay with me. With Val away, your family doesn't need any more . . . changes."

Good idea, Aunt Az. Take her to *your* house. I stared at my hands, folded on top of the book in my lap, waiting for Mom's reply.

"Oh, no. She's insisting on staying here, in the house where she grew up." Mom stood up and walked around the kitchen now. "It'll do me good, actually, to have a distraction. Get my mind off of Val . . . and believe me, I'll still need plenty of help from you."

My head popped up. Had she said that while looking at me, or my aunt? Or did she mean us both?

"So, how long do you really think she'll stay?" My aunt didn't sound convinced that this dying-in-a-few-months thing was really going to happen.

"I don't know. If she never actually goes back to England, she'll live with us until the end, I guess."

My jaw dropped. *The end?* It sounded like my grandmother was nothing but a DVD that would be taken back to the video store when the final credits came. But no, obviously, "the end" for a human means something completely different.

I'd heard enough. "I'm gonna go read for a while." I jumped to the floor, slid the book under my arm, and went outside, a lump forming in my throat.

I love big ideas and big words, so the book in my hands should have kept my interest. Sitting sideways in a wicker chair on the front porch, reading about Sir Isaac Newton's 300-year-old discovery of light diffraction, I could almost believe it. The trees above caused dappled sunlight to dance upon the pages. The warm air felt good on my skin. I looked out and saw the rolling green carpets of the neighbors' manicured front yards, leading up to porches lined with shady trees and American flags waving in the breeze. It was a beautiful day, but that sick tickling feeling of worry wouldn't leave me alone.

Everything is perfectly normal. Stop thinking about what you just heard and concentrate.

But I couldn't ignore a gnawing sense of dread.

I thought about the day Val left to join his band of brothers. I was sitting on his bed while he was whistling a song, packing his duffle bag. He grabbed the framed picture of the two of us from his bedside table. It had been taken over a year ago, when I turned twelve.

"I'm gonna take this with me so I can see your goofy face whenever I need a laugh," Val teased. For some reason, he especially liked making stuff up about my face.

I usually had a quick comeback about his ears, but today I sat in silence.

"Don't worry, Care Bear," he'd said. That was the nickname he'd given me the day I came home from the hospital, when I was only two days old. He said I looked like a small teddy bear all bundled up in my little pink blanket. "I'll be back home before you know it. You just have to believe that everything will be okay."

But believing isn't so easy. I already knew that death could strike at any moment—the news was filled with images of Humvees driving the dusty roads of Baghdad and soldiers in their camouflage missing an arm or a leg. Val was about to put himself in the middle of roadside bombs and bad guys who wanted to kill American soldiers. How could I believe that everything would be okay?

And now I'd soon have a crazy grandmother to deal with. When I was really little, I desperately wanted a loving grandma and grandpa like everyone else seemed to have. But Grandma Faye was all I had, and she couldn't have cared less about us. While other kids were getting birthday cards and eating homemade cookies from their grandparents, she was off in her own world—a world she never wanted to share. And now she was coming to our house . . . to die?

I scrunched lower in the chair with my book, so there was no chance anyone could even see the top of my head.

My mom was an expert when it came to old people. She worked at Golden Oaks, the old folk's home on Abrams Road. I'd made the mistake of visiting her at work a couple of times, like on my school's Take Your Daughter to Work Day. Other kids went to a bank or a law firm. I spent the day talking to people in their pajamas who didn't know what day it was and serving them cups of runny canned fruit salad. The strange moaning noises and geriatric smell of old people mixed with Pine-Sol made me queasy.

I just wanted everything to be normal. So, it was times like now that I turned to Sir Isaac Newton. Give me the facts. Figures. Tell me about the Law of Motion, gravity, or the orbit of planets. These things didn't have feelings. They didn't depend on people coming home or not. People living or dying. They just were. And *these* were the things that made the world normal.

After rereading the same paragraph four times and not comprehending a thing, I let out a sigh and closed the book, thankful that the boxwood shrub along the edge of the porch did a good job of hiding me from people walking by.

Unfortunately, the wicker chair was a creaky thing. I set my book down on the ground, and that was all it took. *Squeeeeak!*

"Hey there!" At the sudden sound of a boy's voice, I nearly jumped out of my skin.

I made a visor with my hand to block the rays of sunshine and found myself face to face with a pair of mischievous bright blue eyes. I instantly froze. My palms grew sweaty, my tongue felt thick—it's what happened to me around guys.

"I almost didn't see you there," the boy laughed, leaning comfortably against the porch pillar. "Do you know which house Mrs. Newman lives in?"

She was my neighbor, but all I could manage was to point to the right. It was this loss of speech that made me sure I'd never have a boyfriend. Why couldn't I be more like Lacey? She'd know exactly what to say.

"Thanks. I work at Tom Thumb, and I usually don't deliver groceries, but she just had a hip replacement and can't . . . anyway, I couldn't make out the address. Pickle juice." He smiled, holding up the juice-soaked paper, and then just stood there.

Again, I didn't have a reply. But it didn't really matter—a boy that good-looking, with such dark, wavy hair, wouldn't care about me anyway. I wished he would, but I was too plain and nerdy.

"Ah, well, see ya," he said, giving me a wave as he turned back down the stairs.

Then a rush of panic came over me. Now I'd have to avoid him whenever I went to the grocery store this summer. What if he recognized me and tried to make conversation? He was way too cute—I might keel over on the spot.

I needed to go immediately into the house, in case he came back, so I went up to my room. As I entered, a strong breeze wafted against my face, surprising me. That's funny, the window was closed. I stopped, opened and closed the bedroom door briskly several times, but couldn't replicate the same gush of wind and the feeling it stirred within me.

Strange.

The winds of change. It was an expression I'd read once in a novel, but I pushed it aside. My house is more than eighty years old, so it definitely has its quirks. After setting the book on my window seat, I flopped onto my bed and stared at the lumpy white ceiling. I often lounged here, on lazy weekend mornings, searching for pictures formed by the hairline cracks. There was a lady's face that I could pick out immediately. She looked like a Victorian woman, her hair in a bun and her eyes closed . . . oh great, just like the grandma who was on her way to stay here. A future of wiping drool and cleaning out bedpans flashed before my eyes. Or worse, racing to restrain the bony arms of a frantic, delusional woman screaming in the middle of the night.

All I wanted was to continue to perfect my new ability to be utterly unseen around the house. It wasn't hard, with Dad always away on business, Mom always at work, and a brother in the armed forces.

When I tell people that my brother Val is serving in Iraq, they always act like I just told them he was on vacation in Florida. "Oh, how wonderful!" they would say. It was hard to bite my tongue. Didn't they know that he was in danger? Didn't they understand that he might never come home?

My family's shared worry about Val hung in the air, but we never spoke about it. In our own practice of denial, my mom and I had our nightly routine. We ate dinner, washed the dishes side by side, and then each did our own thing. I didn't want to freak Mom out by talking about my worries, and at the same time, I worried that if I talked about the things that frightened me they might come true. Most nights, my mom busied herself by paying the bills or reading in the living room, while I escaped to study or draw.

"Wow, Claire!" Mom would often say, looking over my shoulder as I sketched while sitting on the couch. "You are really good at drawing. There are so many details."

"Thanks, Mom. I want to capture the precise perspective and accurate shading of my subject matter," was my usual response.

Tonight was no exception. "You're practically photographing with your fingers," she had said, after we'd finished our spaghetti and meatballs.

I felt myself grin in a big way. "I was afraid you were going to say I was 'another Picasso.' We just learned about him in art class. Here's what I don't get. He was brilliant at drawing in the classical style, but actually gave it up for *cubism*. Noses on foreheads and ears protruding from chests! That's just bizarre. He must have been delusional."

"Well, I think he just had a great imagination," Mom said. She returned to her favorite chair, where she'd left her book balanced on the arm.

"If you ask me, wild imaginations are better replaced with concrete, educated thinking." I hesitated before deciding to say, "Today Lacey and I heard insect wings and strange voices coming from beneath one of the stone bridges over Turtle Creek. And then these wild winds started up. I can't figure out a scientific explanation for it, though."

Mom picked up her book and opened it where the page was marked. "Science can't answer every question, you know."

"I disagree. That's what it exists to do." I had tapped my pencil in cadence with the last four syllables of my statement for emphasis. And it was at that moment I decided that what I had experienced under the bridge was just a large swarm of insects. My fear had made me hear words in the fluttering of the insect wings and I'd convinced

Lacey to hear words too. The power of suggestion. And winds could pick up at any time, and they often did in Texas. It was the most logical explanation.

Later that night, I took my sketchbook to the old oak desk in my room, plunked down in my swiveling desk chair, opened the large bottom drawer on the right, and took out my painter's palette. Popping off the airtight lid, I dipped a clean, soft brush into a glass of water, then into the paint, and began blending the watercolors to make a perfect prism spectrum. There was actually a hint of magenta when the colors were blended correctly.

3

Returning Home

"Home, the spot of earth supremely blest,
A dearer, sweeter spot than all the rest."
—Robert Montgomery

 hile eating breakfast Monday morning, I looked closely at my mother's face, the beautiful Amy Collins. Although I'd often been told that I look just like her, I knew I was really just a plainer version.

Mom's wavy blond hair fell softly around her face, framing her bright blue eyes and creamy skin. In contrast, my dark blond hair was stick-straight around my grey eyes and freckled face. "Angel kisses," my mom called them, but I wasn't a believer in heavenly apparitions, let alone ones that left small brown specks on a person's face. Why did people feel the need to make up stories about what was technically just *epidermis pigmentation*?

My mom had a special talent: the gift of gab. She'd talk to a complete stranger in an elevator, and, five floors later, have managed to exchange quite a bit of personal information. And the worst part was, Mom used anything apparent to get the conversation started, such as: "Isn't that a purse you're carrying?" or "That's a fine watch on your wrist, isn't it?"

Like I said before, she's the Universal Queen of Stating the Obvious. And it had never failed to make my face burn with embarrassment.

I longed for the day that someone would answer sarcastically, "Of course it's a purse. What else would the bag-like object I'm carrying over my shoulder with a strap be? A meatloaf?" Or a good basic reply like, "It's a Rolex, so I should hope it's a nice watch."

But with one look at Mom's kind face, people always answered politely, starting down the road of a big conversation.

Once, when my mom was enthusiastically . . . ah, a better word would be *zealously* helping a complete stranger shop for the perfect tie, an old lady sorting through boxer shorts noticed my beet-red face. She made her way toward me and then leaned in close.

"People's faults are their strengths in excess," she said softly, then winked and walked away.

In Mom's case, this was certainly true.

Last Monday, when we were at the bank, my mom met an attractive middle-aged lady with a toy poodle in her cheetah print tote bag. And because of that, last night, at around 1 a.m., I woke up in a cold sweat.

I'd dreamt that I was reliving my mom's encounter with the woman and the tiny white dog, except the woman in my dream was ancient, with a humped back, bending over a cane. Underneath her transparent skin pulsed grotesque blue veins, and her breath smelled like musty licorice.

"Come closer, dearie," she gestured with a spindly finger. "Don't you want to see the cute doggy in my purse?" I stepped nearer, but the old woman grabbed my arm and forced me to stand pressed against her skeleton-like body.

To my horror, there was no dog in the bag—in fact, there was nothing but a deep, dark hole that swirled and pulsed. The strange churning air began to move faster, drawing me closer and closer no matter how much I struggled to pull away. As I neared the black crater, the force became more powerful, sucking my hair into the abyss. Frantically, I dug my heels into the floor, trying to keep myself from disappearing into the unrelenting hole, but even as I did, something in the endless tunnel caught my eye.

As I gazed hard into the darkness, there was a moment of stillness. Fluttering within a radiant bubble-like orb was a beautiful, glowing butterfly. My jaw dropped. It was amazing, with sparkling wings that flashed a rainbow of colors. I reached out to catch the enchanted sphere in the palm of my hand. Then I woke up.

I thought about the meaning of my nightmare as I brushed my hair that morning. I knew that dreams were manufactured by thoughts in one's subconscious—Freud would've had a field day with this one!

I'm sure Freud would have said that the scary old woman represented my grandmother. After all, she was a stranger with whom I was about to come face to face.

But what about the butterfly? Why did a beautiful creature appear in the middle of such a terrible nightmare? That part was a mystery.

I went downstairs and grabbed my book bag off the kitchen counter. I had deliberately skipped breakfast because my tummy was in a twist; if Mom noticed, she'd force me to eat, so I tried to sneak out. But just when I had opened the door, she stopped me.

"Just a minute, Claire."

Darn! "Yeah, Mom?"

"Dad's coming home from his trip this afternoon, so we'll all be having dinner together tonight. Don't make other plans." Something about the anticipation of Dad coming home made her smile even prettier than usual.

"I won't. Dad's been gone over a week this time. It'll be good to see him," I said, turning and stepping quickly outside.

"And don't forget that your grandmother's coming after dinner," Mom hollered, just before the door slammed behind me.

Forgetting that wasn't going to happen.

I had a difficult time concentrating in school that day, and not just because my stomach rumbled from hunger; thoughts of the dream kept popping into my mind. At noon, eating lunch quieted my stomach, but I had nothing to stop—*quell*—the thoughts in my head.

That night, I sat between my parents at the kitchen table. Mom served us a dinner of Dickey's barbecued ribs and my favorite smoky potato salad, speckled with chopped sweet pickles. She had obviously served our favorite dinner to soften us up before my grandmother came. Also, probably because my father was home. He'd arrived late that afternoon after attending a financial conference in Washington, DC. He was a certified public accountant, or CPA, for a big firm. Val and I always teased him by saying that the letters "CPA" stood for "Counting Pennies Abroad" since he traveled so much.

Now that Val was away, Dad took even more trips. Just being in his company made me feel better. He was the rational, steady one in our family, and he and I were the most alike. We never allowed our emotions to make us do silly things, like cry or cheer loudly in public.

"Well Stu, things were pretty quiet around here this week, until we got the news," Mom said as she plopped a large scoop of potato salad on her plate.

"I can't believe Faye is finally coming here, after all these years," Dad said, taking the large bowl from Mom. "It's just like your mother, Amy. Not only is she coming to visit for the first time in fifteen years, but she's coming to *live*. She always did things in a big way."

"I think it will be nice having her here, no matter how long she stays. The family has been a little . . ." Mom paused to find the right word, ". . . disappointed that we haven't seen her in such a long time."

Dad moved the napkin next to his plate onto his lap. "It sounds like you don't think it's a permanent thing."

"Well, the doctors say she's a healthy eighty-seven-year-old. I predict that she'll miss her home in England and eventually go back." I heard disappointment in Mom's voice.

"Well, what do you think, kiddo?" Dad asked, turning his attention to me. "You probably don't remember your grandmother, do you?"

I pushed a chunk of pickle around the plate with my fork. "Nope, I don't."

"Well, she's always been quite a character," Dad said with a crooked smile.

When people say someone's "quite a character," I never know if that's meant as a compliment or not. I decided to change the subject. "I got my honors history quiz back today. Got an A."

"Honey, I'm so proud of you. I know Val would be, too," said Mom.

"Nice job, kiddo." Dad got quiet after that and the conversation was minimal throughout the rest of the meal.

After dinner, I retreated to the front porch to digest. The thing about eating ribs is that there always seems to be a small, stringy piece stuck between your teeth. I toyed with mine, grateful I no longer had to deal with braces.

I heard the telltale squeak of the screen door and the shuffle of my father's shoes as he came to sit beside me on the stairs, pressing his shoulder against mine, his way of showing affection. I waited for him to say something as I enjoyed the familiar scent of his aftershave.

He was a man of few words, but when he spoke, it mattered. He traveled so much that I'd gotten used to him being gone, and since Val left, he habitually kept to himself. So I barely noticed when he *was* home.

I thought back to when my father had been more social, when he would tell a dumb joke now and again. Then I remembered the change. The physical change of the light in his eyes when he realized Val was really gone. Gone to the war. I actually witnessed the exact moment that it dawned on him. We'd gathered for dinner for the first time since Val left, and Dad had stared at the chair in which my brother would have sat, his place setting missing.

Nearly a year had passed since then. Here Dad and I were, sitting on the porch, both missing Val but not saying a word about it.

"I guess there are only two more days of eighth grade left," he finally said. "Your mother told me you'll be bringing home another nice report card. Straight As."

I could see in his eyes that he was proud of me. "You've worked hard," he said. "A break is much deserved."

"I can't wait to spend the summer drawing—and reading books I want to read," I said, picturing myself on the swinging bridge over the lake, sketching the turtles while they swam and made bubbles.

"Enjoy yourself, darlin'. You're young for only a short time."

We gazed out into the yard—which was still sunlit, as daylight savings time was in full swing. The first hints of the scent of a humid Texas summer was in the air, a smell that I love. Cicadas chirped in shifting harmonies, randomly flitting from tree to tree in the waxing twilight. Whenever I traveled away from this house in the summer, I missed the cicadas serenading me at night with their song; upon my return, they would sing their refrain, telling me I was finally "*home, home, home, home.*"

"Grandma's on her way," Dad said, "and I bet you're thinking about how much it will change things around here."

I managed a half-smile.

"Claire, I need you to keep in mind that although it will be a change for all of us, it's a much bigger one for your mother. This is a sacrifice. A sacrifice of love."

"And you're about to tell me that I need to help," I said, bracing myself for a lecture about giving Mom a hand. I knew it was the right thing to do, but it made me physically nauseated to even think about dealing with . . . all the old person stuff.

"No, being thirteen means independence. You shouldn't feel obligated to help out all the time. Mom's fewer job hours should help everyone continue to do whatever he or she needs to do." He smiled, gently tapped my knee with the palm of his large hand, and then stood up and walked into the house.

Was this reverse psychology? Had he just told me <u>not</u> to help, in an attempt to get me to jump in and do the opposite? If so, I was on to him. Or maybe, he meant that I needed to enjoy my life—the life my brother was fighting so hard to protect.

I lingered on the porch a few minutes more, watching the shadows grow long and dim, light reflecting brightly on the edge of every car, curb, and roofline. Lightning bugs gathered in the shrubs, flashing in the darkening underbrush.

Then, it came upon me again, that strong urge to draw. I needed to reach my goal of capturing each stage of every flower I could find, from bud to bloom, like Audubon himself would have done.

I got up, with every intention of hurrying to my room, but suddenly, a figure appeared in front of me: a woman holding a floral patterned hatbox. Her white gauze top and white hair were lit by the streetlight behind her. She looked like a glowing angel.

"Grandma?" I gasped.

"Oh, my Clairy! What a lovely young lady you've become!" she said, swooping in on me, giving me a big kiss on the cheek. *Smack!* Some things never change.

"I can't wait to catch up, but I'm so tired from traveling. Can we chat tomorrow?"

"Sure," was all I could say before she disappeared into the house.

Mom went by me next, a small tote bag in her hand. She was smiling from ear to ear. Then came Dad, carrying a large, old-fashioned blue suitcase.

"Need my help?" I asked.

Dad huffed and puffed as he went up the steps. "No thanks, kiddo. This is all she brought. But I swear, she packed her entire house into this one suitcase." I jumped up and held open the door for him.

Well, it was really happening. My grandmother was really staying in my house.

I went upstairs to my room. Studying wasn't going to happen with the new arrival on my mind, so I decided to work on the pink, white, and green caladium leaves I'd been painting. Dip, dip, brush, brush—after about an hour, the water had turned murky brown, so I cleaned up and called it a night. As I stood at the sink to wash for bed, I looked in the mirror—a bright pink pair of lips was imprinted on my cheek.

4

Familiar Stranger

"Come forth into the light of things, let nature be your teacher."
—❧ *William Wordsworth* ❧—

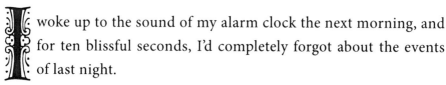

I woke up to the sound of my alarm clock the next morning, and for ten blissful seconds, I'd completely forgot about the events of last night.

I walked to the bathroom down the hall, passed the guest room, and stopped just outside for a minute. I took a deep breath. The ruckus of my parents getting my grandmother situated echoed from behind the door: the crackling old-crone voice, the moving around of a suitcase full of clothes and belongings, and the rattling sound of large amber-colored bottles of prescription pills. The thought of walking through that door felt like the entry into an unknown world.

I needed to get the heck out of there before someone caught me in the hall. But I was too late. Mom appeared.

"Claire, Dad and I are going downstairs to get some breakfast for Grandma. Why don't you go in and say good morning?" Mom swiftly pulled my arm until I was in the middle of the guest room and deposited me there without a second glance.

I kept my eyes fixed on the daisy-patterned sheets. If I lifted my head, I'd finally be face to face with my new nemesis. It had to happen sooner or later, so I bit my lower lip and forced myself to look my grandmother in the eyes—but all I could see was the backside of a silver-haired woman who was sitting on the vanity chair, facing the window.

I needed to get in and out of that bedroom as quickly as possible. Did she know I was there? What should I say? "Hey, how's it going?" or "What have you been up to the last dozen years or so?" Well, I needed to say *something*, but I didn't want to scare her.

Awkward moment number one.

While I stood frozen in thought, the tables were turned when my grandmother spoke first, startling *me*.

Awkward moment number two.

"When this was my home, there weren't any leaves to see from the second floor. There were a few ever-so-small trees just starting their lives. My! They are mighty now. I can hardly believe I'm seeing the tops of them. Amazing what time can do."

She paused for a moment and then began again. "*Arbor Vitae*, the tree of life, giving us food, shade, and offering Earth's creatures shelter. Remarkable things, trees. Don't you agree?"

I noticed she had a very subtle Texas accent (I had expected to hear more twang) mixed with a proper British one. Most people who live in Dallas suburbs like Highland Park really don't have heavy accents anyway, myself included, but we do say things like "y'all" and "fixin'"—as in, "I'm fixin' to go to the market, y'all need anything?" My aunt Az was guilty of purposely saying words ending in "ing" without the "g," but I consciously tried not to use that kind of slang. It would make it easier for people to pinpoint where I was from and I liked being more "universal."

My grandmother was talking about the three old, large pecan trees in the backyard. Grand, strong, and usually full of pecans, these prolific beauties enticed a large number of squirrels. Sure, squirrels are cute, in a "rat-with-a-fluffy-tail" kind of way, but they spend all day sitting on the branches, eating pecans, and dropping the shells on the ground. If you have ever stepped on a pecan shell with bare feet, you'd understand the pain. My mom called it "the agony of da' feet."

I often forgot that I lived in the original family home, built by my great-grandparents. Probably because I've never known what it was like to live anywhere else. It had been updated over the years, with a modern kitchen and fresh paint every five years or so, so I never thought of it as old. My Highland Park neighborhood, although filled with true southern hospitality, had a bit of that "keeping up with the Joneses" feeling. Our house was nice and modest, but still—when the trend had been to paint your dining room deep red, Mom did it at once.

Now I wondered for the first time what other changes my grandmother might be noticing. After all, nearly every inch of her old home had been changed, be it paint color, furniture, or other decorations.

"What was life in this house like back then?" As soon as the question left my mouth, I wanted to kick myself. Wasn't it my plan to say "good morning" and leave?

"Come have a seat and I'll tell you," she said as she gently tapped the arm of the chair with her spindly hand, causing her bracelet, which was made of tiny silver bells, to make a tinkling sound.

"I've got to get to school," I said, looking at the clock.

"It's only—" she looked at the tiny, ornate watch on her wrist, "—five after seven. Could you spare a few minutes for your old grandma?"

I still had an hour before I had to be at school, so I reluctantly replied, "Sure," and cautiously took a seat on the edge of the bed.

As the old woman spoke, I gradually allowed myself to observe her bright shining eyes, which were focused on the window, and her smooth, age-spotted complexion. She was probably quite pretty in her younger days. Her hip, ethnic clothes surprised me. She wore white linen pants with a bright pink and orange chiffon tunic top which had been decorated with shimmering pink sequins.

"Well, this house was finally finished in 1927. The piles of brick, barrels of concrete, and planks of wood were all made to fit together to create my parents' dream—a house of their own. This whole area," the old woman swept a clawed hand from left to right, "originally was flat, barren land with miles and miles of dirt and brush.

"Cows and bulls roamed freely, so when people began building, the livestock didn't know what to do. I remember the builders chasing the cows away from the patches of grass that grew on our property. If you've ever been face to face with a stubborn cow, well, you'd know that getting a 900-pound animal to move is nearly impossible! As a young girl, it made me laugh to see the men waving their hats, throwing water, clapping their hands . . . but nothing worked. The cow usually left when it was good and ready, often after eating someone's brown-bag lunch!"

She chuckled quietly.

"But by 1930 or so, houses began cropping up everywhere. Friends and family you once visited by horse were within walking distance. It really felt like a community.

"Schools were built, a small shopping district was opened, track was laid and a train station was erected. Suddenly, it was the place to be. The founders made sure that a large amount of the city's property was left for parks, hence its name, Highland Park. Parks were where all the socialization happened back then. I have so many cool memories of those parks!"

Had she really used the word *cool?* I rolled my eyes at the childish energy brewing inside of this eighty-seven-year-old woman. Weren't grandmothers supposed to be soft-spoken and proper? I hoped she was done speaking, and rose to leave, but she started again. I settled back down, trying to be polite.

"Life was so very different back then. We watched every penny, and our priorities then were unlike today's. For instance, my father bought the three biggest pecan saplings we could afford—he said that the only thing that could make Mama's pecan pie better was if the pecans came from her own trees. Only having one pair of play shoes was fine, as long as Mama had her trees."

She stopped watching out the window and looked right at me. Her eyes were clear and blue, just like my mom's.

"After establishing Highland Park in 1913, the founders tried to entice even more people to move here. What was the slogan again?" She paused and glanced at the ceiling. "Oh, yes. 'Ten degrees cooler.' At least they *said* it was ten degrees cooler here than anywhere else in Texas, true or not." She paused again. "Now where was I going with this?"

"Ah, pecans?" I said, trying not to sound impatient. I shifted on the bed and crossed my arms.

"Right, Mama's pecans. Well, as I said before, the parks were the center of the town's social scene, and that's where everyone went to enjoy their Sunday supper. Oh, how I looked forward to Sundays as a young girl! My favorite events were the evening hayrides and moonlit picnics in the park by Exall Lake. Accompanied by the melodic sound of a small band, men rowed boats out on the water while women sat behind them, twirling their lacey parasols.

"A colorful array of handmade quilts were scattered all over the grass, each topped with a large basket full of home-baked goodies. Of course, you tried to sit by the good bakers just in case they decided to share their delectables. Naturally, everyone crowded around *our* blanket when Mama brought her pecan pies!" The memory of the pies was almost visible in the old woman's eyes. She sat, enveloped in her thoughts, until out popped "sulfur!"

"Sulfur? The pie was made with sulfur?" I asked in disbelief.

"Oh, no. That's the smell of the memory. Memories are often related to smells, aren't they?"

I decided to treat that as a rhetorical question, but yes, she was right. Memories and smells are definitely associated. I read that psychologists refer to it as "cue-dependent memory."

"The pie's smell was wonderfully brown-sugary," she continued, "but the spigots along the lake side produced sulfur-smelling water. People would fill up bottles and drink it. Believed it would cure irregularity, arthritis, even lying and playing hooky! Simple times back then. Not so focused on technology and science like today."

She'd found my Achilles' heel. "Didn't people get sick from drinking that sulfur water? I'll bet they did. Science isn't bad at all—it might have kept those people from getting ill. Drinking bad water can give you bacterial infections; it doesn't keep you from lying or playing hooky," I argued.

"Yes, simple people, simple times." She didn't seem to catch on to my angst and just kept talking. "We even used kerosene lanterns back then to light our way to and from the park, and we used them in our houses at night. The cause of many homes going ablaze . . ." She trailed off, and suddenly the spark of glee in her eyes faded into sorrow.

The silence grew thick between us.

Then, much to both my joy and dismay, my grandmother decided to change the subject. "Why, let me take a look at you, Claire! Please, stand in front of me. Turning my neck isn't easy these days, as rusty as I am."

I got up from the bed and stood between the chair and window.

"My, my, my . . . how much you have grown up! You're thirteen, is that right?"

I nodded.

"The last time I saw you, you were five or six. Do you remember visiting me in England?"

I shook my head.

"Ah, you were too little to remember," she sighed. "I miss being there already. I miss my little fairy friends most of all. They told you I was coming, didn't they?"

The moment I'd been dreading had arrived. The old woman really *did* believe in fairies! Worse, she referred to them as if they were as common as peanut butter and jelly!

My heart began beating at a frantic pace.

"Ah, I've got to get ready for school . . ." I stood up to leave. Then I noticed a dramatic change in the way she was acting—a change in her *demeanor*. "I'm sorry. I'd like to stay, but . . . hey, are you okay?"

She sat there with a blank expression and had gone from focusing on my freckled face to a place far away; she stared silently, and sadness filled her eyes.

I tried to get her attention by repeating "are you okay?" several times, but the old woman remained in a fog. Then, one solitary tear ran down her wrinkled cheek.

And just when I was about to gently shake her, she suddenly reached out her knobby fist, rapped upon the bedside table three times, pointed a crooked finger, and brushed it this way and that.

I felt my face screw up in a mixture of fright and utter confusion.

"My goodness, Claire," Mom entered the room as though she'd never been gone. "Could you try to smile *once* for Grandma? Mother, Claire uses her smiles sparingly, but they are quite a treat when they appear!"

"Oh, I think she is lovely either way," my grandmother answered without a beat.

What had *that* been all about? She'd gone completely comatose, but then snapped out of it the second my mom appeared!

I felt my red face radiate.

Grandma just smiled.

"Visiting time is over. Mother, you must be exhausted, and Claire, you need to get ready for school. You two can catch up later," Mom said, shooing me away with both hands.

I gladly retreated to my room.

When my mom stopped in to see me half an hour later, I was packing up my schoolbooks, paper, and pencils.

"So, how'd your visit with Grandma go?"

"It went okay," I said. "She started telling me about the history of this house, which was pretty cool, but then she became, well, kind of . . . *incoherent.*"

"Well, she's old, sweetie. Patience is key when dealing with someone her age. Everything she's said to me has been quite sharp. She remembered all the names of our neighbors and asked about each one. She even remembered that Mrs. Stewart had laser eye surgery and that Mrs. Newman had a hip replacement—she inquired about their recoveries. I was pretty impressed."

Huh. My grandmother knew more about the neighbors than I did. Well, I did know about Mrs. Newman, at least, thanks to the handsome grocery guy who had come by.

Remembering him made my stomach do a flip.

"So then, do you think that what she told me was true?" I asked. "I mean, as far as the family history and all that. Does she know what she's saying?"

"Yes, you can believe most of the things she says."

The word "most" was an interesting choice.

My mom sat down on the bed and leaned back on her hands. I sat next to her.

"Mom, I know we visited her in England once, but I don't remember very much about her."

I had a vivid memory of London and all the sights. I could see Big Ben in my mind as if I were still that six-year-old girl gazing up at its grand face as it watched over the beautiful city, but I was hazy when it came to memories of spending time with my own grandmother. Except for those bright pink lips.

"I had always pictured a life where my children would grow up knowing their grandparents," Mom answered. "But before you were born, she and your grandfather decided to move to England so that she could illustrate books on gardens for some British publisher."

"Why didn't we see them more?"

"They became very attached to their little cottage there, refusing to ever leave it, and after that one visit, whenever I'd ask when we could visit again, they always said we wouldn't understand their lifestyle. They didn't want any of the family to come." Mom shook her head from side to side. "When my father—your grandfather— died, she wouldn't even let any of us come to his funeral. She actually refused to tell any of us the date, time, or place."

"That seems pretty strange," I said. "Why didn't you just go anyway?"

"They had moved to an even more remote cottage in the country- side a couple of years prior, but wouldn't give us the address—only the phone number." Both corners of Mom's mouth turned downward. "We've all been pretty angry with her these past ten years for that. People, even the ones you think you really know well, can surprise you sometimes."

"But she gave us her house to live in. She must have cared about us."

"You know, even with all of the strange behavior, I have always known how much your grandparents loved us." A small smile returned to Mom's face. "That's why I'm willing to let bygones be bygones."

That was so much like Mom, forgiving and forgetting so easily. I'll bet Aunt Az will have a harder time with that.

"And during that one time we did visit her, I was amazed by her gorgeous garden," Mom added. "I really got into English gardens myself. Remember all of the hollyhock seeds we planted in the back- yard after we came back home?"

I smiled and nodded. I did recollect the rows and rows of pink, white, and red flower-towers along the wooden fence. They were twice as tall as I was, with crepe paper petals.

And after thinking about it, I did remember more about Grandma. She wore thick gloves and pushed a wheelbarrow full of spades, hoes, and other gardening tools. She had shown me how to make a fancy woman from a hollyhock flower and a bud. Using a toothpick, she'd connect the just-bursting blossom to the base of an upside-down, fully opened flower. The petals really looked like an elegant chiffon gown, the bud just like a head with a colorful headpiece on top, and the toothpick made the outstretched arms. I loved floating those "ladies" upon the surface of a bucket full of water, watching them dance as the breeze caused currents.

"So that's how our backyard became such a jungle—the influence of a wild English garden. I get it now," I teased.

She smiled back. "Do you remember Grandma teaching you how to make those ballroom ladies out of flowers?"

"Yes, now that you mention it, I do." I stood up and stretched, arms overhead. "So she agreed to finally leave her gardens, eh?"

I watched Mom grow visibly uneasy. "She thinks she's going to die. Soon. But there's no medical reason for her to think that. Perhaps she just wants to make amends."

"Well, she got a little sad earlier while talking about her home in England. She actually got weird and said she missed her 'little fairy friends.'"

"Never you mind what she says about 'little whatever friends.' She's very old and may be slipping a bit now and then." Mom's smiling mouth didn't match the sadness in her eyes. "But you can believe in the family accounts. No one knows them better than she does."

I gave Mom's hand a squeeze. There had been enough emotion for one day.

"I've gotta get to class, and then after school, I'm going to Lacey's to study." I slung my backpack over my shoulder. "Finals tomorrow and Thursday, eighth grade graduation on Friday, and then I'm done with middle school," I announced, doing a silly victory dance to lighten the mood.

"Okay, Claire. Keep an eye on the time. Dinner with Grandma is at six o'clock sharp." She rose and kissed me on the forehead before disappearing down the hallway.

I stepped outside, and after breathing in the sweet smell of freshly mown grass, relaxed a bit. I got through my school day without thinking too much about my grandmother. I waited about five minutes for Lacey by my locker, before I got a text:

Had ortho appt. Meet @ my house.

I texted back "K" and started to walk toward Lacey's.

The weather would be blistering hot soon, so I needed to enjoy the perfect day. Stopping by the creek for a few minutes on the way wouldn't cut into my study time too much. To get there, I'd have to go back five blocks, down the concrete sidewalks of the neighborhood. When I felt like a peaceful walk, I'd go down Stratford or Maplewood Avenue—quiet streets where people watered plants, sipped iced tea on their porches, and kids rode their bicycles, waving as I passed. When I wanted to marvel along the way, I'd walk down Beverly Drive, where large mansions stood in perfectly kept yards with fancy cars parked in the driveways. Today, I walked down Stratford. In his driveway, old Mr. Henry, a retired Highland Park teacher, was buffing his pristine 1972 Cadillac Sedan de Ville—turquoise with a white top. He gave me a nod as I passed by.

At last I came to the place where the sidewalk ended. There was nothing but stretches of green: periwinkle vines, live oak trees, and ferns—and beyond the green was the creek. Plopping beneath an old oak and studying its canopy soothed me, especially watching how the rippled reflection of sunlight from the water danced upon the branches above.

As I lay back in the grass on my elbows, I noticed a curious thing. A shimmering green hummingbird, with a ruby throat no larger than my thumb, landed on the white rubber toe of my right Converse high top.

"Why, hello, little guy," I said gently, not moving so I wouldn't scare him.

Wow! Hummingbirds never hang around humans. I decided to study him for a drawing.

As if he read my mind, he seemed to pose for me, left wing out-stretched and tail fanned. Then he flicked his skinny tongue out six times before turning his head as if he was studying *me*. Suddenly, he flitted his wings, slowly lifted off my shoe, and hovered closer and closer in the air until he was two feet from my face.

A shiver went down my spine because, like under the bridge, I heard a voice. Or I could have sworn I did. I looked in every direc-tion, but there wasn't a soul around.

Follow, it whispered. Things were getting weird again. Was this all in my head?

Or was this what people called *intuition?* Intuition is the ability to understand something without the need for reasoning. The funny thing was, I didn't question my sanity. The warm feeling that came over me made it feel entirely natural to receive such a message. And I supposed that intuition was an important trait for scientists to have. After all, if Sir Isaac Newton hadn't allowed his subconscious to take over while sitting beneath that apple tree, he may not have even theo-rized about gravity!

Follow, the voice said again. The tiny hummingbird began to zig-zag toward and away from me, over and over.

"I guess you want me to follow you. But where are we going?" Okay, I'm losing it. I just tried to have a conversation with a hum-mingbird!

I grabbed my backpack and he led me by weaving and dipping in the air, staying about a foot in front of me. I supposed he would have preferred to take a more bird-like path, perhaps zipping through trees and over fences, but he led me down sidewalks, across front yards, and even down an alley—all places a human could go—until we reached the public library. Once we arrived, he landed on the wooden door frame above the entrance and began preening his feathers.

I absolutely must be going insane, following a bird to the library because I'm hearing voices. And I think he wants me to go inside. Really weird! Oh, well. I can study here as well as anywhere.

I got out my cell phone. "Hi Lacey. Seems there's a change of plans. Can you meet me at the library instead to study?"

"Sure. But why?" She sounded confused.

"I'll explain when you get here."

5

Real Faeries

"In all things of nature there is something of the marvelous."
— Aristotle —

The white stucco Spanish Mediterranean building is beautiful, with an ornately decorated cement frieze over the entry. Built in the early 1920s, this is one of the greatest works of architecture in town. Not only does the building house the library, police headquarters, and fire department, but also city hall, which has beautiful paintings and engravings that date from the 1800s to the 1940s. I love browsing the corridors, studying each one. These aren't weird, annoyingly blurry and formless expressionistic art pieces, but landscapes, still lifes, and portraits done in fine detail.

Inside the library, the grand oak reception desk and wooden bookcases welcomed visitors with their chocolate-brown facades. I'd grown too big to sit comfortably at the low tables in the children's section, where I'd once spent so many hot summer days reading. A beautifully painted mural of children playing in local sun-spotted parks wraps around the top of the room, and when I was little, the green marble baseboards reminded me of a fancy kind of indoor grass. The thought still made me smile.

After wandering for a minute, I found an empty out-of-the-way table in the corner—the perfect spot. I sat still in the wooden chair, carefully listening for any more intuitive instruction. Nope, no inner voice telling me to do anything. And then I felt ridiculous that I had even *considered* listening for voices in my head. The stress of finals, the void Val left, and the arrival of Grandma must be getting to me. And what if a voice had asked me to stand in the middle of the library, pat my head with one hand, rub my tummy with the other, and hop on one leg at the same time, would I do that? I needed to get a hold of myself. I was supposed to be studying, so I took out my French textbook.

While keeping an eye out for Lacey, I waited, pretending to read until she entered through the glass-paneled doors. I stood up and waved at her from the small round table. She came over, dropped her backpack on the floor, and leaned on the tabletop towards me.

"How's *the grandmother?*" she whispered, as if my grandma were "The Thing" from the horror movie.

"She seems nice, but . . ." I leaned in even closer, also speaking in a hushed voice, ". . . she believes in *fairies.*"

"A little loony, eh?"

"Maybe. She said she missed 'her little fairy friends' at home and even asked me if I had received their message that she was coming."

"What? Does she think they can e-mail or text or somethin', too?" Lacey smiled big but laughed quietly.

"Maybe," I chuckled. "But I was thinking, what about what we heard under the bridge the other day? The voices said, *'She's coming!'* Do you think those were . . ." I cleared my throat, ". . . *fairies?*"

"What? Naw," Lacey said, sliding back into her chair. "You, if anyone, Ms. Science Diva of Dallas County, should know that fairies don't exist."

"Well, what if we did a little research about them? Just for fun. After all, we're in a library full of information. It will only take a few minutes."

"All right. If you really want to," Lacey said with a shrug.

To prevent potential snoopers from seeing what we were researching, we tucked ourselves, side by side, into a solitary wooden desk upstairs with a nearby computer. But while staring at the empty search box on the screen, I hit a roadblock.

"Should I look under 'folktales?'" I asked Lacey.

"Or maybe 'psychological disorders,'" she replied, rolling her eyes.

"Very funny. I'll just type *F-A-I-R-Y.*" I hit the return button. "Look at that! This can't be right . . . *Fairy Myths and Lore* and *The Guide to All Fairies.* These two books are listed in the *nonfiction* section!"

"I'm confused." Lacey looked at the screen, my face, then back at the screen again. "Fairies are *fictional.*"

"Let's go take a look," I said, jotting down the call numbers on a scrap of paper. I scanned the tall bookshelves. "Here are the 398s—there they are." I grabbed the two books and handed *Fairy Myths and Lore* to Lacey.

"What am I supposed to do with this?" she asked, cocking her head to one side.

"I guess we'll skim through them. See if there's anything interesting. Scientific."

I sat on the floor with *The Guide to All Fairies* and Lacey sat next to me. We read quietly for a few minutes; the only sound was the turning of pages.

"I can't believe it," I said, breaking the silence. I scanned the words again, making sure I hadn't misread. "This book actually has documented accounts of people who claimed to have had 'real' encounters with fairies."

I flipped to the front of the book to see the copyright date. "And this book has been written within the last decade."

"Very interestin'," Lacey said, focused on her book.

"Interestingly ridiculous. What's your book about?" I said, lifting my head to look at her.

"Funky things that people do to get fairies to visit them."

"Hmmm. Sounds pretty strange." I focused back on my book. "I'm not sure I believe all of this, but listen a minute." I pointed to a passage. "There's a bunch of stories about little beings with gossamer wings living in mounds of earth, natural forts of fallen trees, or overgrown wooded places. They're usually described as looking and acting like teensy humans, playing music, and dancing. Many were seen in Ireland or England, but there are detailed accounts from America as well."

"Really? Read one to me." Lacey closed her book, keeping a finger to mark her page.

"'In 1977, a Colorado woman saw a female fairy that was six inches high, with dragonfly wings and long silvery hair, holding a tiny wand with a gleam of starlight on the end. She described the fairy as having the ability to hover like a hummingbird,'" I read. Hummingbird? Oh boy, I'd forgotten to tell Lacey how I had ended up at the library. She was gonna think I'd lost my mind, and I wasn't so sure I hadn't.

"Well, I just read stories about 'fairy rings' made of mushrooms that were mowed down, only to reappear the very next day. '*Within these circles of fungi, fairies dance while tiny fellow onlookers rest upon the surroundin' spotted caps*,'" read Lacey.

"Seriously. Who writes this stuff?"

"My book also says that people believe the best time to see fairies is the first day of each season, Midsummer Eve, May Day, Christmas, full moons, and durin' dusk or dawn."

"I learned about animals in biology that were out only during dusk or dawn, and there was a cool word for it . . . not *nocturnal* since that means 'active during the night,' and not *diurnal,* which means 'active during the day' . . . *crepuscular!* That's it!" I said, loving that one word could convey so much.

Lacey grew more excited, "Oh, and listen to this: '*Fairy-encitin' rituals should be performed faithfully, and with sincerity and humility in your heart because the little garden keepers can see into your soul instantly. If you don't truly believe, or if you don't respect the environment, they know it and will not show themselves.*'"

"Well, maybe that's why we only heard them and didn't see them—we're nonbelievers."

"So you're believin' all of this?"

"That's not what I'm saying." I cleared my throat. "I'm just trying to hypothesize that *if* what we heard were fairies, then maybe that's why we couldn't see them. But I don't believe."

"My book also has a whole mess of rituals for tryin' to see fairies." Lacey was on a roll now. "One suggestion is to 'wash your eyes with the sweat of the stars,' which is actually mornin' dew. Another says a combination of herbs should be gathered and burned upon charcoal blocks. Even teas and wine made of violets, strawberries, and thyme can '*help open the portals of perception if sipped in a fairy-haunted place at midnight'."*

"Fairy-haunted? That's ridiculous. These people are such victims of their own vivid imaginations!" I slammed my book shut. I'd given up believing in anything except for scientifically proven facts at the young age of seven, after an incident that I swore never to think about again. I should have learned from that not to trust any type of bird, be it a hummingbird, mockingbird, or any other feathered creature for that matter. "These may be in the nonfiction section, but I don't think there's any scientific proof here." I put my book back on the shelf. "Why don't more people realize that logic can explain everything? The people in these books are far from logical."

"But still," Lacey said dreamily, "it would be fascinatin' if fairies were real."

"Too bad there's no chance of that!" I took Lacey's book from her lap and slid it next to mine. "We've wasted enough time. Ready to study?"

"Sure," Lacey said, lacking the enthusiasm she'd just had while reading about the silly fairy junk.

We went back to our table and I opened my French book again. But as I struggled to conjugate, my mind kept wandering back to what we'd read.

Stop thinking about that mumbo-jumbo and concentrate on French verbs, Claire!

Lacey opened her French book to the same page. "Compose a sentence for the verb 'to believe,'" she quizzed in her library-voice.

"Okay . . . What about, Croyez-vous dans les fées?"

Ergh! I'd done it again. The translation: "Do you believe in fairies?" I buried my face in my hands.

"Sounds like you've got fairies on the brain!" Lacey snickered.

"It was all so stupid. I mean, what about evidence? None of those books documented that the remains of a fairy had ever been found. Wouldn't something be left behind, like their bones, houses, writing, or clothing?"

"You're right, Claire. Fairies don't exist and that's that."

All of a sudden, a green book flew off a nearby shelf and landed on my foot. "Ouch! Someone must have pushed it through from the other side." I reached down and rubbed my ankle.

Lacey jumped up and ran behind the bookcase to see who had accidentally injured me. A few seconds later, she came back, elbows bent and palms up, "No one's there."

"Well, how could this have . . ." I began, picking the book off the floor. My jaw dropped. "Uh, Lacey, look!"

"Shhh!" the librarian shushed, holding her pointer finger across her lips.

I held the book up to Lacey so she could read the title: *Real Faeries.*

❧ 6 ☙

The Mantis

"Look deep into nature and then you will understand everything better."
—❧ *Albert Einstein* ☙—

The golden lettering gleamed.

Lacey whispered, with a look of complete confusion on her face, "How did a book on fairies, the subject we were just researchin', fly off the shelf and . . . ?"

"I don't know." I scratched my head. "Well, coincidences do happen, and that's what the appearance of this book must amount to—a coincidence."

I took a deep breath. This was certainly too strange to get my mind around. We both sat there in disbelief. "Actually, the title cracks me up: *Real Faeries*. Real?" I crossed my arms in front of me. "Kind of misleading, to use such a term. Definitely false advertising."

"Why didn't we see this book in the e-card catalog?"

"Well, maybe because of how they spell 'faeries.'"

Lacey dragged her chair right next to mine and took the book from my hands. "That's funny. It doesn't have a Dewey decimal number on it anywhere." She flipped it open. The binding was stiff and crackled, as if it had never been read before. "There isn't even a place for the stamped due date inside the front cover."

"Look. The copyright date was last summer, and the author has a PhD in history and science—she's a college science professor." A very intelligent-looking woman by the name of Dr. Cecelia Du Pont, sporting blond hair pulled into a ponytail and modern black-rimmed glasses, looked back at us from the flap. Below her picture was a brief bio.

"Let's check out the Table of Contents," Lacey suggested.

"Good idea." I turned to the front page and a word caught my eye: *mummy*. I found page 22 and we began to read silently to ourselves. The passage seemed so straightforward that I swore I was reading something more clinical than folkloric. My kind of book! The chapter was about a mummified "little person" found in the Matilija Mountains of the United States, and there was an actual photo of it! It was a five-inch shriveled body, preserved like an Egyptian mummy after spending centuries in a bog. The scientists said it was a perfect miniature woman, with stems of preserved cartilage where wings could have been. Testing couldn't tell her age at the time of death, but they knew she was full-grown and not an infant.

Other scientists discarded it as a mutation of nature and refused to recognize her as anything else besides a human, but the fairy-believing scientists, well, they were ecstatic. To them, this discovery was bona fide proof of the existence of fairies.

"This book is actually pretty interesting," I had to admit.

"Let's turn to chapter four. The Table of Contents said it's about a couple of kids who discovered somethin.'"

"Sounds cool." After finding chapter four, we read how two young boys were playing in an old countryside church ruin in Ireland and found an airtight box below a loose floorboard. Inside the rustic container , they found a bunch of old seeds. At first, the children planned to plant the seeds to see if they would still grow, but their wise parents thought the box and its contents might interest a museum due to its antique nature.

They contacted a local professor who taught art history at a nearby university. He put the "seeds" under a microscope and discovered they were really tiny shoes made out of woven grass threads! Here, once again, were photographs, only this time they were blown-up images from a powerful microscope. The craftsmanship was amazing! The shoes were carefully done in a minuscule basket weave.

In that same box were also some small, thin sticks, which under careful scrutiny turned out to be tiny musical pipes made out of mouse skin! Again, an enlarged photo was included, but this time it also had the comparison photo of a recorder, like the one I'd learned to play in third grade.

"Fairy flutes? Lordy, how could this be?" said Lacey, puzzled.

"I don't know, but I think we should look up these so-called experts on the Internet and research their background."

We went back to the computer and looked up several of them, but try as we might to bust—*debunk*—each person's expertise, all of them seemed to be legitimate archeologists, professors, or anthropologists.

All of a sudden, Lacey jumped to her feet. "My goodness, Claire. Look at the time!"

"I should have been home twenty minutes ago. We'd better go." We quickly gathered our schoolbooks and pushed in our chairs. Picking up the *Real Faeries* book, I hesitated. "What should we do with this? Put it back on the shelf?"

"Sure, I guess."

I put it back onto the bookcase, and when I turned my back, *plunck!* The book fell on the floor again. I picked it up and put it back, and once more, the book fell by my feet.

My voice shook a little. "Ah, Lacey, did you see that? The book won't stay where I put it."

"Maybe there's somethin' wrong with the shelf. Stick it somewhere else." She was bouncing from foot to foot now. "And hurry up! We gotta go."

"I'll just leave it on the table and let the librarian deal with it." I set it down flat and reached for my book bag on the floor when *Real Faeries* dropped from the table right into my bag. "Oh my God! Did you see *that?*"

"Uh huh," was all Lacey could get out, frozen and awestruck.

My cell phone began to vibrate and I saw the caller was Mom. She was probably really mad that I wasn't home yet. I quickly pushed the book deeper into my bag, zipped it up, and rushed toward the exit. Lacey gave me a funny look.

"Well, it's not a catalogued library book, anyway. It obviously wants me to take it home with me," I said, knowing full well my logic was completely fuzzy. Today, I thought a hummingbird was leading me somewhere on purpose, and now I was acting as if a book had the ability to command that I take it home. I guess I'm more stressed than I thought.

Lacey and I walked briskly down the sidewalk and parted ways at the corner. I couldn't stop thinking about all of the strange things that had been happening lately. I also went over and over what I'd read.

Those seemingly sane, rational, scholarly people were fairy believers. Science and fantasy had met somehow. But still, my gut feeling told me that there was a catch to these stories. There just had to be.

As I arrived on our back stoop, I felt another peculiar wind pick up, similar to the one beneath the bridge.

"Dang it!" I threw my arms up in a vain attempt to capture a pile of loose papers as they blew right out of my book bag.

I had zipped it up. I know I did!

After one more strong gust—which spread my work even farther across the side yard—the air went still again.

Gathering my notes and sketches from the ground, beneath bushes, and underneath a nearby car, I saw that one paper had gotten stuck on a branch near the top of the back door. Stretching as I reached up, I grabbed the paper, and behind the sketch, I discovered something surprising.

A green creature was standing still upon the branch, watching me with an alien-like glare. It had an equilaterally triangular head with large eyes. Fine spikes lined its long, bendy arms. Its green body had wavering stripes of brown along the shell of its back, contrasting beautifully with the burgundy leaves of the Japanese maple tree.

A praying mantis!

I shoved my papers into my pack, ran to the shed, and retrieved a plastic peanut butter jar that I had previously washed out and poked holes in for such a creature-catching emergency.

Carefully grasping its thorax between my fingers, I lowered it into the jar. It flipped around and beat its paper-like wings, but settled down after a minute. Gingerly, I added a small branch of the tree with a giant, perfect leaf sprouting from it, then I tightened the lid and looked at my specimen more closely.

What an amazing creature of nature! I couldn't wait to draw it!

"There you are. You're half an hour late for dinner," Mom complained through the screen door, arms folded. "Go wash up and make it quick."

She held open the door for me and I dashed in, hiding the jar beneath my arm. Mom wouldn't like me bringing a bug in the house. "I promise I'll be back in a jiffy!" I liked the word jiffy because, in the world of electronics, it's actually a measured amount of time, one-sixtieth of a second—though it took me longer than that to even say the word.

Inside my room, I put the jar on my dresser and stared at the mantis.

"I promise I'll only keep you long enough to get some good sketches," I told it. "I'll definitely let you go in the morning."

I washed my hands and went down to dinner. Upon entering the kitchen, my nervous feeling returned.

"Where is everybody? I thought you'd all be waiting for me." I was relieved to have a few minutes alone with Mom.

"Dad's taking a phone call. Work. And I'm going up to get your grandmother in a minute." Mom hummed as she set a fork at each place on the table.

"Mom, there are a couple of things I've been wondering about."

"Ask away."

"Are you sure that . . . is Grandma, well, OK . . . like, in her mind?" I began to fill the glasses with water from the pitcher.

"Her mind seems pretty sharp to me. Her short-term and long-term memory are both quite good." Mom set the salad on the table and tossed it several times with a pair of tongs. "Any other questions before I go get Grandma?"

"Well, you work full-time. How can you take care of her and go to work?"

Mom set the tongs down and absent-mindedly wiped her hands on the red floral apron tied around her waist. "I'm figuring that out with my boss, but it looks like I'll be taking a temporary leave of absence."

"For how long?"

"I'm not sure," she said. "Grandma may be here a week, a month, or a year, for all we know. We'll just have to see."

She still may be living here in a *year from now?* It was gonna be difficult to swallow my food tonight with the sudden development of this golf ball–sized lump in my throat.

"Anything else?" Mom headed toward the door.

I could only shake my head.

"Be right back." Mom dashed out of the room.

I plunked down in a chair and rested my head in my arms on the table. All I wanted to do was get through this meal tonight. Then footsteps came from the direction of the den. Dad. I sat up and he kissed my head before sitting next to me. His usual place.

A minute later, I heard the shuffling of feet. Mom entered the room holding my grandma's right arm, leading her to a chair. Grandma still had on her sequin top, sparkling in the overhead light, and she'd put on her pink lipstick again. "Honestly, Amy, I can still walk," she was saying.

"I know, but I just don't want you to fall going down the stairs." Mom let go and pulled out a chair. "You sit here, next to Claire, Mama."

But that's Mom's spot! I thought surely she'd sit in Val's old seat across from me, but no. We were right next to each other.

"I'd love to sit by Clairy. We're already getting to know each other better," said Grandma, with a beaming smile.

I politely smiled back.

Mom sat and started passing around the food. "Now, help your grandmother. Some of these bowls are heavy." Handing me the mashed potatoes, she asked, "So, Claire, what did you do today?"

"I met Lacey at the library. To study."

"I thought you were going to her house," said Mom.

"Ah . . . change of plans." What if I told the truth, that a hummingbird led me to the library instead? They'd all think I was nuts!

"Who's Lacey?" Grandma asked.

"She's my best friend."

"Oh, I had a wonderful best friend when I was your age. Her name was Anna," said Grandma. But then, the elderly woman leaned over to me and whispered, "Her fairy name was Glorianna."

"Fairy name? Glory Anna?" I asked, looking over to see if my parents had heard. Nope. They were deep in their own conversation.

"Well, I was the only one who called her Glorianna, really. Glorianna, Queen of the Fairies! I was already born with a fairy name, since Faye actually means *fairy*, and it just wouldn't be fair if my dear, kindred spirit didn't have one too."

Our conversation wasn't off to a good start, and I'd already heard enough. I just wanted to stand up and walk out, but I knew I had to stay. Then I got an idea. I decided to take the opportunity to poke a hole in her fairy references.

"There are no such things as fairies and, therefore, no Queen of the Fairies either." Reality check!

Without missing a beat, my grandmother's eyes glimmered from behind their creased façade as she asked, "Do you like to read, dear Claire?"

"Oh, Claire loves to read, don't you, kiddo?" Dad chimed in.

Now my parents were listening, when the conversation was normal.

"Of course. If you can read, you can learn about anything. Reading is an important skill. I read a lot. It's an important part of my day."

"Then look up *The Faerie Queen*, spelled f-a-e-r-i-e, by Edmund Spencer and tell me what you think. Queen Glorianna and all of her friends are mentioned," Grandma said. "I think you'd enjoy it."

"It's a fine piece of Victorian literature," Mom added.

"Surely this piece you mention is fictional, right?" I asked.

"Well, fiction often comes from truth." Grandma winked.

"So are you saying that fairies are *real?*" I said, glancing over to my parents. It was time for them to see how cuckoo she was. "Besides, I observe nature every day when I draw, sometimes for hours on end, and I've never seen one."

"Now Claire, Grandma's not saying . . ." Mom began.

Grandma interrupted, "An English writer, Hazlitt, once said, 'We do not see nature with our eyes but with our understanding and our hearts.' I think he was very wise."

"What a lovely quote, Mama," said Mom. Dad nodded in agreement.

I'd been outwitted by this eighty-seven-year-old again!

Dinner went on with small talk about Dad's work and Mom's plans now that she had decided to take a hiatus from her job and stay at home full-time for a while.

"I'll help you landscape the backyard," Grandma said. "It looks pretty dreary out there now, if you don't mind me saying so. You used to send me photos of such magnificent flowers."

Mom frowned. "As soon as Val left, we quit watering and weeding it."

It was true—as if we weren't allowed to have such a beautiful place while Val was in such a horrible one.

Once the meal had ended, Grandma walked stiffly but steadily to sit on the couch in the other room while Mom made coffee and cleaned up. Dad went into his study to watch sports highlights on television.

"Go and keep your grandmother company." Mom nodded in the direction of the living room.

"I have finals and I really need to go study." The truth was, I was afraid of what she'd say to me while we were alone.

"Come on, just visit for a few minutes while I finish." Mom turned and started drying a pot that was upside down on the counter. "Besides, didn't you and Lacey study at the library today?"

Oh, if she only knew that we looked up fairies all afternoon instead! But I knew I had no choice in the matter, so I sauntered in to join Grandma.

"Oh, dearest Clairy, come sit by me." She tapped her old, bent hand on the cushion. "I want to talk to you."

Uh-oh.

"I can tell that you don't believe in fairies yet, and that will take some time, but I want to ask you a favor." Don't believe *yet*? She's not gonna let this thing go!

"Okay," I said, sitting on the edge of the couch, ready to leave the second Mom entered the room.

"Could we keep our fairy discussions just between the two of us?"

"Well, Mom and Dad should know . . . ah, *learn* about them too, don't you think?" They needed to realize how zany she was.

"They don't understand my life with the fairies. It would be detrimental to your fairy education if they were involved right now." She paused a long time before adding, "Besides, they might ruin everything."

What did she mean by that? Did she really have some secret plan? Or maybe she was afraid my parents would find out that she was senile and not let her stay with us. I needed to do further research. "So do you really think fairies exist?"

"They absolutely do. I have known that nearly all of my life. I had three of the most remarkable fairy encounters."

"But if they are real, wouldn't a lot more people in the world have seen them?" I felt like we were two arguing kindergarteners.

Grandma waved it off. "That's easy to explain. Fairies only show themselves to true believers."

"Science is the only way for seemingly mysterious incidents to be explained. If science can't back something up, it doesn't exist." I tried to sound convincing, but what I had read about the fairy artifacts, and the educated professors that backed them up, popped into my head and made me feel surprisingly unsure of myself.

"Well, Anna and I both saw them," said Grandma. "If two people can see something, couldn't that make it real?"

I thought about that. Both Lacey and I had heard the voices under the bridge.

"How do you know she wasn't just saying that to make you happy? People do that. And, well, if you believe in fairies, why doesn't my mother? Didn't you tell her about them so that she could grow up believing, too?"

"It had been made abundantly clear to me that it wasn't proper for a young mother to teach her children such things. I was told—well, commanded really—to stop believing in them, although that could never happen after what I experienced. I just quit *noticing* them . . . for a while, until I was in a place in my life where I was with my husband living among the flowers."

Grandma stopped a minute to smooth her white linen pants, then continued. "Nonetheless, the fair ones have been around me, and are around all of us, the whole time. It wasn't until I was in England that I could start actively believing again . . . but when they recently told me that I only had a few more months to live, I knew I had to leave them." A sense of urgency was in her voice. "It's crucial that I share all I can about the fairies with you, Claire. That's why I'm here."

I wasn't sure what to make of all this. "There is really no way there are fairies," I said under my breath.

Grandma took a long look at me. "At least, dear Clairy, let me tell you more. Someone in our family needs to know about them. From the day you came to visit me at age six, I knew you were the one."

"I'm not so sure . . ."

"Besides, your generation is so much more open to uncharted ideas than mine was." She put both hands on her knees, a serious look in her eyes. "Most importantly, though, the fairies can help you, even in this modern and crazy world. That's the problem, you know. The world got hectic so fewer people believed, and so we are losing touch with nature's powerful ability to heal!" There was definite conviction in the old woman's voice.

I guess it wouldn't hurt just to listen. "All right. I'll hear you out."

"I hope you ladies are enjoying your time catching up. Here's your coffee, Mama," Mom said, entering the room and setting the steaming cup on the coffee table. "Claire, you can go and study now, if you'd like."

I suddenly remembered the praying mantis I had waiting for me. "Yeah, sure. I should go now."

"It's been lovely talking to you, Clairy. Perhaps you'll have tea with me tomorrow?" Grandma said, eyes twinkling.

"Sure. Sounds like a plan. Night." I went quickly up to my room to check on my little green friend.

It was nearing 8:30 and the house was dim. As I approached my bedroom door, I noticed a green glow illuminating the gap beneath it and the floor. What did I leave on in there? My computer? I opened the door to see, and boom, out went the green light. The strange thing was that my computer wasn't on, nor were any of the lights in my room. And for a millisecond, I could have sworn the glow was coming from inside the praying mantis jar.

7

Tea For Two

"I am beginning to learn that it is the sweet, simple things of life which are the real ones after all."
— *Laura Ingalls Wilder*

"Oh, great. I found a radioactive praying mantis," I joked out loud.

I stood by the light switch and flipped it on. Everything looked normal. I turned the light off again and waited in the dark for at least five minutes, but nothing glowed or anything. All of the crazy fairy talk my grandmother had been doing must have been getting to me.

Or maybe there are praying mantids that glow, like fireflies. I figured I should check it out. So, I logged onto my computer to do a little research.

I found out that the term mantis was Greek for prophet or clairvoyant, which made sense because they always look as though they're praying. And although there was no information about any that glow like a glowworm, I did find out that mantids ate things like crickets and moths, and captured their prey by going through a special ritual.

A ritual, eh? That's something I'd like to see.

Using an empty bedside water cup, it didn't take more than a moment to capture a moth on my window. A quick slide of paper between the pane and the rim of the cup had the unsuspecting moth fluttering inside. Then I let it go in the peanut butter jar, where my insect friend was hanging out, to watch what happened. The mantis waited patiently for its victim to come closer, swaying back and forth like a leaf in the breeze, its prey not suspecting a thing. Then suddenly, the creature's bent arms snapped straight out, grabbed the moth, and devoured it headfirst.

Awesome!

Wanting to learn more, I wheeled around my desk chair and steered it with my feet back toward the screen of my computer. The article said that young mantids shed their exoskeleton many times before living their full lives, becoming bigger and stronger each time, but remaining the same individual in look and general character. It made me wonder . . .

A person going through change in his or her life is so often compared to the metamorphosis of butterflies. But butterflies go through only one great transformation in a lifetime, which takes the original being and alters it into an extremely different one, in character and looks—from a sluggish, furry worm to a beautiful and graceful winged insect.

But for humans, our experiences don't change us into completely new beings.

More realistically, people go through many changes in one lifetime:

they remain the same in appearance and basic personal traits, but become a newer version of themselves. So, wasn't it more accurate to say that people go through a series of metaphoric shedding of skin due to growth? Isn't a human more like the mantis?

Therefore, the butterfly analogy didn't work for me anymore. Another myth busted! I grinned, proud of my discovery. But I knew I'd have to find more specimens to be sure—no true scientist bases their conclusions on one trial—since the beauty of science was in comparisons.

My fifth-grade teacher, Mrs. Shay (whose first name was Cher, like the singer, which always made the students laugh when they heard someone say it), inspired my need for "comparisons."

Patting down her puffy black hair with one plump hand, Mrs. Shay would always say, "Observation is how great ideas, inventions, and scientific discoveries come to be."

"Everyone," she said, passing around stacks of blank paper, "I'm handing you each an ordinary peanut, still in its shell. Look at your peanut carefully, then I want y'all to sketch every little detail of your peanut on your piece of paper."

Well, drawing was right up my alley, so I sketched it the best I could.

"Now, I'm coming around to collect your peanuts." Mrs. Shay put them all in the same brown paper bag, and gave it a shake.

"I named mine Fred," said Ed, a boy in my class. "Goodbye forever, Fred!"

"Is it goodbye forever to your peanut friend? Maybe not." Mrs. Shay then dumped the bag of nuts on her desk. "Using your sketches and observations, come find your peanut!"

For a lot of my classmates, finding their peanut friend wasn't easy.

"Hey, that's mine!" argued Veronica, trying to pry one from Steven's fingers.

"No, mine had a scar across the top. See?" Steven showed her his drawing.

Ed, on the other hand, picked up each one, saying, "Fred, is that you?" His drawing was only an outline and some dots—no real details.

My sketching skills didn't let me down, and after less than a minute, I found mine.

Once things settled down, Mrs. Shay said, "Some of you were very good at observing and recording what you saw. Others aren't sure if they have the same exact peanut they started with or not. The point of this exercise is the importance of true observation."

I never forgot it, and never again took for granted that two items that looked the same at first were exactly identical. Each was uniquely different, and I loved discovering how.

Of course, my mom would argue that it was also because of Mrs. Shay that I became such a slow shopper. It once took me forty minutes to find the best rainbow twisted lollipop at the Texas State Fair in a lineup of four-dozen. Sure, I'd eventually lick all the lines away, but I was happier knowing that I was licking the prettiest one.

So, I sketched my little green extraterrestrial for a while, and then studied physics until I was tired.

Before going to bed, I opened my bedroom window and let in the warm air that hummed with insect wings. The wafting warmth carried the promise of summer vacation beginning. How I longed for that free feeling of having no school to rush off to in the morning; no pressure to get my homework done at night. It always took about a week for that momentary panic of needing to work on something for school to fade away completely.

I thought about how Grandma had asked to keep our fairy discussions just between the two of us. Weird. I was interested to hear her side, but my plan was to argue the logical, scientific side. I felt embarrassed about the research I'd done with Lacey at the library. We should have been studying for our exams instead of wasting our valuable time. How silly to even begin to believe what those so-called scientists had to say.

I got up, took the green book out of my book bag, and put it on my bookshelf. I half expected it to jump to the floor like it had at the library, but it stayed put. It would have to be disposed of somehow, or snuck back to the library. I'd figure out what to do with it later, but I didn't need to be carrying it around.

Just to the right of where I had slid in the book, the empty journal that had mysteriously arrived in the mail on my last birthday caught my eye. The return address on the package was a stationery company in Colorado, and there was a card enclosed that said "To Claire," but the card wasn't signed by anyone. For nearly six months, it sat on my bookshelf collecting dust.

It seemed like a shame not to write some of my family history down, with everything my grandmother told me about the founding of Highland Park and the building of this house. Knowing I'd forget the details if I didn't jot them down right away, I pulled the pink and green striped journal down, opened its cloth cover, and began to write.

I imagined the pecan trees, purchased to supply the town with the best pecan pies around, baked by my great-grandmother, and how wonderful they must have smelled browning in the oven downstairs. Maybe the trees weren't such bad vegetation after all. Trying to remember everything made me even more tired, so I went to bed, my mind still going even after I turned off the lights and snuggled under my covers.

I'd need to talk with my grandmother again to get more family history.

I rolled on my side and closed my eyes.

Please, praying mantis, live through the night.

I awoke early the next morning and looked in the jar. The praying mantis was still alive! I was anxious to take it down to the creek as soon as possible.

I dressed quickly, grabbed the jar, and crept out of the house. The streets were quiet on that early Wednesday morning; the only sounds were the chattering of squirrels and birds and my feet hitting the pavement. I arrived at the edge of the creek, where three white-flowered dogwood trees grew with lots of thick azalea bushes at their bases. Those azaleas were magnificent in their prime blooming season—shiny green leaves difficult to see among the voluminous fuchsia and white blossoms.

After unscrewing the lid, I tilted the jar over a thick growth of foliage. Slowly, the mantis picked its way down the Japanese maple branch in the jar before finally stepping warily out into the world. As I watched it climb onto an azalea leaf, a wave of relief washed over me.

I emptied the jar in preparation for the next nature critter I found, pulling out the Japanese maple twig with its large leaf still attached. There were scratch marks on the leaf. Did the praying mantis do this? The leaf was perfect when I'd put it in yesterday. I studied the marks. No way! It couldn't be, could it?

The leaf scrapes spelled out these words: "YOU ARE READY."

Ready? Ready for what?

I stared at the leaf in total disbelief. Praying mantids can't write! And who would have snuck into my room while I was asleep and written that? Not my mom or dad. Would Grandma? I put the leaf sprig back in the jar and screwed on the lid. I wasn't quite sure what I was going to do with it, but I needed to save the evidence.

I returned to the house and got ready for school. I was ready for my day of finals.

I had studied and so I did the best I could on each test, but my mind kept wandering to the glowing mantis and the writing on the leaf. I couldn't come up with one single logical reason for it, other than a possibly senile grandmother who wanted me to get a message, which didn't make any sense. She could just tell me.

Lacey had a different schedule that day, so I didn't get to share my strange experience with her. I ended up going straight home and just vegging out in my room, but not for very long. At four o'clock, there was a knock on my bedroom door.

"Hey, Mom." She had a rattling tray full of hot tea and biscuits in her hand.

"Hi, Claire. It's time for your teatime with Grandma," she said cheerily.

"What are you doing with the tea up here? I thought British people have it in the parlor." I paused. "Do we even have a parlor?"

Mom laughed. "Our living room would be the closest thing, but Grandma has requested tea in her room today."

Of course she did. She wanted to discuss her crazy ideas about fairies being real with me, alone.

Mom shoved the tipsy tray into my hands and disappeared down the stairs.

Great. I was on my own, I guess. I was a little nervous.

I reluctantly walked to the door of the guest room. I took a deep breath. Balancing the tray in one hand, I turned the knob as the teacups clinked with the shaking of my hands. I entered, noticing the dust specks floating in the flow of sunshine that was coming through the window.

The room was tidy and bright, which made me feel surprisingly welcome. There, in the overstuffed armchair in the corner, was my grandmother, smiling vibrantly. She was dressed in jeans and a long sleeve, fitted t-shirt decorated with giant yellow roses that showed how frail her body was. She looked timid and sweet; certainly nothing to be frightened of.

I caught a glimpse of myself in the dresser mirror and noticed the sour look on my face. I tried to smile. Surely Grandma saw the adjustment, but she kept on grinning.

"In England, we enjoy tea every afternoon. I'm glad you're joining me," she announced.

I set the tray on the footstool in front of her, studying what was on it. "But there's only one cup." I dragged the vanity stool closer and sat down.

"Oh, it's okay, dearie. You'll probably enjoy a saucer of tea more." The old woman pointed her bony finger at me. "It's like a saucer of milk for a kitten, and in fact a kitten would probably like it better: milk with a bit of an Earl Grey kicker."

Her old hands shook as she set the teacup aside, filled the bone china saucer until it was nearly brimming with cream, and then added a big splash of tea.

"Got a sweet tooth?"

"Oh, no thank you." I actually loved sugar in my tea, but I didn't want to draw things out any longer than necessary. She added one cube anyway.

Stirring the mixture with a spoon, she held it out to me, her quivering hands nearly tipping it. Quickly, I grabbed the tilting saucer and saved it from spilling onto the carpet.

"Well, taste it . . ." Grandma said with a thin-lipped smile.

I was now obligated to put the dish to my lips and sip. I had to admit that the richness of the cream tasted delicious, and the tea gave it a pleasingly smoky flavor.

"Good, isn't it? When I was in Japan, everyone picked up their bowls to drink their soup. No one even offered you a spoon. What you are doing reminds me of that—and by the way, in Japan, the louder the slurp, the more flattered the chef is. Slurping means that you liked it. Now let me hear you!"

I could feel my face turn crimson. But I wanted to move things along, so I obliged, slurping more loudly than intended.

My grandmother laughed, "Sounds like you like it quite a bit!"

She gestured toward the vanity mirror. I looked at my reflection and saw that I'd managed to get a bunch of white froth on my upper lip, just like in those "Got milk?" ads. And though I tried to restrain myself, I had to laugh, too. I wiped the cream off with the back of my hand.

"That's the first genuine smile you've given me since I got here, but it was worth the wait," said Grandma. "What a lovely girl."

Embarrassed, I changed the subject. "Well, what did you want to talk about?"

"Hmmm." Her eyes rolled up toward the ceiling. "Where shall we start?"

"Oh! I wanted to show you something." I jumped to my feet. "Can you wait a minute while I run and get it?"

"I sure can."

"Great. I'll be right back." I dashed to my room to get the leaf in the jar, and then returned to the guest room. "I found a praying mantis yesterday."

"Magnificent insects, aren't they?"

"Yes, and this one was more remarkable than most."

"Is there one inside of that jar?"

"Not anymore." I couldn't believe what I was about to say next. "It may have scratched a message on this leaf while it was in the jar, though." Or more like someone snuck into my room and did it!

"Let me take a look," she said, without flinching. I unscrewed the jar lid, pulled out the twig, and handed it to her. "YOU ARE READY," she read out loud. "Hmmm . . . very interesting." She leaned forward, studying it.

Okay, Grandma. Time to 'fess up.

"I'm positive that the leaf had no scratches on it when I put it in the jar with the mantis, and in the morning when I let the insect go, I found the message."

Grandma looked serious as she asked, "Was there anything else unusual about this mantis?"

"Actually, when I went to check on it after dinner, I thought I saw it . . ." Am I really going to say it? "Glowing."

"Well, that makes perfect sense," she replied with confidence.

"It does?"

"Absolutely. The praying mantis was enchanted."

"Enchanted?"

"Yes, the praying mantis was a messenger from the fairies. Apparently the fair ones are planning something big for you." She handed the leaf back to me.

Of course she'd think that. What else had I expected her to say?

"But you have much to learn before that special day comes. We should begin!" She leaned back in her chair and put a hand on each of its arms. "I think I'll start by telling you more about Anna. Now sit down, child."

I didn't know what to say, so I decided just to listen. I sat back down on the vanity chair.

"Anna was small for her age, with brown hair, and the bluest eyes you've ever seen." Grandma looked across the room at the window while speaking, as if seeing ghosts pass by the glass. "We met in grammar school, and back then, communicating with fairies was all the rage . . ."

8

Glorianna

"A rustle in the wind reminds us a fairy is near."
—❧ *Unknown* ❧—

"Spiritual beliefs started in the mid-1800s," Grandma began, "when three sisters—let's see, their last name was . . . Fox. That's right, the three little Foxes. They lived in New York and said they communicated with spirits by clapping their hands. The way the spirits conversed back was by rapping upon the doors and walls. People actually witnessed the girls communicating with 'the other world' in this way, often through séances they held at their home."

She turned her attention to me.

"This helped begin a movement called 'spiritualism.' Many of the immigrants who came to America back then held similar beliefs in spirits, so they also had a hand in influencing the nation. But as years progressed, scientists began discovering many new things. The world was more and more exposed to new scientific explanations. The line between science and spiritualism became quite blurry. People didn't know what to believe."

"So, science eventually proved this spiritualism was phony . . . a *farce,* right?" I asked.

"No, quite the contrary. Science made people more confused than ever. Was there another realm where spirits dwelled that was about to be discovered? No one was sure. Science certainly didn't prove that it *didn't* exist. People had to decide for themselves. I chose to believe there was a fairy realm based on the fact that nature is so inexplicably amazing. Growing and tending flowers, trees, and animals is too big of a job for God alone. He needed helpers! But not everyone believed as I did, especially my parents' generation."

"I guess you were an independent thinker," I said.

"I'd like to think I was, and still am." She gave me a wink. "Why go with what is forced upon you as the truth? Even if you are among the few who believe differently, it doesn't necessarily mean that your truth isn't right."

Grandma now looked right in my eyes as she spoke. "Life has so many unexplained miracles, even today, that the most skeptical soul must puzzle over the phenomena they witness. Being open to recognizing small moments of wonder, *epiphanies,* is the key to happiness."

How could this seemingly meek woman be so insightful? So well-spoken?

I felt a bit of admiration start to grow.

"With science being such a big deal back then, why did people still believe fairies existed?" I asked.

"Well, I can think of a reason to support each side of the 'science versus spirituality' argument in the early 1900s. For example, when

I was about eight years old, two girls, ages ten and sixteen, photographed some fairies in England-"

"The Cottingley fairy story!" I blurted out.

Yikes, I had just tipped my hand about my own fairy research.

"I . . . just read about them in . . . some silly book once," I added.

"Why, yes! Sir Arthur Conan Doyle, a very famous writer of the time-"

"The one who wrote the Sherlock Holmes books?" I interrupted.

"Yes. He showed an interest in what they'd found, which led to a booming public awareness of fairies. He even wrote a book about them, *The Coming of the Fairies*. I'll never forget seeing a copy of the photograph of Frances Griffin in a magazine with four dancing fairies in front of her! This was a time long before computers or photo retouching, so you could only believe it was real."

"I've seen that photo before." It was in one of the books that I had found at the library.

"Didn't you think the fairies, holding flowers and dancing, were magnificently beautiful? I remember thinking that no human could have created such amazing little ones—and there were no strings or wires to be seen. Although many decades later they were found out to be fake photos after all, to me, that didn't mean there still weren't *real* ones. The fairy frenzy started by those girls caused people to go outside and try hard to see the wee ones. It made people truly believe, and you know what? People actually <u>did</u> see them!"

"Humph," was all I managed.

"Their existence was something real, I knew it in my bones," she continued, "so I set out to discover authentic ones myself, and once I saw my first real fairy, I knew they were indeed fake photographs taken in Cottingley. They look nothing like those drawn fairies posed upon leaves."

"You've seen a real fairy before?" I asked, accentuating the doubt in my voice.

"Oh, yes. Believe me, at first I thought it was difficult to do. Then, I realized how to see them quite easily." She leaned closer to me. "You must have a strong desire and an open mind, beyond your subconscious. You have to truly, *truly* believe. No doubts casting shadows! With your psyche wide open—while showing respect for them and nature—you will be granted the gift of being able to see fairies." She tapped her chest three times with her right hand. "But you also must listen with your heart. They have messages for you and powers to share that are magnificent." She settled back into her chair again.

"And what about the people who believed in *science* back then?" I wanted to hear my grandmother's explanation of the other side of the argument, as promised.

"Well, in 1925 there was the Scopes Monkey Trial. You learned about it in school, I'll bet."

I nodded.

"It certainly signified the debate between science and spirituality, the argument over whether evolution or creation should be taught in public schools. The clash was between the older generations of creationists and the younger generation of new thinkers. Even if you were a solid believer in God, scientists like Darwin brought information to the world that was difficult to ignore.

"Based on my personal experience with fairies, let me tell you the truth. There's a tangible spiritual world that is close at hand, but we've moved far away from it in today's beliefs. Just see a fairy yourself; you'll know what I am saying."

I impulsively said, "Oh, I don't plan on trying to see . . ."

But the aged woman had an ember in her eye, and like a locomotive not wanting to stop at its destination, she steamrolled me. "Those Cottingley girls were excellent artists. You have to appreciate how skillfully they drew, cut out, and posed those fairies. They not only encouraged my belief in fair ones, but inspired me to become an artist. They piqued my interest in England as well.

"Anna believed too, and together we set out to see them. Ah, to be thirteen again. Those were good days without much responsibility. Back then, turning sixteen made you old enough for marriage. Anna and I wanted to spend as much time as possible being young girls, out among the flowers."

I gasped. If this was 1925, I'd only have three more years of independence left!

"We'd study anything written about the enchantment of the little folk," Grandma went on, "but mostly focused on learning how to attract them to us. Often, we'd be outside performing some new ritual, thinking it was surely the one, *the* ceremony that would make them visible to us."

She shook her head from side to side. "I don't think there were any other girls in the world that devoted so much time, thought, and energy to attracting fairies."

"How did you attract them?"

"Well, for instance, we used a plate of butter as an offering at the base of an old oak tree, down by Turtle Creek, every Sunday before church. We recited poems and sang songs—all part of our fairy enticing ceremony."

"Can you remember one of your traditional chants?"

"Oh, yes, I'm sure I can. Let's see." She cleared her throat before reciting:

Little folk, little folk, we are here to please thee—

with a treat and a dance, all we ask is to see thee!

"Okay." She chuckled a bit to herself. "That may not have been the best rhyme, but we chanted and danced anyway."

"Did you tell people what you were doing?"

"Oh, no, especially never any adults. The adults were too busy anyway. They never noticed what made the natural world so amazing; the beauty of a dragonfly when it landed on a reed, its rainbow-bubble wings shining in the sun. There was no way they'd be able to take a moment to open up their hearts and see the fair ones. Besides, if they saw one, their beliefs would have to change, which would cause them to have to rethink *everything,* and people aren't very open to change, generally speaking."

Crossing her arms, my grandmother's face turned serious when she said: "I can feel there has been a change in this family, since your brother left for the war. Change can be hard. You have to trust that everything will be okay, and that seeking the fairies' help to soothe your fears is the first step."

"So are you saying we'd all be better off wandering around looking for fairies every day?" My skepticism was crystal clear in my voice. What did she know about my family anyway, after never having been around?

She scooted to the very edge of her chair and got right in my face. "Claire, every day holds the possibility of a miracle."

I turned my head to get out of her gaze and tried to block out the words, but they lingered in the air and seeped into my mind until I really heard them.

Every day holds the possibility of a miracle.

Every day I hoped that Val would surprise me and show up on the doorstep. I *had* to believe in miracles, didn't I? I realized that I couldn't argue with a statement like that.

"I need you to promise me two things and then I will beg your pardon for a while. This old body needs to rest," she said, standing up and moving to sit down on her bed. "First, promise me that you'll come back tomorrow at the same time, four o'clock, for tea again. I haven't even begun to tell you all that you need to know."

"Okay, I will." I had a lot of unanswered questions. "The second thing?"

"The fairies are asking for ladyfingers, you know, the dessert. Please bring me some."

"What? I don't know . . ." I'd never heard of such a thing before, but just as I was about to ask for further explanation, the old woman laid down on her bed, closed her eyes, and fell asleep.

Apparently our visit was over.

Just when I stepped out into the hall, tea tray in hand, Mom called from downstairs. "Claire?"

"Yes, Mother?"

"I need you for a minute."

I found my mom in the kitchen making homemade biscuits.

"What did you want to see me about?" The tray rattled as I set on the counter.

"Did you use a pound of butter? Perhaps in one of your science experiments?"

"No, I didn't use any butter." The fact that my mom assumed I had used it for a science experiment made me smile. Other mothers may have assumed their daughters had baked cookies, but she was right, a science experiment would be more likely for me.

Then, I remembered my aunt saying that my grandmother had been "sneaking into the kitchen in the middle of the night to get butter and sugar, explaining that it would entice the fairies to visit her."

Was Grandma stealing the butter at my house now too?

"I could have sworn that I bought a brand-new box just two days ago," Mom said, scratching her head. "Well, be a dear and go to the store to pick some up."

It was the first day in a long time that the weather had reached over 90 degrees, and it was quite humid. As I walked to the store, I passed the grand houses on Beverly Drive, their enormous windows allowing me to gaze through and see families enjoying their air-cooled rooms. The temperature made me want to run to the creek and sketch. Yep, summer was beckoning me. I'll join you soon, summer! Soon!

The chilly grocery store was a welcome relief from the heat—even cooler was the open refrigerated section on the back wall, where I grabbed a yellow box of butter. Ah!

I figured that I might as well fulfill Grandma's request while I was here too. Nearby was a sign that listed "cookies" on an aisle. I turned down the row, passed the boxes of crackers, and found the rows of sweets.

Let's see . . . ladyfingers, ladyfingers. I scanned the shelves. The only package with an "L" was Lorna Doons.

Not right. Darn it! I'll have to track down an employee and ask for assistance. Great. Every teenager's dream.

"Excuse me," I said, tapping the shoulder of someone dressed in the standard green apron and white collared shirt, with a black pen behind his ear. He was sitting on a blue plastic crate, scanning items on a shelf with a beeping machine that was shaped like a bulky gun.

"How can I help you?" He swiveled around.

I lost total control of my jaw. Oh my God—it was the cute guy from my porch!

9

A Boy and Ladyfingers

"Just living is not enough . . . one must have sunshine, freedom, and a little flower."
— *Hans Christian Anderson*

I completely panicked. Here I was—a nerdy girl who froze like Frosty around people of the opposite sex!

"I . . . I . . . need help . . . finding something." I could barely talk! And though I wasn't one to get all "gaga" over anything, especially a boy, his handsome face made me feel like jelly inside. And my heart was beating in a way I'd never felt before, which made me feel lightheaded.

"Sure. Let me see if I can guess—you've got butter in your hand. You must be . . . looking for the sugar?" His blue eyes twinkled.

"No," I managed, a little bothered. He had to guess *sugar*, the only other ingredient for Grandmother's crazy fairy rituals? I was overthinking this and needed to calm down. But then I got a little defensive. Did he think I was such an idiot that I was not capable of finding sugar in the baking aisle?

"I'm looking for cookies called ladyfingers," I blurted. He looked startled. My neck grew hot—it was only a matter of seconds before it crept up to my face. "You probably don't have them." I turned and started to quickly walk away, staring at the floor.

"Oh, wait! We do have them, but only the cakey-kind," the young man said, jogging to catch up to me. I stopped and looked at him peripherally. He pleasantly continued, "The crunchy ones are my favorite, but we don't have those. I can show you the right place, just follow me."

My, he is tall! Following behind him, I noticed his hair, so shiny and dark brown . . . and thick . . . and wavy.

I loved the contrast between his dark hair and bright blue eyes—so different from my dull grey eyes and stick-straight dark blond hair. And his tanned skin was so luminescent under the store's fluorescent lights; mine just looked washed-out and pale. But I didn't tan. I only ended up with more freckles and a sunburn.

As we walked, the pen he had stuck behind his ear dropped to the ground. He stopped in front of me, bent over, and his gorgeous hair was only about six inches away from my face. I had the inexplicable urge to run my fingers through it.

What was I thinking? He would never think of me in that way—no matter how much I wished he would. Still, having a romance would be such a wonderful thing . . .

I shook my head and straightened myself up. He's just a member of the male species, nothing more. And I was so awkward that I would probably never have a boyfriend. Hadn't I decided long ago that was okay? What was going on with me today?

"Here you go . . . they're here, with the cakes. My aunt makes this great dessert with them for my birthday every year. It's my favorite. A fairy cake. It has whipped cream and . . ."

A fairy cake? Are you kidding me? Now this was too much!

"Ah, thanks," I interrupted, taking the package out of his hands. Wow, his hands made mine seem so small and feminine.

Stop thinking about that stuff! I scolded myself.

I felt like I'd stepped into the Twilight Zone! What else could explain the automatic—*intrinsic*—impression of a boy who spoke of fairy cakes and butter with sugar? The only thing I knew for sure was that my stomach felt like a hundred ladybugs were crawling around inside. I clearly needed to go home and lie down.

Unavoidably, my face was the color of a ripe strawberry. I quickly scooted to the shortest checkout line, and for a brief second, I glanced in his direction. Was he gesturing for me to come back to him? I'd looked so quickly, I couldn't be sure. Maybe he wanted to know my name. Maybe he wanted to talk with me longer. No, who was I kidding? He was probably relieved to be rid of the crazy girl who could barely speak straight.

I felt jittery on the way home. Why had I acted like such a dork? I should have just smiled prettily, like I'd seen Lacey do a dozen times, and ask him questions. Did he like working at Tom Thumb? Where did he go to school? I couldn't even ask the most basic one, what was his name?

What was his name? Then, I remembered his nametag: G. Walker. I had seen it when I had peered at him out of the corner of my eye. Greg Walker? George? Gerard? Gary?

I decided to call him "G" as in "Gee whiz!" since that's how I felt around him, and because he seemed like an old soul. In fact, the last time a clerk delivered groceries to someone's home must have been in the 1950s. But his kindness made it hard for me not to like him, at least secretly.

G, you're a swell kinda guy!

I giggled a bit at my retro phrase. Giddiness was a new feeling to me, but I enjoyed how it made me feel. It was as if my feet didn't touch the ground all the way home.

The next day, I went to my middle school classes for the last time and took the rest of my finals. Total and complete brain drain. And when the bell rang at the end of the day, I used up my last ounce of energy by cheering.

Once home, I wanted to eat, draw, watch television, and curl up with a good book . . . then I remembered my promise to have tea with Grandma.

Oh well, twenty minutes of listening to her talk about fairy non-sense and then I'd be free to chill.

And at precisely four o'clock, Mom called, "Claire, Grandma is ready for tea now."

As I gathered the plastic package of ladyfingers and headed upstairs, I realized that I was actually looking forward to hearing more stories from her. And when I saw Grandma sitting once again in the overstuffed armchair in her room, her face looked quite happy to see me as well.

"Here are the ladyfingers. What will you do with them?" I held the package out toward her and waited, curious to see just how an offering was made.

"Thank you, my dear. Why don't you open them up and put a few on the edge of the windowsill? The fairies will be so happy! They've been craving something delicious."

I did as she asked, setting the leftover ladyfingers on the dresser next to Grandma's hatbox. Then I sat on the vanity stool, studying her for a minute.

"What's on your mind, Clairy?" she asked. "You know you can ask me anything."

"You wouldn't know anything about some missing butter, would you?"

"Well, dear, I have been mind-speaking with the fair ones and they asked if I had any. I told them 'no,' but suggested that maybe they could look in the kitchen. They probably just helped themselves."

"Uh . . ." I mumbled. That wasn't exactly the response I'd expected. Maybe it'd be best to change the direction of the conversation a bit. "Why do you call the fairies so many things, like 'little folk' or 'fair ones,' for example?" I asked.

"Well, Anna and I read that people in Ireland, Scotland and England used to fear them in the ancient days of Ireland, Scotland, and England, so it was best not to offend them. You see, fairies never want to be referred to directly, because it's quite rude. It would be like saying 'hello, human!' to us, since that's technically what we are." I smiled and she went on, "Instead, we used courteous nicknames like 'little folk' or 'wee ones'—equivalent to saying 'kind gentleman' or 'young lady' to a human."

"Do the fairies *want* humans to see them?" I poured some tea and handed the steaming cup to her. It was too hot of a day for me to have tea, so I just helped myself to a slice of banana bread.

"They don't want to be blatantly acknowledged. If someone yells, 'I see you, fairy!' they'll disappear in a flash. They want humans to respect their discretion. That's why they make humans work hard to see them. We have to demonstrate genuine belief in the fair ones. We must earn their trust."

They wanted to be known, but at the same time, they didn't? It seemed pretty inconsistent to me.

"Anna and I also read about how much they loved dancing and music. Neither of us had learned an instrument one could play out in nature. We both knew how to play the piano, but rolling one down by the creek was impossible!" The smirk on the old woman's face was like a child's. "So, we'd dance around to the music we could make with our voices. We tried all sorts of musical genres, from classical to modern melodies of the time, not knowing what kinds of songs they wanted to hear."

"So, you and Anna went outside and danced and sang?" I'd have been way too embarrassed to do something like that.

She sipped her tea. "Yes, of course. We also jumped, twirled, and laughed. That's what I remember the most—we'd get carried away, feeling the pure joy of swishing our skirts in the sunshine. And it wasn't all silly fun. We also danced with fervent gravity at times too, with the depth and emotion of Isadora Duncan. Have you heard of her?"

"No," I replied.

"She was the end-all, be-all of dramatic dancers, with her bare feet and interpretive modern dance technique—it was all the rage! And the greatest part was that her style meant 'anything goes,' just like the old song by Cole Porter:

In olden days a glimpse of stocking,
Was looked on as something shocking,
But now, God knows,
Anything goes . . ."

Her voice was a little raspy, but I could tell that Grandma could really carry a tune!

"Well, enough of my mediocre singing and back to Ms. Duncan." She set her teacup on her bedside table. "The 1920s were a new frontier after the stodgy nature of the turn of the century, let me tell you! We discarded our high-necked blouses and restraining corsets for short dresses, bobbed hair, thinly plucked eyebrows, and red painted lips."

"Wait a minute, wait a minute. Grandma, you were a *flapper?*"

"Oh, yes! King Tutankhamun had just been unearthed in Egypt at the time and the treasures found in his tomb influenced fashion. We used charcoal, *kohl,* to line our eyes in black, just like the ancient Egyptians did, and the stylistic designs of the Art Deco movement began, based on ancient Egyptian decoration."

"I didn't know Egypt had such a big influence on '20s style. What was it like being a flapper?"

"Well, we were all about having fun, and we used terms like 'nifty' and called ourselves 'jazz babies'. What do you know about the 1920s? They must have taught you about it in school."

"Well, I know it was a time of prohibition . . ."

"Yes, it was. You want to know what we called bars and alcohol?"

"Ah, sure."

"'Whoopie parlors' and 'giggle water,'" she said grinning from ear to ear.

"Why, Grandma!" I said teasingly. It was pretty funny to hear her use those terms, and with such a goofy smile on her face.

"Now how did we get on that subject? I do tend to go off on tangents."

"You and Anna danced and sang during your fairy rituals," I reminded.

"Ah, yes! We also constantly created special 'visionary oils' from ground-up plants mixed with mineral oil. We'd leave the concoction in jars for weeks, strain out the solids with cheesecloth, and then anoint our eyelids. Every single time we were sure we'd finally created the magical potion that would allow humans to see little sprites! It never worked, but we didn't give up."

Didn't work? Well, that was no surprise.

"One of my favorite memories from childhood was snuggling down in the tall yellow-green grass, dotted with red ladybugs. Usually, the smell of warm sugar cakes wafted through the air. These sweet indulgences were a special gift for the fairies, much like the ladyfingers you brought today."

"What are sugar cakes?"

"Delicacies we'd bake by sneaking ingredients from our family kitchens and slipping the fresh batter into the oven while our mamas baked their weekly biscuits."

"So, what exactly did you do with the cakes?"

"Well, after singing and dancing, we'd put our freshly baked offerings at the base of a tree and spend hour upon hour sitting perfectly still, waiting for the fairies to show themselves to us."

"Did you ever bring other friends along?"

I figured that the more eyewitnesses there were, the more believable this story may become.

"Oh, no. We'd never bring anyone with us, even if someone swore they were a true believer. We couldn't see into their hearts to know for sure, like the fair ones could. We didn't want to jeopardize a sighting by breaking the fairies' trust. This was also the reason we didn't tell our other friends or family about our beliefs, at first. Any negative energy given off by a skeptic may inadvertently be carried by one of us and sensed by the pixies."

I wanted to cut to the chase. "So, did you ever see any fairies?"

"Well, for many months, we saw nothing . . . and usually we'd end up in trouble for being terribly late to dinner, mostly because we'd spend many of those hours waiting, pencils and paper in hand, observing nature."

"Was Anna an artist as well?"

"An artist, yes, but she didn't draw. Her artistic calling was poetry. She'd write a poem and I'd illustrate it. We started using her original works in our rituals, thinking fairies would enjoy it."

"But you didn't answer my question. Did you ever see-?"

My grandmother interrupted, "Would you like me to recite one of her poems for you now?"

"Sure," I shrugged. Maybe there would be a clue in it somewhere.

"We had a favorite Glorianna original. Let me see, can I still remember it? Ah, yes:

> *Brighter than the sun, deeper than the moon*
> *my devotion is to thee,*
> *Alas, I cannot come to you, but you must come to me.*
> *So little ones with hearts of gold, who tend the flowers fair,*
> *Please show yourselves, with all your grace,*
> *and make me so aware!*

Oh, I remember it! We said it so often, I'm really not surprised that it's burned into my memory."

"You and Anna sound like good friends. Where is she now, do you know?" How I'd love to get in touch with her!

"Anna was my best friend, but in one single moment, our relationship was changed forever." Clouds rolled across my grandmother's soft blue eyes.

She looked so sad! I reached out to put my hand on hers but thought better of it. I didn't know what to say, so instead I watched the wall clock slowly count down one minute with its thinnest hand.

Thankfully, before a full minute had passed, she shook her head gently and began again. "Now, you know who Isadora Duncan was."

"Yep."

"Well, she helped your grandfather and I meet."

"Really? How?"

"I will tell you all about that very soon, but I'm still a bit jetlagged. Can we pick this up later?" She yawned.

"Sure. Of course." But now my curiosity had the best of me. I wanted to know more.

10

The Pixie Sisters

*"Forget not that the earth delights to feel your bare feet
and the wind longs to play with your hair."*
— *Kahlil Gibran* ❧

There were two words to describe the eighth grade graduation ceremony: "long" and "hot." I wished Mom hadn't talked me into the silk dress I was wearing because it stuck to the sweat on my back. I didn't like fancy clothes anyway and hardly ever wore skirts or dresses.

Mom, Dad, and Grandma took me to lunch afterward at a nice local restaurant where they served us tall glasses of sweet tea with lots of ice. So refreshing! I looked around the table and wished Val could be there too. My grandmother was seated next to me, so I was on alert for those hot pink lips. I hoped they wouldn't kiss or whisper at me.

So far, so good.

Conversation was pretty normal, and Grandma told us that her botanical illustrations have appeared in twenty-five published books. Wow! She must be some artist. She loved plants so much that she also took classes to become a certified master gardener.

As she spoke, I kept staring at the strange necklace she was wearing. It had tiny silver hands, hearts, legs, animals, and crosses on it, all tied together with multicolored satin ribbons.

"You like my necklace?" Grandma said to me, with a twinkle in her eye.

"Yeah." I kept my comment to that—I didn't want to say anything rude since I actually thought it was weird. Didn't Mom and Dad worry that she was wearing a necklace made up of some kind of voodoo charms?

"Do you know what these little metal figures are called?" She looked right at me, and so did my parents. They acted as if everyone in the world knew the answer except me.

"Nope."

Grandma lifted the bottom of the necklace to give me closer look. "The charms are called milagros and are found in Latin America— they're used in Europe, too. They are usually hung with ribbons from altars and shrines. The word *milagro* means *miracle*. I wear them for protection and good luck."

Once again, somehow her craziness made sense. After that, lunch went along pretty normally, and once my tummy was full, all I wanted to do was get home and get that dress off.

At home, I enthusiastically changed into shorts and a t-shirt, and then Lacey came over. She was wearing a pink sundress; that was casual for her.

"What do you want to do?" she asked.

I glanced over at the journal on my desk in which I'd been writing, ah, *inscribing*, the family history my grandmother had told me. It gave me an idea. "Are you game for a little attic search?"

"Sure. What's up there?"

"A box marked 'old stuff' that I'm dying to look through, now that Grandma has been telling me about her life."

"Great idea!"

We pulled the rope hanging from the ceiling in the upstairs hallway. Inside was a retractable ladder. I pulled it down and climbed up first. Once I yanked on the chain that turned on the single light bulb, I could see all of the plastic bins and cardboard boxes full of memories. Mom and I had organized it last April.

"There's no room to stand up, so I'll have to crawl," I said. "I know where the box is—I made the label for it myself last spring. Here it is." I grabbed the old shoebox and dust danced through the air as I slid it toward me. "Ready? I'm going to hand it down to you. It's a little bit heavy."

"I'm ready." Lacey climbed halfway up the ladder. As she took the box from my hands, she coughed. "So dusty!"

"Sorry about that." I turned off the light and then climbed down the rungs myself. "I'll close the attic door before any more of that dirt escapes with me."

We took the box down to the kitchen table where I wiped the top with a damp paper towel. We also washed our hands in the sink before sitting down. We just stared at the faded orange shoebox for a minute.

"Have you ever looked at what's inside before?" Lacey wondered.

"Yes. There are mostly just pictures in there, but I didn't know who some of the people in the photos were—they just seemed like strangers to me then."

Inside, there was a faded old envelope with about fifty black-and-whites of people I now recognized as my grandma, and grandpa and my mother and aunt as children, all smiling at the camera and dressed in 1940s and 1950s attire. Many of the snapshots were taken around this old house, and the familiarity of it gave me chills.

"Your grandma was mighty beautiful when she was young. She looks a lot like you." Lacey smiled.

"Huh, I guess she does. That surprised me, too. After Grandma came to live here, I realized where I get my good looks from." I flashed a teasing grin.

"Don't let it git to your head, now," Lacey teased back.

Then I came across a photo of my grandmother in a wild English garden, holding my hand when I was a little girl. This was one of the few color photos in the box, and on the back, in my mother's handwriting, was: "Mother and Claire, England, 1996." I was only six years old.

I flipped it back over, studying the picture. I wore a turquoise t-shirt and yellow shorts, and my hair was in two braids on either side of my head. My grandmother wore a red checkered apron and held a trowel in her other hand. In my other hand, I was holding up a bright pink hollyhock lady.

I slipped the photo into my pocket.

"Look at this, Claire." Lacey pulled out an old leather-bound book.

"It's a diary," I said, reading the first page aloud. "'This belongs to Faye Grace Davis, 1929.' It's Grandma's from when she was young."

"How old would she have been then?"

"Let's see . . . thirteen."

"Like us. You gonna read it?"

"Yes . . . I mean, no. I'd love to, but a diary is really personal . . ." As I spoke, a very yellow newspaper clipping slipped from between the pages and fell onto the floor. I picked it up and laid it on the table:

> **Learn to Dance Like Isadora Duncan!**
> Modern Interpretive Dance Classes,
> every Tuesday for five weeks at the
> Highland Park Community Pavilion
> ~Only $1 a lesson~

"Ever heard of Isadora Duncan?" Lacey asked.

"Yeah, from Grandma. I guess 'Izzy' was a big deal in her days."

Her eyes lit up with an idea. "Fan the pages of the diary and see if there are any more loose papers."

"Oh, you are so tricky sometimes, Lacey."

"Well, we're not actually readin' the diary, but we can still get a little information."

"You're right," I said, flipping the pages with my thumb. Out popped only one more aged newspaper article:

> **July 20, 1929:** The home of Mr. and Mrs. Jasper Connelly burned to the ground at 3:59 p.m. on Thursday. Mr. and Mrs. Connelly and two of their three children perished. They are survived by their 13-year-old daughter, Anna Connelly. Funeral to be held at the Greenville Methodist Church on Saturday at 1 p.m.

Lacey's fingers touched her parted lips a moment before she asked, "How awful! Do you think your grandma knew these people?"

"Yes, I think she did. Anna was the name of her childhood friend."

"Could this horrible thing have happened to her?"

"I think so."

I slipped both articles back into the diary, which I set aside. Lacey had to go home, but before she left she helped me put the photos back into the shoebox, and then back in the attic.

I wanted to find Grandma, so I went upstairs and knocked on her door, but there was no answer. I peeked inside her room, but she wasn't there. I searched all over the house, and finally found her in the throbbing heat of the backyard, looking at our old garden with Mom.

"I think peonies would be lovely here in the spring." Grandma saw me and smiled. "Why, hello, Claire."

"What are you two doing out here in the burning sun?"

"Grandma's giving me gardening ideas," Mom said. "What are you up to, honey?"

"Look what I found." I held out the diary. "Ah, Grandma?" The old woman was standing there with a monarch butterfly on her finger. "Is she *talking* to it, Mom?"

"I know. It's all good . . ." I heard Grandma say.

Mom walked over and touched her on the shoulder. "Mother, Claire has something for you."

"Thank you. Goodbye," Grandma said to the butterfly as it flapped its orange wings and flew off her finger and over the fence. "Now, what was that you were saying, Amy?"

"Claire found something of yours."

"My old diary!" Grandma took the book from my hand. "Where ever did you find that?"

"In the attic." I threw a quick look at Mom.

"Oh, I shall enjoy reading this. Thank you for finding it, Clairy."

"Sure."

"I think you've had more than enough hot sun now, Mother." My mom shrugged her shoulders at me, and then led Grandma away by her arm into the house. "Claire, are you coming?"

"In a minute." I looked up at our big brick house, then at the giant pecan tree, wondering what Grandma wrote about in her diary.

Just then, a ladybug landed on my arm, tickling me. "Hey there, little lady! You have one, two, three . . . seven dots on your back." And then it flew away. I watched its blurry black form float up toward the trees and disappear, and then I went inside. I found Grandma sitting alone at the kitchen table.

"Where's Mom?"

"She's helping your dad pack for his next business trip."

"Oh, yeah. He's leaving tonight." I saw the diary sitting next to Grandma's hand on the table. "When I picked up your diary, a couple of newspaper clippings fell out of it."

"Oh, really? What were they about?"

"One had to do with community dance lessons."

"Yes, I remember those classes. Anna and I were so obsessed with Isadora Duncan that we planned to leave Highland Park and move to Los Angeles to become a famous pair of interpretive dancers. We were going to be known as 'The Pixie Sisters.'"

"Why didn't you do that?"

"Well, I met your grandfather. He changed my mind with one smile." Her face glowed at his memory.

I sat down in the chair next to her. "Did you and Anna take the dance lessons together?"

"Well, we wanted to, but we had to scrimp and save our money."

"The article said it only cost one dollar each." I thought a moment and then added, "But I guess that was a lot of money back then, like ten dollars or so today." I remembered the teacher saying something like that in social studies.

"Oh, yes, it was a lot. I was actually able to earn my money working for my father in his coal furnace business. He installed and repaired heating systems, although on a hot day like today, it's hard to believe how icy Texas winters can get! It was just before the Great Depression, when free enterprise was booming. People were spending money and businessmen were doing well."

"How did Anna make the money?"

"She didn't. Unfortunately, she had no way to earn even an extra penny, and if she had, she'd have felt obligated to give it to her parents."

"Why?" I wondered.

"Her father had contracted tuberculosis after working in the garment industry in New York City for most of his life, and he was unable to provide for his family for years. It wasn't until 1920 that the Worker's Health Bureau of America helped make those stifling, lung-infecting job conditions better, but it was too late for him. Anna's family had moved here in hopes that the air would be fresher, and better for his health."

Grandma shifted, reaching for a glass of water sitting on the table. "Her mother worked days at the Dallas City Market, leaving Anna with two younger brothers to look after. All they focused on was keeping food on the table and a roof over their heads."

"So, what did you two do?"

"We were faced with a dilemma, especially when the local newspaper announced that the class was nearly full."

I dragged my chair closer.

"At first, we were going to try and split up the classes. However, if we each took two lessons, who would take the extra one? After much deliberation, Anna insisted we'd both learn much more if I took all five lessons and taught her what I had learned immediately afterward. She felt I had a better memory for retaining it, and after all, I had the money."

"That was really nice of her."

"Yes, that was Anna. Besides, she hoped that once our career as The Pixie Sisters took off, she'd be able to support her family and never have to worry about money again. It was all about the big picture, the means to an end."

"My friend, Lacey, she's like that. She puts her family first, but our friendship is important too . . ." I stopped myself.

"You're a lucky girl, to have a friend like that. Not everyone finds his or her kindred spirit, you know." Grandma gave me a sideways nod.

"You're right."

"Well, going back to the dance class, on the first day our instructor, Miss Dabble, announced that we'd be performing a recital on the Highland Park Pavilion stage at the end of the five weeks. Anna and I were supposed to perform in public *together*. I worried she would feel left out, so I planned to not be in the recital at all. But, oh, Anna was a loving and encouraging friend!

"'Of course you'll perform!'" she said, 'You'll get the world excited about what's to come when The Pixie Sisters hit the stage!'"

"That was nice," I commented, wondering if Lacey would have said that to me if we were in the same situation.

"It made me work hard to remember what I learned each week. I taught it to Anna faithfully, and we added these dances to our fairy rituals. Surely the wee ones would appreciate the pure freedom of expression in our dance." Grandma looked deeply into her water glass.

"Anna was a perfectionist in helping me fine-tune my barefoot moves as the recital neared. She was determined that I would be at my best. The performance would kick off the town's summer activities of picnics, concerts in the parks, parades, the public pool opening, and so forth. Everyone would be there. Everyone would see."

"That's a lot of pressure."

"Yes, it was. So, I practiced night, day, and in my sleep. I made sure that my kicks were higher than everyone else's, my movements had remarkable fluidness to them, and my hands were the most graceful."

Grandma lifted her gnarled hands and we both watched her fingers flutter to imaginary music.

"Finally, after what seemed like an eternity, the night of the performance arrived!"

I scooted to the edge of my seat.

"Mother, it's time for us to leave," my mom said, entering the room in a flurry. Her perfume filled my nose—it was the one she wore on special occasions.

I looked at Grandma. How could she leave me hanging like this?

"Where are you going?" I asked.

"Remember, your aunt Az is having a small get-together with some old friends, in honor of Grandma." Mom looked at her watch. "And Dad's leaving on his trip in ten minutes." She looked up at me. "Why aren't you ready to go?"

"Would it be okay if I skipped the party?" I gave my biggest grin.

Mom paused. "Well, I guess you'd be bored in a room full of adults. But you'll be home alone tonight."

"It's all right." I tapped my foot quickly.

"Mother, I'll go get your purse." Mom rushed out of the room.

"Here." Grandma flipped open the diary and slid it over to me.

"This page will tell you more about what we were talking about."

"I don't know. A diary is a private thing." I said, pushing the book back toward her.

"I *want* to share this with you." She tapped the table three times with her knuckles, slid a finger one way and then the other—such a strange thing to do!—and then stood up. And just before she turned to leave, she said, "But don't read anything else in the diary yet. Each part will be revealed to you at the right time."

I slowly reached out and picked up the book. I ran my fingers over the black bumpy leather knowing just where I wanted to go to read it—by the creek.

11

Dancing on Air

"The bird a nest, the spider a web, man friendship."
—❧ *William Blake* ❧—

Being there by the creek made the start of summer vacation official. I'd been too busy to enjoy it, but on that day, I could wallow. Reading and sketching by the creek was what I had planned to do for most of the summer. The sweltering Texas humidity was extreme, but I loved the heady smell of heated organic dampness.

The creek changed quite dramatically from winter to spring, summer to fall. I looked at it as a theatrical show of seasons, each slowly pushing one another away to take over the stage like a leading lady.

Autumn brought falling leaves to the scenery, which floated down the creek like little boats. The mockingbirds picked through the ones on the bank to find bugs hidden beneath the moist undersides. It was a time of leisure for the animals as they saved their energy until their instincts cued them to prepare for winter.

Soon, heavy rains would knock down the last of the crinkled brown leaves, but these deciduous trees had a beauty of their own, twisting and turning, dark against the backdrop of a bright grey sky. The only ones that held onto their leaves were the great live oaks; however, they hosted a guest that would eventually drain their energy away, as longtime visitors tend to do—boughs of white-berried mistletoe, which beckons lovers to kiss beneath it.

Winters were cold, with intense winds that bellowed fiercely through the twisting creek bed, parted by torrential waters thousands of years prior. And even though Highland Park is built on a desert, there are occasions when the weather turned a cold shoulder and brought on ice storms.

In the spring, dragonflies and butterflies fluttered, showing off their colored costumes. I would catch glimpses of orange, yellow, or iridescent flashes of light, which instantly imprinted an afterimage in my eyes.

Golden orchestras of low-lying forsythia, as well as the pink, purple, and white backdrops of crape myrtle trees all played roles in the extravagant show of hues. My goal was to capture the moment when an orange monarch landed upon the bluest Texas bluebonnet, creating the perfect duet of complementary colors. The audience of purple-blue periwinkle faces bloomed along the banks, and the supporting cast of tiny yellow moths flew to and fro.

Even the turtles, encouraged by the glorious weather, forgot their inhibitions and came out of hiding. Yes, Turtle Creek got its name from the occasional unhurried cavalcade of turtles sighted along the slippery river rocks, stopping to eat algae along the way, slow due to their genetic disposition. They made excellent subjects for my detailed sketches.

But now it was nearly summer and the hot, moist air felt thick. The blooms around me were becoming dry and discolored, beginning their rest—*respite*—until they put on their show again next year.

In my hand was Grandma's diary. I had less than an hour before it got too dark to see. I opened it to the page she had allowed me to read. The binding cracked, letting out a musty smell.

March 3rd, 1929

Tonight I danced just like Isadora Duncan! It was so wonderful!

I want to remember every detail . . .The wooden stage was beneath a thick area of oak trees in Pavilion Park. The pillars that supported the pergola overhead were wrapped in ivy and fresh flowers. I brushed my hair with a hundred strokes so it was extra shiny and placed the silver tinsel crown upon my head. I wore a gossamer white empire waist gown, with silver braiding at the waist, neck, hemline, and cuffs of the quarter-length puffy sleeves.

As I stepped behind that stage with the nine other dancers, preparing to begin, I was very excited. At first, my nerves made me a bit nauseated, especially when I peeked from behind the white chiffon curtain and saw how many spectators I knew: Mrs. Goodhue the librarian, Miss Tole my teacher, my parents, my friends . . . practically everyone was there!

But as soon as the music began, I felt like I wanted all of them only to see me. I was one with nature, expressing myself through music and dance beneath the stars on a warm early summer's night. I floated, and then flew, across the stage, stopping just in time to hold a graceful pose. Stage left. Stage right. Round and round. The silver foil fairy wings flapped between my shoulder blades as if they were aiding me in every move.

Anna was there watching from the front row, and her wide-eyed, encouraging face made me try even harder to be big and bold in my performance. She mouthed "Pixie Sisters!" to me whenever she caught my eye. That made me dance with even more animation. I picked up one of the wands—which were my idea, by the way, and the audience just loved them—and swished around the silver-glittered star upon the end of it, tiptoeing and spinning in the part of the dance we referred to as "The Fairy Finale."

It was all too ethereal to be true! I didn't want it to end!

And there, glued to the next page, was a wonderful old black and white photo of Grandma as a young girl, dressed like a fairy, just as she'd described. She had on ballet slippers, a chiffon gown, aluminum wings, a silver crown, and was holding a tinseled wand. It made me smile in a big way.

Oh, I want to read more! But, no, she trusted me to read only this.

Suddenly, I saw something hovering close by from the left corner of my eye. I turned my head to see what it was, but there was nothing there. I looked back down at the photo, and again, I could peripher-

ally see something flittering, but when I looked directly at it, it was gone.

Hmmm. I'll just take a picture of it with my phone. *Snap!* I looked at the image on the screen, but all I saw was a bunch of bushes with the light of dusk gleaming through the leaves. Oh well, it was going to be dark soon, and I was hungry, so I headed home to fix myself some mac and cheese.

At around 9 p.m., Mom and Grandma entered the house laughing and talking. After a few minutes, I heard each one close her respective bedroom door, and just when the house went quiet again, my cell phone buzzed. A text message from Aunt Az:

Hostess has flu. Can u and a friend work 1 to 5 tomorrow? Missed u tonite. L-AA

I called Lacey. "Hey, tomorrow's the first full day of summer vacation. I'd like to spend it with my bestie!"

"Sure, me too. What do you wanna to do?"

"Well, Aunt Az needs help at the tearoom tomorrow. Will you seat people with me for a few hours, during the rush?" Lacey was silent. "We'll get a free deluxe tea, with sandwiches and scones," I added. "It would be much more fun with a friend . . ."

"Free gourmet lunch?" Lacey was a foodie, even at the age of thirteen. "I'm in!"

I slept in late the next morning and hung around the house in my pajamas until noon, but then I had to get ready to go help Aunt Az. I reluctantly pulled on a skirt. My aunt believed in dressing nicely for work.

"Don't worry, jean shorts. I'll be back soon," I reassured them from their place at the end of the bed. They looked so comfy that it was hard to leave them there.

Lacey's mom dropped her off at my house and we walked to the tearoom together.

"So, Lacey, you know that diary we found?"

"Yeah, your grandma's." Lacey was wearing red low-heeled sandals that clicked on the sidewalk.

"Well, she let me read one entry."

"No way! Only one? It was probably pretty boring. Being a teenager in 1929 couldn't have been much fun." Then a playful grin came over her face. "But still, diaries are so secretive. I'm dying to know what it said."

"Well, it was about a dance recital and . . . oh no!" I stopped dead in my tracks.

Lacey saw what I did—and the look of horror came over her face. "Is something in the tearoom on fire?"

A plume of smoke trailed up into the sky, just above the restaurant's back door. We ran, with Lacey keeping a slower pace due to her fancy shoes.

"P.U.! It smells like sulfur!" I pushed through the back door.

"Oh, Honey-Claire!" Delta, the cook, threw her hands up at the sight of me.

"Is there a fire?" My heart was beating quickly now. Lacey caught up.

"No, no, Claire. I was boilin' eggs for da egg salad sandwiches and I guess I got a little distracted." She pointed to the soap opera that was playing on a small television.

"After working here for twenty years, you still break Aunt Az's 'no television while cooking' rule," I said smiling, feeling myself calm down.

Delta patted her curly grey hair, pulled back with rhinestone clips and covered with a black hairnet. "An' I just done my hair. Now it's smellin' like rotten eggs."

"Well, how can we help? Lacey or I could run to the store and get more eggs . . ." I offered.

"No thank you, darlin'. It's crazy out front. They need ya'll to seat da customers." Delta wiped sweat from her brow with the back of her hand; her usually flawless make-up was running. "Besides, da eggs are on their way. Now scoot, you two. Miss Azalea'll be so happy to see ya!"

We'd only taken one step into the dining room when Aunt Az swooped in and put an arm around each of us. "Thank heavens you're here!" she said, quickly kissing me on the head. "Thanks for helpin', Lacey doll. We're swamped."

We each grabbed a stack of menus.

"Next party, please," Lacey announced.

I greeted the next in line, "Right this way, Mr. and Mrs. Hampton. Table for two?"

I got swept up in the chaos of customers, menus, and refilling ice water—that's why I didn't see the tall figure behind me until I crashed headlong into him.

"Hey there. I thought that was you." A deep, familiar voice was speaking to me. "The ladyfingers make more sense now. You work at the tearoom."

It was the cute boy from Tom Thumb! My heart skipped a beat. My mind raced with the things I wanted to say but couldn't, like, "I don't usually work here. My aunt just needed help today," and, "The ladyfingers weren't for me but for my grandmother."

Yes, great idea, Claire. Tell him about your grandmother's fairy fetish!

"Uh, are you here for tea?" came tumbling out of my mouth. Well, at least I managed to say something.

"No, no. Official egg deliverer, at your service." He nodded his head, as if bowing to a princess. His handsome smile made him look like Prince Charming himself.

I'm sure I blushed. "Thanks."

"By the way, I was wondering what your name—"

Suddenly, Lacey appeared next to me. "Is table four free?"

"Ah, let me check," I tried to hide my face, which surely matched the red vinyl menus, by walking quickly to the podium and studying the seating chart. "Yes."

"Great." Lacey looked from me to the boy and back at me again. The boy kept looking at me and so I couldn't move. "Um, Claire, there are several people in line and . . ."

"Oh, I should let you get back to work." His face beamed as he set the sack of eggs on the counter and said, "See you around." He disappeared into the crowd. I took a deep breath and was able to move again, using the excitement I felt to fuel me.

Later, when things calmed down, Lacey asked, "What was *that* all about?"

"What?" I asked, knowing perfectly well she was referring to.

"That tall, handsome delivery boy. You two seemed to be into each other. You never told me you were crushing on anyone." Lacey seemed hurt that I'd kept him a secret—and she genuinely thought that boy could actually like me? No way. They always like her, which was understandable. She was outgoing and pretty, unlike me.

"I'm not crushing on him. He's just a guy who works at Tom Thumb."

Lacey just stared at me. It was obvious she wasn't buying my story. Then suddenly she asked, "Do you ever think about being in love?"

"Well, scientifically speaking," I told her, "coupling is part of the natural world."

"You mean having a boyfriend is natural, but love isn't?"

She said the word "boyfriend." I really envied the girls my age who had one, but it wasn't in the cards for me.

"That's not what I'm saying, Lacey," I told her. "When animals connect in nature, it's merely to continue their species. No love involved. So, love must have been *created*, since it seems to be exhibited by humans alone."

"I don't know—my dog really seems to love me."

"Lacey, pets can be *loyal,* but that's just because they know who feeds them every day. Ivan Pavlov, the famous physiologist, proved that merely blowing a whistle before feeding a dog each day causes it to become *conditioned* to know that 'whistle equals food'—hearing the sound makes the dog salivate and come running. Maybe that's all love is—cultural conditioning."

"Y'all's tea and sandwiches are ready!" Delta called from the kitchen.

"I'm starving! Let's eat," I said.

Phew! Saved by Delta!

I got home after Grandma's teatime, at around six that night.

"Where's Grandma?" I asked Mom.

"She went to bed early. I think she's still pretty jetlagged."

No stories tonight. I felt my shoulders sink in disappointment.

I kept thinking about G and how he had bowed to me, his blue eyes sparkling. And about Grandma and Anna, wanting to hear more.

Hoping to fill the void, I sat at my computer and looked up *The Faerie Queen* by Edmund Spencer. Hmmm. A three-book allegory about Elizabeth I. Sure enough, the name of the fairy queen was Glorianna. The story dealt with six main virtues: holiness, temperance, purity, friendship, justice, and courtesy.

Wow, Grandma was pretty well-read. I hoped I'd be the same way at the age of eighty-seven, after nearly a century of reading, learning, and living. Pretty amazing!

Then I remembered the photo I took of the peripheral image that I couldn't see straight on, so I downloaded the latest pictures from my phone. Making it as large as possible, I still saw only splatters of sunlight between the leaves of the bush next to me—but three of the blotches were interestingly formed. They were clearly butterfly-shaped, with a line extending from between each of the wings, like arms. But there were no other details there, no matter how much I zoomed in.

How curious.

I shut down my computer.

I tried to draw, but my concentration was about as solid as a hollow gumball. I went down the hall to brush my teeth, having given up on doing anything productive, and saw that my grandmother's light was on in her room. I was feeling pretty wound up, so maybe a brief chat with her would get my mind back on track.

I grabbed her diary from my desk and brought it with me. "Knock, knock! Having trouble sleeping?" I opened the door.

"As a matter of fact, I am. I fell asleep early and now I'm wide awake." She smiled, sitting in an upright position in bed, wearing a light pink nightgown with a crisp white sheet over her legs. "Would you like to visit a bit?"

"Sure," I said, gravitating to the vanity stool—my official seat.

I looked around for the ladyfinger cookies. Not even a crumb was left on the windowsill and the package on the dresser was gone.

"Are there any ladyfingers left?" I asked.

"Oh, no. The last one was eaten this afternoon."

"You had it with your tea?" It was only logical. "You must have really liked them."

"No, I didn't even eat one, but the fairies were extremely grateful to receive such a nice offering."

"*They* were grateful?"

Grandma ignored my inquiry and changed the subject. "Did you read the part of my journal about performing on the pavilion stage?"

I set the book on the vanity. "I did. I enjoyed it."

"Oh, what a magnificent night that was!" She started to hum a tune and sway.

"In your entry, you mentioned 'The Fairy Finale.' What happened during that part of the dance?"

Her eyes went to a faraway place. "I spun and danced, floating on air with my shiny wings flapping just like a fairy's. Glitter was tossed high from ladders behind us, filling the night with shimmer before landing upon the stage. All eyes were on me. And without a doubt, due to an inexplicable tingling sensation I felt throughout my body, I knew that the fair ones, hiding in the surrounding plants and trees, must be watching, cheering me on."

I could tell by the flicker in the old woman's blue eyes that she was doing the fairy dance in her mind. She swung her bent fingers continually to and fro to the music she hummed again. She seemed genuinely content in her distant place.

It was when she bolted out of bed and onto her feet that I got scared!

"Grandma! You need to be caref—"

She got carried away, trying to dance like she had as a young girl on that starry night, but her body didn't comply. Her feet slid from beneath her, and down she went upon her back, her silvery head hitting the floor last.

She lay there upon the hardwood floor, motionless for a moment. I began to shake, panic setting in.

"Are you hurt? Maybe I should get my mother . . ."

"No . . . darling . . . just pick me up." Her voice was as shaky as my body was now.

Still, I froze. I was afraid to touch the woman, but knew I had to. I carefully helped her back into bed, her tiny bones feeling frail in my hands.

I pulled the sheet back over her spindly legs, breathing a sigh of relief. But once Grandma was safely back in bed, she turned her face away. For the first time, she looked extremely sad.

I glided over and grabbed the cold, bony hand from upon the covers, holding on tightly.

"Are you hurt? Shall I call my mother?" I whispered.

She sighed. "No, I'm fine, my dear. Age just gets in my way these days. In my mind, I'm still that young girl in the iridescent fairy dress with a twinkling wand flailing about, but . . . but my body won't cooperate anymore. Getting old is terribly frustrating. It's hard to accept the limitations. It's hard to accept that soon there will be no more fairy visits, no more watching the miracle of flowers blooming, no more time for me on this beautiful earth."

"But Mom says you're still really healthy and . . ."

"My time is limited," she said, then broke into a poem that I recognized as Robert Louis Stevenson:

. . . And does it not seem hard to you,
When all the sky is clear and blue,
And I should like so much to play,
To have to go to bed by day.

She looked at me now, her eyes teary. "Appreciate your youth, dream big, and then, my beautiful Clairy, fulfill those dreams. You are a lovely girl, and a smart one at that. You can *manifest* anything with true belief. Don't just listen to my words but take them into your soul. Reap the joys of life as much as you can." She smiled through her tears. "You are so very special to me. I wish you such wonderful things in your life."

Then, Grandma closed her eyes and turned her head away, but gave my hand a squeeze as if to say, "I don't mean to be rude, but I need some rest now."

I gently let go of her hand and tiptoed out, nearly reaching the door before Mom rushed into the room. Her face was flushed. "What happened? I heard a crash."

"Shhh, Mom, Grandma's sleeping. She had a little . . . fall. But she's okay."

"I'd better check her . . ."

"No, she's fine. She just needs some sleep."

"All right. I'll check on her a little later then." Mom looked tired. "Turn the light off, please."

"Okay, I will."

And just after Mom left the room, I reached to flip the light switch off and heard, "Oh, and one more thing." The old woman opened her eyes long enough to say: "I really flew that night, on the stage. Everyone thought I used invisible wire, but it's simply not true. Real fairy dust must have been mixed into that glitter. The fair ones helped me fly and only Anna understood the truth . . ."

I sighed. "Sweet dreams, Grandma." I turned off the light and left the room.

Well, I had to admit she had a very vivid imagination.

As I walked down the hall, I replayed this last visit, and once in my room, I wrote everything down in my journal. Her memories and these times we shared were part of my family's history. Without a record, they could be lost forever. Maybe one day *my* granddaughter would want to read mine.

I wrote for an hour straight, my right hand cramping up every so often, giving me the need to shake some feeling back into it. Midnight had chimed on the grandfather clock downstairs by the time I was finished.

When I got to the end of my entry, I paused for a moment recalling Grandma's inspirational words about "reaping the joys of life" and how special she said I was to her.

How could a woman who I really just met wish wonderful things for me? We barely knew each other.

But then a thought crossed my mind: The well-wishes come from the unconditional love born from simply being my grandmother.

12

A Letter Home

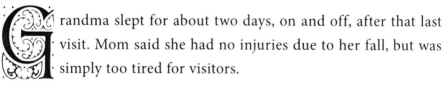

"Nobody has ever measured, even the poets, how much a heart can hold."
— *Zelda Fitzgerald* —

Grandma slept for about two days, on and off, after that last visit. Mom said she had no injuries due to her fall, but was simply too tired for visitors.

The first day was fine; I read and drew and went to the movies with Lacey, enjoying my time, but by the second day, I grew antsy.

I decided to visit Aunt Az and Delta at the tearoom. When I entered the kitchen, they were both sitting on tall barstools, drinking lemonade.

Delta jumped to her feet and grabbed an empty glass. "Can I get you some, Honey-Claire?"

"Sure, thanks, Delta."

"Business is slow as molasses today." Aunt Az crossed one leg over the other. "What's goin' on with you, sugar?"

Delta handed me a tall glass, filled with ice and luscious lemony liquid.

"Nothing. Just hanging out."

"Aw, somethin's up." Delta sat back down. "Come on, ya know ya can talk to your auntie and me about anythin'. Now, what's on your mind?"

"Well," I hesitated. "Do people know when they're going to die before it happens?"

Aunt Az chuckled. "If they knew that, couldn't they avoid dyin' altogether?"

"I guess." I took a long sip, feeling the cool liquid run down my throat. "Can someone will themselves to die?"

"Where's all this talk about dyin' comin' from, child?" Delta looked concerned.

"I know," Aunt Az interjected. "Grandma Faye is livin' with Claire and my sister. What crazy story has Mother been tellin' you?"

"She says she knows she's going to die soon."

Delta just listened, eyes wide.

"Aw, honey, she doesn't know what she's sayin' about that." Aunt Az patted my knee. "The doctors say she's doin' just fine."

"And she talks about fairies as if they're real." I stirred my lemonade with the straw.

Aunt Az reached out and put a hand on each of my shoulders. "Now you listen here. She's in her eighties and Lord knows what age can do to a mind. Don't worry about it, sugar. Really."

I smiled. "Thanks, Aunt Az." I felt my body relax. "You're right."

"I had a cousin who said she'd come back as a cat with one blue eye and one yellow one," Delta chimed in. "And though I check out every cat that crosses my path, I ain't ever seen no crazy lookin' cat like that!"

We all laughed. Maybe everyone has a crazy relative in their family.

Ding-ding! Delta jumped off her stool. "That sound means an order's up. Gotta get back to workin.'" She grabbed a piece of paper off the pass-through and started making a tuna sandwich.

"Well, sugar, I got some work to do myself," Aunt Az said, pulling a pencil out of her pocket and walking over to a stack of papers by the sink. "Can you believe it? They forgot to deliver the lemons I ordered again."

"How many do you need?" I asked.

"A dozen or so should do for now."

"I'll go over to the store and get them for you."

"Would you, sugar? That would be mighty kind of you."

"I'm happy to help." Of course, I had an ulterior motive. I wanted to see G somehow, but without him seeing me.

Walking through the store's automatic sliding doors, I panicked. What should I say if he caught me in here? "Hi there!" or "So, I've been wondering, what does the 'G' stand for?" Gosh—too dorky! I need to be cooler than that!

As nonchalantly as possible, I went to the produce section. While picking out lemon number ten of twelve, I saw him, about twenty feet away, leaning against the metal shelves. My stomach dropped. He was talking and laughing with Sally Parker, a pretty redhead from my class. Sally flicked her hand against his chest, so obviously flirting that it made me want to puke. I retreated, quickly checking out before he could spot me.

I was crazy to think for even a second that G was interested in me. Of course, a cute guy like that had girls swarming around him. He could pick anyone and had lots to choose from.

—◌◌◌—

I arrived home from the store to find that a letter from my brother had arrived in the mailbox. I held it in my hands, half excited and half nervous about the information it might contain.

I had a picture of Val on the bulletin board in my room, right next to the one of Albert Einstein and the ones of my three favorite celebrities: Steve Martin, Natalie Portman, and Cindy Crawford. All three of them are really smart; all graduated at the tops of their classes. My idols. And Val is my idol too. Since we are four years apart in age, we had pretty much lived separate lives and, therefore, little competition existed between us.

He was practically a celebrity in Highland Park. Valedictorian, and a gifted athlete, Val was always kind and generous—and the girls went wild over his muscular arms and handsome face. He had it all.

I often heard others describe him as "such a lucky person," but I knew how hard my brother had worked for all he had, and that luck had nothing to do with his success. He earned it.

When Val chose to risk such a bright future by joining the army, our whole town was shocked, but for Val, life wouldn't be complete without serving his country. He felt it was his job to try to create peace in the world, even though he knew it wasn't an easy thing to do.

When people asked him why he wanted to be part of the horrible war in Iraq, he answered, "I'm not campaigning for war, I'm promoting peace. Although I personally didn't start the combat, soldiers are needed to end it."

I had trained myself never to think about the risks my brother faced daily. It was better to focus only on his goal of calming the chaos. I didn't watch the news or read the newspapers. It was pretty easy to avoid, so I couldn't understand why my father didn't skip over the war news, too. I guessed he just couldn't help himself.

Dad believed in defending one's country. He always said, "Serving your country isn't an obligation, it's a privilege" but he had different feelings when his only son was one of the soldiers. He still believed in the fight for freedom, but he prayed for the war to come to an end as soon as possible.

Yet, Dad still read the newspaper every morning. I could tell when he got to an article on the war. His face grew paler. He'd get up and leave the room without a word, disappearing into his study with the door shut. No one disturbed my father when the door was shut.

But letters were different. Everyone knew they were reading the truth, although it was tough to take sometimes. So, the great thing about getting word from Val was that it meant he was alive and hanging in there. The problem was, after everyone had read it, a somber mood took over the household.

I slipped the letter into my back pocket and covered the part that still stuck out with my t-shirt. I wanted to read it before my parents did. When I read his words alone, it was as if he was speaking directly to me. I also wanted to make sure there wasn't any really terrible news that I'd have to break gently to my parents before they read the letter.

Having just returned from his business trip, I saw Dad, with Mom at his side, pass by the front window, so I snuck around back to find a quiet place. I climbed up into the clubhouse at the top of my old slide. Val and I had spent many hours playing on this old wooden swing set when we were little.

I sat on the floor and pulled the letter out of my pocket. The black marks all over the outside of the envelope showed that it had gone through a lot while traveling to us. I poked my finger under a loose edge of the envelope, tore at the flap, and opened it.

Dear Mom, Dad, and Sis—

Still stationed near Fallujah. Being in the army has got to have the longest workdays in any field . . . I just got off of a twenty-hour shift, which consisted of being on my toes at every moment. Resting too long can be deadly around here.

We tried out our new bulletproof flak jackets. They weigh about 40 pounds. Can you imagine? And in this heat, they can be unbearable, but we have to wear one to have a better chance of survival if something goes wrong. I could name a dozen examples of men whose lives were saved by this heavy, sweaty thing. They help keep the nerves down too, especially when you hear any sort of "boom" from nearby.

Explosions instantly trigger a million questions in your mind, you know. Who got hit? What type of weapon was that? How far away did it happen? Are they coming this way? We just hope for the best, otherwise it can make us go crazy.

I think so often of home. Mom, thank you for the care package. I shared it all with my brothers. We feel so isolated here that it's nice to have reminders of home.

The candy was especially a hit. Who knew Lemonheads would be such a coveted item, like a fine bottle of wine to a sommelier? We also appreciated the Silly String. Most of it will be used to spray for invisible wires and booby traps before entering any unfamiliar buildings . . . but I have to admit that a can or two was used on a couple of sleeping soldiers as a joke. We sprayed Joe Salinger, from St. Louis, and he woke up saying, "Ma, why didn't you give me a plate for my spaghetti?" We laughed about it for days.

Yesterday an EOD tech passed through camp. This basically means he diffuses bombs. So often these bombs are in a hole or an abandoned structure with trip wires. He has to be one of the bravest men I have ever met, going into unknown places with the chance of being blown up. I gave him a few cans of the Silly

String (as you can imagine, he needs it!) and he told us about an experience he had just last week.

He was trying to discharge a bomb before it injured anyone. His platoon of men was protecting him all around from enemy invaders. And sure enough, a bad guy was hiding in a carefully camouflaged hole and set off another bomb right next to them, causing all of the men to fly into the air. Luckily the EOD had already disengaged the first bomb or it could have been much worse. The only injury was to the sergeant who had both of his knees blown out. Thank God for the medic there who performed first aid on the spot and saved his life. This qualified him for a Combat Medic Badge. A big deal around here. Stories like that deepen my desire to become a doctor when I return home.

I don't write this to scare you, only to enlighten you with the truth. I worry that the papers don't report with accuracy about this place. We don't feel victorious, we don't feel defeated, but when we protect the civilians, especially the children, we feel needed.

The Band of Brothers is what we are all about here. We look after and take care of one another. Something that amazes me is, every time there's a call for the donation of blood, which is quite often, the line is so long that it take hours before you get your turn to donate. Ironic, right? Or maybe not. It's all about patriotism around here. When I see things like that, I know I enlisted for all of the right reasons.

So, thank you for your last letter. Sounds like all of you are keeping busy, Dad and Mom with work, and little Sis with school. Another nice report card, Claire Bear—wish I could be there for your eighth grade graduation.

Your love and support makes you heroes in all senses of the word. Your belief in our troops makes us proud, and the prouder we are, the harder we'll fight to get back home.

Love to you all—and I miss you terribly!

Val

I closed my eyes, holding the letter over my heart for a long time before I slowly climbed down from the tree house. Val hadn't written anything too harsh for my parents to handle, but the dangers he was facing in Iraq reminded me so much of what happened to Joseph Tucker.

Joseph was another Highland Park graduate, a year older than Val, who had valiantly served his country. But he was one of the unlucky ones. My family knew the Tuckers and found comfort from each other, both having their eldest son fighting in the war. Military families stuck together through the good times and bad, just as their sons and daughters did for each other, half way across the world.

Joseph Tucker's funeral was scheduled for Thursday.

Once inside the house, I found my parents talking in the living room, both with a section of the newspaper in their lap. One look at the red and blue airmail stripes on the edge of the letter caused them to stop their conversation midstream.

Pulling the folded letter out of the envelope, I stood and read it aloud.

By the end of the letter, my mom had begun to weep quietly. Dad went into his study and closed the door. I tried to concentrate on the fact that Val was fulfilling his dream of being a true advocate for freedom in America. Still, as I walked to the kitchen, I felt a hollow place in my heart grow emptier. When were they going to send Val back home?

God wasn't exactly scientifically proven enough for me to be one hundred percent sure He existed, but it still helped to sort my feelings by saying them aloud, in prayer.

"Please, God, keep Val safe and bring him home soon. Assist in making peace and safety in the world," and then I hesitated before adding, "and please . . . make Grandma rested enough to talk to me some more."

I repeated my prayer again just before falling asleep that night.

And the next day, it seemed someone had been listening.

At least to part of my request.

13

Kindred Spirits

*"In every winter's heart there is a quivering spring,
and behind the veil of each night there is a smiling dawn."*
—⌒ *Kahlil Gibran* ⌒—

Mom knocked on my bedroom door the next afternoon. "Claire, darling, Grandma's asking for you."

I looked down at my fingers, which were covered in dried paint. I'd been mixing red, blue, and white to make periwinkle.

Mom was unfazed. "Why don't you take this to her?" she asked, holding out the tray of tea. "She looks forward to spending time with you."

"Well, all right," I said, dramatically so she wouldn't see the excitement I felt.

Mom smiled at me, but I just rolled my eyes, took the tray, and went into my grandmother's room.

Abstract patterns of sun stretched out on the yellow chenille bedspread. The whole room had a bright aura about it. Grandma was in bed like the last time I visited.

"I brought you some tea," I said, flipping down the carved legs of the bed tray and setting it over her lap. My mom used this tray whenever I was sick. Was Grandma sick or just tired?

"So good to see you, Clairy! Come on over and sit on the edge of my bed." The old woman tapped the comforter with her vein-lined hand.

"Okay."

"Your mother said I've been sleeping for two days. It feels as if I only took a tiny nap, just after I told you about the fairy dance recital."

"Are you feeling all right?"

"Yes, I'm fine, and anxious to tell you what happened next." Grandma got a sly look on her face. "My flying fairy dance was what got your grandfather's attention. I knew I must have conjured up some kind of magic that night, with the help of the fair ones, but I didn't realize that the magic of love was there too."

I felt my face flush at the mention of romance.

"However," she went on, "even before that, something monumental happened, which changed my whole life. Why don't you climb beside me and rest on these pillows?" She pointed to the two fluffy ones next to her. "It's a queen-size bed and there's plenty of room, and it's much more comfortable."

I went around to the other side, paused, then climbed on the bed, leaning back on the pillows, ready for more tales. It was quite comfortable after all—much more so than the backless vanity stool. I relaxed and noticed that Grandma smelled of baby shampoo, hand lotion, and mint.

"About six weeks after the recital, Anna and I were strolling by the new theatre that was being built, to see how it was coming along, when the volunteer fire department bell began to ring. These days, you don't really think twice about hearing sirens blare, but back then it meant someone was in danger."

"Oh!" I sat straight up. "The other newspaper clipping that fell out of your diary was about a fire, and a girl named Anna Connelly. Was that . . . ?"

"That was about my Anna. When the fire truck sped by us, we followed it, along with many other children and people who joined us along the way, to Dickens Avenue. When it turned the corner, our hearts were beating frantically. I looked at Anna and saw that her eyes were big as saucers. We both felt the same gloomy sensation."

"So Anna's house was burning down?"

"Unfortunately, yes." Grandma had a strange glaze over her eyes, like she was watching the fiery inferno all over again. "We stood there staring as the tongues of fire singed the roof and doors, until my mother swept us away."

Grandma paused, and did that crazy knocking and cross motion again, this time upon the wooden bed table still across her lap. I really wanted to ask what that gesture was, but didn't want to interrupt her story.

She continued, "Back at the house, Mother gave us homemade ice cream she'd been churning on the front porch, but neither a word nor a smile ever came to our lips. As children, we were helpless and could only wait for some news. Pure dread had created a lump in my throat, making each bite go down in a slow, painful way."

"Terrible," was all I could say.

"At about eight o'clock that evening, the police chief knocked on our door and gave us what turned out to be devastating news. A kerosene lamp had fallen, starting the fire, and Anna's parents and siblings had perished. All of them. Her home was gone, along with everything in it." A tear journeyed down Grandma's cheek, but she continued on. "Anna stayed with us for a while. During the first few weeks she didn't shed a single tear, even when nearly the whole town attended the wake."

"Thank goodness you were there for her during such a difficult time in her life."

"Oh, yes. I loved having her around all of the time, but my sweet Glorianna was so forlorn that she went to bed early every night and only went through the motions of what was expected of her from day to day."

"Did you try to get her out of her depression? Maybe you could have taken her down to the creek . . . to dance for the fairies with you."

"I tried, but she refused to go. Mother told me to leave her alone. Time, she said, was the only healer of such cavernous wounds." Grandma dried her cheek with a napkin from the bed tray. "And I respected that as long as I could, until one night I couldn't stand it any longer. It was eating me up inside to have my dearest friend wandering the world as a shell of herself."

"It must have been horrible for her, losing everyone and everything all at once," I sympathized.

"Yes. Her grief was certainly more than I could imagine, but one night, I exploded. I grabbed her by the shoulders, nearly shaking her, demanding how much longer she was going to be sad and out of touch with nature, with the world . . . with me?

She sat there, quiet and stunned at first, but then, finally, tears began to flow. I held her, stroked her hair, and whispered that it was all going to be okay. We stayed like that for at least an hour."

I felt my own tears welling up in my eyes and fought to keep them back.

But Grandma looked at me and smiled. "Emotions aren't meant to be bottled up, Clairy. They're meant to be expressed, or else they wouldn't exist in the world at all. And how dreadful that would be, everyone walking around acting polite and serious all of the time!"

"Losing one's family and home in a fire is an awful thing, but why can't people move on without excessive hugging, kissing, and crying? All of those mushy feelings make me uncomfortable." I squirmed.

Grandma chuckled. "Too much sentiment for you?"

"Yes, actually," I replied. "I feel like people can be so dramatic sometimes, when things get emotional. Like they're acting out what they've seen their favorite soap opera actor do."

"Maybe, in that case, art resembles reality."

I could see that we weren't going to see eye-to-eye on this subject, and that's when Grandma and I, stubbornly and abruptly, both crossed our arms in unison, like mirror images of each other. Then, we caught our reflections in the nearby dresser mirror—like a matching pair of bookends—and we burst out laughing.

"Well, I guess we can agree to disagree," I said.

"Oh, I won't give up that easily," she said with a smile.

Grinning, I settled back into the pillows, ready to get to the crux of this story.

"After the sorrow eased, although her heart was still broken and would never fully mend, we carried on as the kindred spirits we had always been."

"Did she end up living with you, or did she have relatives somewhere?"

"Well, open the drawer of the side table on your side of the bed." She flicked a finger in that direction.

"Okay." I reached over and yanked on the brass pull. "Your diary!" A rainbow of ribbons hung out of the top and bottom of the closed book.

"Yes—I think you'll get a more accurate picture if you read about it firsthand." A seriousness washed across her face. "I marked the page with the red ribbon."

"Each of the ribbons has a milagro tied to the end." I opened the page where the red one was, and a small silver trinket shaped like two embracing hands was tied on its end.

"I put my necklace to better use. Now go ahead, dear, read."

I flattened the open book with my palm and began:

> *March 12th, 1929*
>
> *Anna and I want her to live with my family so badly! She has no recollection of any living relatives, anyway. We planned to get odd jobs, like babysitting and selling coal for my father, to help with the cost of having an extra child in the house, in an attempt to convince my parents to let Anna stay. However, when we told my parents our plan, they said they're waiting for a telegram from Anna's aunt in Pennsylvania, before any decisions will be made. Anna has never met her aunt, so we're sure luck is on our side.*
>
> *And so far, we've had a couple of lucky omens too. The first was when Anna found a dollar on the grass at the park. At first, we figured it would be the beginning of our savings, but then we got a better idea. We took that dollar, plus the quarter that I had hidden in my sock drawer, and purchased a bottle of perfume from the local dime store. It's called "Starlight." Who wouldn't want a bottle of starlight? Plus, the label has a crescent moon with a fairy sitting on it, holding a wand that trails stars across the label. It smells exactly like violets—we figure it will attract fairies for miles around!*
>
> *The next step of our plan—to lure the fairies and ask them to magically make us true sisters, the wish we share in our*

hearts. If this dream comes true, we will be together always!

So, today, we drenched ourselves in the thick, potent liquid, and baked two sugar cakes, the batter enfolded with rose and nasturtium petals. We anointed our eyelids with morning dew mixed with sage, and performed the most theatrical show of poetry and song we'd ever done. Now, although not a fairy flittered, we actually received the second lucky sign. Just as we were holding hands during the silent part of our ritual, a dragonfly landed where our pointer fingers touched, and it didn't fly away for a long time. It had a shiny peacock-blue segmented body and rainbow iridescent wings— the most dazzlingly colored dragonfly we had ever seen. Then, after several minutes passed, it hovered above our heads before flying away toward the sky, and vanishing into thin air.

We are sure it is a true sign from the wee ones! The fairies sent us a winged messenger to tell us something. Maybe to let us know we were getting close to a breakthrough, that we finally figured out the proper itinerary to entice the tiny folk! I'm convinced that if we try again, on a moonlit night, we'll meet the fairies face-to-face and they'll grant our wish!

"And that's the end of that entry." I looked up, feeling puzzled.

Grandma's eyes were glassy. "That was our last fairy ritual together."

"The last one because all you saw was a dragonfly and no fairies, and after all of the rituals you performed, logic told you that fairies simply *didn't* exist, right?"

"Oh, but we knew they truly did exist! We knew it just as sure as we had known that Anna's home was on fire <u>before</u> we even saw it. Do you know what *prescient* means?"

"No." I answered, annoyed with myself for not knowing the definition.

"Prescient means a foreknowledge of events, and later, after my real fairy experiences, I realized I'd known all along that I would eventually see them. I had prescience when it came to fairy sightings.

"And, of course, after that, I never doubted their existence. A world in miniature exists, parallel to the world we know, made of the unity of humans, animals, plants, fairies, and angels, all in the hands of God."

"So, even in your world of fairy belief, God exists?"

"Of course! Fairies are God's creations. They protect earth's nature and animals, watching over the elemental realms of earth, air, fire, and water, too. They heal the environment and want to work with humans to keep the earth a beautiful place, and in return, they gift humans with such things as well-being, fortune, and happiness."

"But isn't that supposedly what angels do?"

"No, angels work with humans on spiritual paths. It's well known that if we communicate with angels, we are linked to God, right? But humans haven't accepted the fact that if we communicate with fairies, we are linked to God as well. Fairies and God are connected through nature. So you see, fairies and angels work together to assist humans and make earth a more blessed place."

"So, assuming a person could actually see one," I challenged, "how do you know if you're seeing a fairy or an angel?"

"Oh, that's easy. Fairies have dragonfly-like wings and angels have bird-feather wings," she answered, without missing a beat. "The fair ones show their gratefulness to those who believe in them by healing nature and giving abundance. You know, cultures that believe in fairies grow better produce, have more parks, and have a more lush, beautiful environment."

"Are you saying that Highland Park has a large population of fairies? Twenty percent of the land around here consists of parks, and it's a very green town, with lots of plants and trees."

"You could be right! This town may be full of fairies and believers at that."

"But I don't know of any fairy believers who live around here."

"Well, the fair ones are extremely peaceful and fun-loving little folk who are constantly trying to get humans to tend to nature, but few listen. Instead many people litter and pollute."

"You say that fairies are peaceful, but aren't there evil fairies who fight each other, and have wars? There are lots of stories written about fairy warfare."

"Fairy wars are fictitious," Grandma replied, flicking her hand downward. "In the human realm, conflicts are solved by combat, and in the process, the human acceptance of war has become a part of life for humankind. Humans then project their warfare onto the fairies, writing outlandish stories about them battling, but fairies would never be at war with anyone. They truly are non-aggressive, peaceful creatures."

"But wars are necessary sometimes. Val's fighting in the war to try to help create peace. I guess that's kind of saying opposite things—an *oxymoron*, but it's true."

"Yes, he's a very brave and dedicated young man, isn't he? I do support our troops, and I pray for your brother every night. But, it just isn't a fairy characteristic to fight." She shrugged. "Destroying each other, or nature of any kind, is not the fairy way. Living in harmony and peace is. Littering, oil spills, cutting down too many trees are the ways humans ruin our environment. The more people who believe in fairies, the more people there are taking care of our earth."

"Are the fairies angry that there's war in the world?"

"I think it makes them sad, but not angry. And when wars end, healing begins, which fairies are very good at helping humans do."

"So, you say there really aren't 'bad fairies,' but I've read lore about people disappearing for days, and of sprites in houses stealing objects or even babies," I said, finally admitting that I'd brushed up on my fairy knowledge.

"Well, when it comes to dealing with fairies, you must think of it like dealing with a young, mischievous child. They're so playful that their actions can cross the line sometimes. They may play silly tricks on people they like a lot, like taking something and hiding it. We've all done that, just to be humorous, haven't we? But they can also get jealous, so they may even take a baby—but would never harm it; they always return it safe and sound."

"Fairies get jealous?"

"Yes, just like humans, fairies have egos. But they will share themselves with a true kindhearted believer, unless that human is fearful or cruel to the environment or animals, then they may play tricks out of spite. But people can change, and the fairies know that—they actually are counting on the fact that disrespectful humans will amend their ways. Fairies will always give humans who have a change of heart a renewed relationship with them."

"Can they grant wishes?" I felt childish asking that question, but I wanted to know.

"Well, yes and no. Can they wave their wands and give you a brand new house or car? No. But if you ask them to help guide you toward money, happiness, or love, they can absolutely help you find your way to those things."

"But you have to be a believer first."

"Exactly." Excitement returned to her eyes. "Did you know that fairies get energy from believers too? Think of what they could do with even more energy to heal the earth! The rays of sun, the dew on flowers, and the rainbows that stretch out across the sky are examples of messages sent by fairies asking humans to believe in them, to listen to them, to preserve our world."

"*If* you are intuitive enough to be able to listen to them," I added, like a good pupil.

"You got it," said Grandma with a wink.

"Well, *I've* never seen a fairy and I'm always outside."

"Are you sure? Maybe they've been sending you signs. Have you ever noticed anything . . . unusual?"

I immediately remembered the strange gusts of wind, the voices, the hummingbird, the library book . . .

"No," I lied.

"Clairy, you must change your way of seeing things in order for that to happen. I know your scientific mind thinks you have to see something to believe in it, but when it comes to ethereal spirits, see-ing isn't believing . . . believing is seeing!"

"Oops!" I said, changing the subject. "We completely forgot about the tea and it's probably cold by now." I pulled the tray closer and felt the outside of the pot, cupping it with both hands. "It's room temperature—the teabags won't steep."

"Well, these are the kinds of things fairies can help us with. Any-thing having to do with nature or the four elements." She then closed her deep-set eyes for a moment. Blue veins decorated the wrinkled lids, and I could see the movement of her eyeballs through them. "There! The tea will be hot now. My tiny friends have helped. You know, once I ran out of olive oil and needed more for a recipe. All I needed to do was ask and, bingo, the bottle was a quarter full when I looked again."

"Really, now?" I said in a patronizing tone.

There was no way the tea would steep, but I figured I'd humor her anyway.

However, as I opened the lid to place the teabags inside, hot steam rose up and burned my fingers. "Ouch! This is scalding hot! Boy, this teapot must have extra insulation. I didn't feel the heat until I opened the top."

Grandma just smiled a knowing little grin. "Now touch the sides again . . . carefully . . ."

"They're super hot too! What's going on here?"

She didn't answer me, and without batting an eye, Grandma poured the scalding tea in each cup. "Two sugars for you and one for me." *Plop-plop, plop!* She eyed the book still open in my lap. "Go ahead and read the next entry, to find out what happened next."

My heart thumped faster as I picked up the diary.

14

The Train of Tears

"In faith, there is enough light for those who want to believe and
enough shadows to blind those who don't."
— Blaise Pascal

March 29th, 1929

Today is a most unjust day! A telegram came from Anna's Aunt Isabella—she claims to have a legal document naming her as Anna's new guardian! However, she went on to say that she is too old to keep and raise a young girl. Her lawyer is drawing up official papers making Anna an orphan! An ORPHAN! I can't believe the horribleness of her aunt's decision! Anna and I have been weeping all day. She will be sent west on the next orphan train to find a new family to employ her. I am gravely saddened, and can write no more today.

I slammed the diary shut around the red ribbon. "Didn't your family fight that decision? Surely the courts would let them keep her rather than send her off as an orphan."

"Back then, people didn't go to court to fight such matters like they do today. The elders had the authority to make decisions, and the word of a lawyer was the law."

I shook my head. "So, what's an orphan train anyway?"

"Well, homeless children were put onto these westbound trains and sent to farmers who needed extra hands to work their fields. 'Trains of Tears,' they called them. Not only had the poor children lost their parents, but they'd arrive in a strange town where a bunch of unfamiliar people would look them up and down. The farmers would pick the ones they wanted and send the rest out again, on to another station stop."

"How sad!"

"Sad, indeed! Brothers and sisters were separated . . . I read once that more than 35,000 children were put on these trains." Grandma's thin lips turned down into a frown. "However, there were strict rules the farmers had to abide by. For example, they were expected to treat the orphans like family as far as clothing and school was concerned. They had to take their orphaned child to church every Sunday, and make sure he or she attended the local school until he or she was at least fourteen years old."

"All of that's for real?" I could hardly believe it. I couldn't imagine anything like that happening in America today.

"Yes, it's for real. Now read the page with the green page marker," she said, shaking a finger towards the diary.

I slid my finger between the pages, opened the book, and found that the milagro on the end of the green ribbon was a heart with a crack down the middle.

April 6th, 1929

It's been a week since I last wrote because my heartache has been too great, but suddenly something MIRACULOUS has happened and I need to get it documented!

Today started off as the worst day of my life—Anna left on the orphan train. Oh, how Anna and I cried on the train platform, clinging to each other! The burning smell of engine smoke lingering in the air will always remind me of that horrific moment.

The train let out a startling "woo-woo!"—the last call before it left the station, and Mother forcibly pried us apart. Quickly, I slipped a Djer Cosmetics sterling compact, with an important note inside, into Anna's hand. The compact has a gorgeous relief of a fairy couple surrounded by flowers on the front—I had it on layaway at the used goods store for her 14th birthday in December. Sadly, I won't get to spend that special day with her now, so my father kindly lent me the money to pay it off and I agreed to sell coal this fall to pay him back.

Mother then ushered Anna, my sweet, wonderful Glorianna, Queen of the Fairies, onto the orphan train kicking and screaming. My heart shattered. There were other children's faces peering out of windows, all with sad, frightened expressions. Where were they going? Why was this happening to them? Would they be loved?

And when I saw Anna's face peering through the curtained window, I was sure I'd cry every day for as long as I lived. I felt so helpless. Who knows if anyone will adore and appreciate her as I do? I wish this was all a nightmare and that I will wake up soon! But unfortunately, it's all too real.

Unable to bear it, I ran to my place of refuge, the creek. Crying, and then tripping—the tears made it difficult to see—I fell down upon the green banks. I bawled so hard it felt as if I were injuring my insides. But after a long bout, I just wasn't able to cry anymore, so I lay there, feeling the pain paralyze me. It was a while before I noticed, through my blurry eyes, that I had landed near a small natural spring surrounded in baby tear ferns. I'd never noticed this little niche before.

In that spot, the left side of my face, closest to the spring, felt cool. Lying on top of the warm grass, the trickling sound of water seemed to whisper secrets I couldn't decipher, like a message trying to get through to me. I wanted to listen and make out the words, but was too distracted by my sorrow.

And that was when I felt something tickle my left cheek... I thought a strand of hair must have come loose from my ponytail. I went to brush it away, but there was no tendril there. Returning my hand to my side, I felt a tickle on my face once again. This time, it was more of a firm rhythmic pat than a mere touch. Tap–tap–tap–tap! I tilted my head and saw a flitter of something near my face. A swallowtail butterfly? I slowly rolled over to see.

"What was it?" I straightened, alert.

"Keep reading to find out." Grandma settled back, perched to listen.

My hot, swollen eyes were difficult to focus, but between me and the tear-shaped foliage was a tiny fairy dipping a pecan shell into the water! Her glistening yellow-gold wings brushed against my cheek every time she plunged her jagged brown vessel. Then, she looked over her shoulder at me and flickered her wings, purposely giving my face a sweep.

My first real fairy encounter!

I stopped and looked at Grandma, but her eyes were closed.

The fairy was like an organic image that nearly blended into the natural plant growth around her, yet she stood out due to the luminescent glow surrounding every curve of her form. As she was somewhat transparent, I could see through the small human-like figure, which stood only about three inches tall. Her four elongated oval wings, two on each side, had the effect of a dragonfly's. They grew from her shoulder blades, above where she bent her tiny waist in order to reach the spring to fill her shell.

She didn't wear clothes per se, but she was shaped like a human and made up of parts of a pink flower. Fine filaments for hair growing long over her shoulders, leaves in tight rows like a layered designer gown starting by her neck and blending into petals as they went down her tiny body, and jointed plant stems for legs and arms. Her face, though, was the most amazing part of all. Definitely modeled on the human form, she had two eyes, a nose, and a mouth, but her complexion was smooth, opaque, and difficult to describe. The most beautifully diminutive face I've ever seen!

She was using a pecan shell as a pitcher, filling it with water, and it seemed heavy to lift once filled to the brim. I feared that once she completed her task, she'd leave. I held my breath, not even blinking, my artist's eye taking in every detail. She then turned to me and smiled, so I was assured she knew I was there.

Suddenly, her wings moved rapidly, until she was hovering over my head. She tilted her pecan shell ever so slightly, and a drop of water fell directly on my chest where my heart thumped below. At that very instant, a warm feeling of contentment washed over me and I no longer felt the throbbing sadness. And suddenly, I knew Anna was going to be all right.

I'll never forget this day of extreme pain and blissful joy!

I closed the diary and set it aside. "The fairy took away your sadness?" Grandma opened her eyes, looked directly into mine, and took my hand in hers. "My dear, that was a miracle from the fairies. I was instantly healed. I don't know how else to explain it. And somehow, the tiny one knew I was better. She had a look of contentment on her face, and nodded as if her duty was complete. That was when she flew away, disappearing into the air above." The old woman let go of my hand and leaned back, smiling peacefully.

I sat there in awe.

I didn't understand why I wanted to believe such an outrageous story, but somehow, I really did.

Before my cynical nature began casting shadows of doubts in my mind, my grandmother continued. "I haven't shared these fairy experiences with anyone in decades, and even then, not many even tried to understand them." She sighed. "Thank you for listening, Claire. It's nice to finally tell someone the truth. After all these years . . ."

Her weary body slumped with relief, as if the weight of the world had been lifted from her shoulders. But I wasn't about to let Grandma stop there. I was hooked. I was like a reporter, ready to get the scoop. It was time to ask more questions; collect more facts.

"So, when you were in England, did you see fairies there too?"

"Oh, well, I never saw them as clearly as when I was young, living here.

"In Somerset, I had the grandest garden you ever saw—a wild English-type with peonies, daffodils, sunflowers, hollyhocks, and foxgloves. I knew the little folk were there because they tended my flowers so nicely. They spoke to me in my head, you know, telepathically, telling me how much they loved my garden, sharing their wishes that all humans cared about preserving our world. They often asked me to spread the word. And as they communicated, I frequently saw them flying about out of the corner of my eye . . ."

"The corner of your eye? How's that possible?" I interrupted, remembering the other day when I'd seen something, but only peripherally.

"Well, I think fairies try to be discreet when they check up on humans they care about. They don't want the person to see them, but peripheral vision allows humans to see into the place between the fairy realm and ours. It's the part of your sight where you can see with your *eyes* and *intuition* at the same time. Perhaps it was due to my old age that my direct fairy vision had deteriorated and I could only see them peripherally.

"Thanks to the fair ones' visits, I was never lonely. Working alongside them when I weeded or pruned helped me feel empowered. To plant a garden is to grow faith in tomorrow."

I smiled. Grandma sounded like a public service announcement.

"I learned so much from the little ones during those days. For example, do you know why weeds so often grow in gardens?"

I shook my head.

"Well, that's what happens when you don't give the fairies enough to do! Humans should continuously plant flowers, shrubs, and trees or else the fair ones will find tiny seeds cast by weeds and grow them to keep up their skills."

"Really?" Somehow, it really made sense.

"Yes! And did you know that ladybugs with seven spots are honored fairy pets? Fairies are very superstitious and like the lucky number seven as much as we do. Actually, they originally taught people that number seven is lucky, starting the trend."

"The other day, when you were outside with Mom looking at the garden, a ladybug landed on me and . . ."

"It had seven spots?"

"Yeah."

"Well, the fairies were all around that day, listening. If you want plants to grow their best, calling on fairy powers will help a lot."

"Is that what you were doing when you spoke to the butterfly that landed on you? Sending a request to the fairies to help Mom with her garden?"

"Yes, I sure was. And they told me if she wears a fairy stone on a string around her neck while gardening, fairy magic will be shared, giving her extra intuition as to where certain plants should go for best growth."

"What does a fairy stone look like?"

"It's a rock with a natural hole in the middle."

"Really? I found one of those a little while ago."

"What a blessing! You should give it to your mother to wear."

"I will. I want Mom to have a beautiful garden. Flowers make her happy."

"The fairies also love it if you hang crystals around the yard, like amethyst and quartz—and light tea candles at night. In England, I built a stone altar and kept such items on it at all times. Oh, they also especially love chocolate!"

"Chocolate? Why choc—" I was interrupted by another one of Grandma's recitations:

Dear Flower Fairies, near and far—
Please tend the plantings in my yard.
Bless these fragrant herbs and flowers,
With your magic loving powers.
When the sun or fireflies glow—
Please do your best to help them grow!

She smiled and then added, "Humans really can learn a lot from the wee ones."

"Speaking of that, why humans? Why would these creatures, surrounded by amazing natural forms, be human in appearance and not something entirely different? I'm sorry, but it seems kind of self-centered—*egocentric*—of humans to always describe a fairy's likeness as resembling their kind. It feels, well, contrived."

"Humans exist. Animals and plants exist. These are the earth's creatures that all humans can readily see. Angels and fairies exist as well, but they are seen using your mind's eye and your physical sight, at the same time. This is because they simultaneously exist in both their own realm and the *human* world."

I narrowed my eyes, but Grandma continued, "Now, fairies are part organic and part human. Their forms are made up of plants, but to keep healthy and balanced, their bodies need food and water, and their minds need work and play. Like humans. But most of all, like humans, they thrive on love."

"Love?" There she was, getting all gushy on me again.

"Now think about it. Of all the creatures in the world, there is absolutely no other whose love is as deep, wonderful, heartfelt, or as complex as human love. Right? The fairies embrace it by taking the form of love's most outstanding source, a human being. Love is the only true magic we humans possess."

I really didn't know what to make of all this.

"Now, where did I leave off again? I'm on a roll today!" Grandma exclaimed happily.

Selfishly, I wanted to hear more, but I was a little worried my grandmother might be getting exhausted from all of the excitement, not to mention the sadness.

"Do you need to rest for a bit?" I asked.

"Oh, no resting. I must tell you more. Sit back and relax, Clairy girl," Grandma persisted, "From the instant I saw that first beautiful little fairy, I was even *more* obsessed, as you can imagine. I wanted so badly to describe what I had encountered to someone who would believe it, but there was no one around to listen. Disbelieving adults could spoil the magic, and I had no kindred spirit whom I trusted— no one like you, Claire."

"What about Anna?"

"I had nowhere to send a letter."

"Did you ever find out where she went? Did you ever get back in touch?"

"She ended up in California. Married a young man with the last name of . . . Larkson. Yes, that's it. *Lark*-son—the name so appropriately close to that of a sweet singing bird. And we did get back in touch, eventually, but that's a story for another time."

I rolled my eyes, but couldn't help but smile.

"So, I began to sketch my fairy every chance I got, spending hour upon hour trying to see another one. My parents took me on an excursion to the new public library in Dallas proper. It was there that I read every fairy legend I could find. I learned even more ways to try to see them! But try as I might, nothing worked, and it was extremely disheartening to try to entice fairies without my dearest friend."

"Were you lonely?"

"A bit, yes, but a new distraction would soon steal my thoughts away. It was strange, really, how a boy I'd never really noticed before could suddenly catch my eye, but catch my eye he did! Your grandfather. You know, he did something extraordinary, especially for a boy."

I immediately thought about G, the grocery boy. Hadn't he, too, been extraordinary in understanding my strange need for ladyfingers?

I shifted on the bed, preparing to hear all about Grandma meeting Grandpa, when I glanced at the clock.

"4:50? Shoot!" I jumped to my feet. "I'm sorry, Grandma, but I've gotta go," I said, putting the diary back in the bedside table drawer and cleaning up the teacups. "I told Mom I'd be ready by now." I left the tray of dirty dishes on the dresser and ran to my room, only having time to pull my black dress over my head before I was called downstairs.

15

Corporal Joseph Tucker

"Can I see another's woe, and not be in sorrow too?
Can I see another's grief and not seek for kind relief."
—◌ William Blake ◌—

There I was, one of a hundred somber faces all saying goodbye to Joseph Tucker. Corporal Tucker had only been stationed a few miles away from my brother when he had stepped on a landmine.

Was Val worried about buried landmines? Was he careful?

A cool breeze oscillated every now and then through the hot air. The day did all its usual things, allowing the sun to rise and give off light and heat, birds chirped, flowers bloomed—the world didn't stop, not even for this hero.

A wave of uneasiness swept through me as I approached the altar before finding a seat in the church. Huge sprays of flowers filled the air with their sweet scents. Upon the altar were Corporal Tucker's military award ribbons, one of his uniforms, and a large photograph of him looking cheerful and unbreakable. People milled in the aisle, hugging and talking softly. This was all that was left of him, was what no one said.

I suddenly had difficulty catching my breath.

The sorrow was balanced with celebration of the young man's life and patriotism during the funeral service. The eulogy expressed how Joseph, like Val, had always dreamed of serving his country and was proud to do it. Chills crashed like waves through my body, and my nose kept prickling. I always got that sensation before I cried, but used an old trick I'd read about in a book to stop myself—tickling the roof of my mouth with my tongue. Luckily, it worked.

After the service, my family followed the other mourners down the town streets to the cemetery—the caravan of cars was escorted by the local police. I looked out the window of the back seat to avoid my mother's tear-soaked face.

It struck me then just how tired, hungry, and isolated the soldiers in Iraq must feel. Did Americans really appreciate all they do for our freedom?

I leaned my head on the cool glass just as my father said, "Well, lookie here!"

Townspeople, having read about the fallen soldier in the local paper, had pulled over their cars and stood on the edge of the streets, hands over their hearts. Boys and girls, women and men stood on the sidewalks, some with flags in hand, showing solemn respect for the man who'd paid the highest price for their freedom.

There were dozens of people, nearly a hundred in all, lining the streets, in sync and in tune, like a nationalistic symphony of salutation. An everyday miracle, just like Grandma had talked about.

I took out my cell phone and took pictures of the patriots. It would make Val so happy to see that the whole town had come out to support his fallen comrade.

We reached the gravesite and my breathing problem returned. The six-foot coffin was draped with an American flag, and I began to sweat as it was lowered into a deep hole in the ground.

Really? Was this the end of Joseph Tucker? The high school's star basketball player, who took the team to the championship with a three-pointer just before the buzzer? The kind young man who served as an altar boy at church nearly every Sunday? The world would simply add him to the Iraq war death statistics?

I looked around at the dozens of other gravestones that surrounded me, all marked with platoon numbers and American flags.

And in that moment, I wanted nothing more than to get away from there.

Luckily, before any involuntary outbursts could strike me, it was time to leave.

Once home, I quickly changed out of my funeral clothes and stayed in my room the rest of the night, Val's safety pressing on my mind.

The next day, I decided it was high time to try and see a fairy or two myself. My accomplice, Lacey, was meeting me at the bench by the creek on the corner of Drexel and Miramar, so I grabbed my art pack, stuck in a half-eaten bag of sour Skittles as a fairy enticer, and headed toward the creek.

But how could I teach myself to see with my "mind's eye," like Grandma described?

I stopped by the library and quickly checked out one of those

Magic Eye 3-D books, the ones where if someone squints their eyes and blurs their gaze while looking at an abstract picture, suddenly, a three-dimensional figure pops out.

"Sorry I'm late, Lacey. I stopped and got this." I showed her the book.

"What for?"

"I thought it would make a good tool for practicing to see fairies." I sat on the bench next to Lacey.

"Oh, boy, Claire. I think you're losin' it."

"No, I'm not. I'm conducting a very logical and scientific experiment, that's all. Grandma says people can see fairies by using what she calls their 'mind's eye.'"

"I'm not sure I follow you."

I opened up the *Magic Eye* book. "Although this phenomenon's advertised as *magic,* there's actually science behind it. You see, our brain collects information from each eye—since the left and right eyes see everything differently—and puts them together."

Lacey closed her left eye and looked around with her right, and then closed her right eye and looked around with her left.

"By looking at the two-dimensional patterns in this book, while blurring the focus of one's eyes, the viewer uses what scientists call 'parallel viewing'—the eye muscles relax and lengthen—and they are able to see the picture in three-dimension." I turned to the first page. "Let's both try to un-focus on this one and see if we can do it."

"Okay."

It was difficult at first, but after a few minutes, "I see dozens of three-dimensional shooting stars!" Lacey exclaimed.

"I see them too!"

"Pretty awesome!"

We tried a few more, and soon we could easily see each of the 3-D images within about 30 seconds.

"It's time to take our skills to looking at trees and plants, to try and spot a fairy hiding in the foliage."

We walked over to a large hedge of coral-colored flowering quince that grew on the edge of the sidewalk and stared into it for about five minutes.

"See anything, Claire?"

"Not yet."

"Y'all look a little dazed, children—might be gettin' heatstroke," said Mrs. Anderson, a friend of my aunt who frequents the Tea Room. She wore heels that were way too fancy for dog walking, a purple polyester pantsuit, and a sparkly silver brooch on her right shoulder.

Lacey and I passed panicked glances between us.

"Oh, we thought we saw a . . ." Lacey stammered.

". . . snake," I lied.

"How awful!" Mrs. Anderson said. "Well, I'll have to walk Pom-Pom later. A snake could be the end 'a her!" The purple lady scooped up the little dog and spun around, her heels quickly clacking down the sidewalk.

Lacey and I snickered.

"I guess we do look a little strange, wanderin' around and starin' at bushes," Lacey laughed.

"Yeah. I say we try this experiment in a more private place, closer to the creek."

By the trickling water, sitting on the grass beneath the shade of a giant oak tree with squiggly roots bulging from the earth, we stared at its leafy boughs and just waited, hoping to see a fairy. All I saw were several mockingbirds and two squirrels.

I leaned back on my elbows. "We need to try something else, I think."

"Well, what else did your grandmother do to entice a fairy?"

I thought for a second. "She recited poetry. Know any poems?"

"Nope. Fresh out."

"I'll just make one up. Let's see . . . Roses are red, violets are blue, oh, dearest fairies, let us see you!"

We sat in silence for a while.

"Nothin'. What else should we do?" Lacey asked.

"Try thinking positive thoughts, like, 'I like fairies! I really want to see a fairy! I am a friend of nature!'"

Lacey's raised her eyebrows at me. "All right . . . but this feels a little strange."

"Just try." I gave her a pleading look.

But after five more minutes, nothing happened. Then, I remembered the sour Skittles. I dug them out of my bag.

"Let's try these." I shook a bunch into the palm of my hand and the sugar crystals on them sparkled in the sun.

"They look like irresistible fairy treats to me!" Lacey announced, taking one and popping it into her mouth.

I smiled, then piled them on top of a thick root, sat back in my spot, said my poem, thought happy thoughts—this fairy enticing stuff was tiring—and we waited silently.

After about ten more minutes of repeating all of this again and again, a large amount of sweat had trickled down my back. Lacey was fanning herself with the *Magic Eye* book.

"This heat's unbearable. I think it's time to go home." So we packed up and left.

We sat together, sprawled out on the couch in front of an air conditioner vent in the family room, the coolest place in my house.

"So, how's everythin' goin' with your grandmother being here?

You thought she was goin' to cause chaos in your house, but it seems peaceful enough." Lacey's dark brown eyes closed as she spoke. Her black hair was pulled back into a ponytail, exposing the smooth, tanned skin of her forehead. It wasn't fair how tan she got, when I would be pale all summer.

"Well, surprisingly enough, it hasn't been all bad. She's been telling me about my family's history."

"Really? Tell me somethin' interestin'."

"Her parents actually built this house," I replied.

"That's pretty cool."

"She also told me about her best friend Anna," I said. "But remember that article about how Anna's house burned down with her entire family in it?"

"Yes. So terrible!"

"Well, that caused Anna to have to leave town on the orphan train."

Lacey opened her eyes. "The orphan train?"

"Yes. In Grandma's day, orphans were sent to other families by train, to be adopted as help around the house, or in the fields."

"Orphans were treated more like 'the help' than a new family member back then?"

"Yes, and to make it worse, the children would get off in different cities along the route and farmers would pick the ones they wanted. If a kid didn't get picked, he or she would go back on the train and try again in the next city."

"No way! That's awful!" Lacey looked stunned.

"Hey, I've been meaning to look up orphan trains on the computer. Wanna surf with me?"

"Sure. I think I need a little more convincin' to believe that these trains existed. The 1920s were civilized times, and these trains sound barbaric."

We went up to my room. I gave Lacey the swivel chair while I grabbed my suitcase out of the closet and turned it on its side to make another seat. Then I typed o-r-p-h-a-n t-r-a-i-n into the Google search box. Up popped articles, photos, books, and even a PBS special—all about orphan trains.

"This really happened! Click on that picture!" Lacey pointed.

I clicked and a larger version of the photo showed boys and girls of all ages hanging out of a row of train windows. Below it was the caption: *Between 1854 and 1932, over 100,000 children rode orphan trains to find adoptive parents.*

"Oh, look at that one little girl. She looks so sad!" Lacey touched her finger to the screen, looking close to tears herself.

"Well, on the bright side, they weren't out on the streets starving. *Oliver Twist* was based on the reality of orphans in the late 1800s, you know."

"You always sound like a talkin' textbook, Claire," Lacey said. "Look! There's a website that gets people in touch with passengers from the orphan trains. Do ya know your grandma's friend's full name?"

"Yes, Anna . . . Connelly." I typed the name into the box and received a message asking me what state she had come from and where she went.

DEPARTED: Texas

DESTINATION: California

"Look, there's an Anna Connelly who fits that criteria. I'll fill out the inquiry form with my name and address and wait for a reply," I said, typing and then hitting "send."

"Which you'll get in eight to twelve weeks," Lacey pointed out. "That's a bummer of a long time, but I'm glad you filled it out and sent the form anyway. You may find out about Anna one day."

"Yes, but you know how impatient I am," I said with a smirk. "With Grandma being a ripe old age, most likely Anna's pretty old too, or no longer alive. Let's try Googling Anna Connelly . . . and what was her married name again? Oh, Larkson."

I typed in Anna Connelly Larkson but nothing came up. The closest we got was an *Anna Clarkson*. Lacey popped her lower lip out into a pout.

But something intuitive told me I'd find out more about her one day.

16

The Language of Love and Flowers

"Nothing can be truer than fairy wisdom. It is as true as sunbeams."
—๏ *Douglas Jerrold* ๏—

That afternoon, I found Grandma in the living room with her tea.

"Have you come to join me?" she asked sweetly.

"Sure." I casually strolled over and sat on the couch beside her. "It's good to see you up and about."

"Thank you, darling. I've been so tired lately," she yawned, stretching her arms forward like a cat. "You want to hear more of my story?" She put both hands in her lap, already poised to start.

"I guess," I understated.

"Well, I believe I was telling you how I met your grandfather."

I traced the fleur-de-lis pattern on the couch with my pinky. "Yeah, I think so."

"Very good. Well then, I was walking home from school one day, alone, when I spotted a vine of purple trumpet flowers trailing out of a trash container, obviously clippings from someone's yard work. I'd been looking for a piece of trumpet creeper to perform a fairy ceremony I had just read about at the library.

"The bin was quite close to the house's large picture window, so I hesitated a moment. If someone were inside, they'd surely see me. But I felt an urgent need to make that garland of lavender-hued flowers for my hair, and as impulsive as I was then, I set my worry aside."

"Oh, I understand. I once climbed someone's fence because the perfect blue bonnet for sketching was growing in their yard. Trespassing for art!" We grinned knowingly at each other. "But go on."

"Well, tiptoeing up to the can, I reached for the blooms, and still standing near the window, I tied them into a wreath. Putting the crown upon my head, I gave it a twist left, and then right, to make it fit just so. I had just turned to leave when I heard a gentlemanly voice recite:

There are fairies fair,
flying in the air,
with purple flowers in their hair!

I nearly jumped out of my skin! But I turned around to see a boy. Graham was his name. I knew him from school. Apparently, it was *his* trashcan I had raided!"

"Ooopsy!" I said.

"*Ooopsy* is right! He was a couple of years older than I, and occasionally hung around with my older brother, but I had never really noticed him. Now I noticed his eyes were a sea green, like the ocean I'd only read about in books. They were so magnificent, I became lost in them immediately."

That's funny. I had the same first impression about the blue eyes of the boy in the grocery store. I shook G from my head as Grandma continued.

"I couldn't speak for what seemed like several minutes, but was probably only seconds. Not only was he quite handsome, and his eyes dreamy, but I was shocked he had mentioned my very obsession, fairies!

"'I saw you dancing in the park show a while back,' he explained. 'With the wands, bare feet, and the flying. You were hard to miss, the way you danced.'

"I was mesmerized by him, and not at all used to boys giving compliments! Nervously I began to smile . . . and that's when I caught a glimpse of my reflection in the window. I looked more like a goofy feral child than a glamorous fairy! The earlier twisting of the wreath upon my head had caused my hair to stand straight up in loops and wisps all around where the crown lay. I was mortified!" She stopped, laughing at herself. "So that's when I *ran!* How's that for a first impression?"

I chuckled along with her. I could totally relate!

"After leaving Graham, and arriving on my own porch, a new feeling came over me. I had found another enchantment to try to attract, where magical forces could be felt all around— the magic of love." Grandma got quiet, looking off into the distance.

I studied her face. Her eyes were droopy, with dark circles today, and her cheeks weren't their usual rosy color.

"Your mom said the funeral yesterday was difficult," said Grandma. "I'm sorry."

"It was fine." I tried to shrug it off. "Makes me worry about Val, of course, but that soldier's family . . . *they* had a difficult day. I . . . I don't really want talk about it. Could we get back to your story instead?"

"Of course, dear." She thought for a second. "Well, after that, I tried to put myself into situations where I might run into your grandfather at school, and for a while, I was content with just daydreams—even a glance from him triggered the happiest thoughts. A smile, or even a nod 'hello,' were fodder for my fantasy."

My face flushed just hearing the word 'fantasy.'

"I began to study your grandfather's habits from afar, and noticed he was very chivalrous, studious, tall, and more handsome each time I saw him. He also, unfortunately, often had one particular girl hanging around him, competing for his attention."

"So, what did you do about the other girl?"

"Well, I wasn't nearly as bold as she—she left me in the dust when it came to flirting!"

"Didn't he notice you at all?"

"Well, whenever he'd walk by *me,* he'd say, 'Well, hello, Fairy Faye,' and wink one of those dreamy eyes. It gave me hope that he might like me. I just didn't know how to take the next step."

"Well, he ended up choosing you. You must have done something right," I said, on the edge of my seat.

"It was a tradition, in those days, to give small bouquets of flowers to people. Referred to today as nosegays, we called them 'tussie-mussies.' These bouquets symbolized one's feelings for another. They were given to friends, family, and lovers as a sort of Victorian-style FTD delivery.

"Although these tussie-mussies could be given to someone special at any time, on May Day everyone sent them. Adults would decorate baskets filled with popcorn or homemade cookies, instead of making bouquets, and leave them on the stoops of special acquaintances and kin. Young people took the opportunity to secretly leave a tussie-mussie upon the doorstep of a potential love interest, because it was the only day when it was acceptable to leave one anonymously."

"So you made one for Grandpa?"

"It was my chance to express my feelings for Graham in a safe way, but the bouquet had to be just right. I searched the town's gardens, fields, and parks for what I wanted." She paused to tiredly scratch an itch on her arm, and then went on. "Hostas, symbolizing 'devotion,' a thornless peach rose meaning, 'your charms are unequalled,' and blue periwinkle for 'friendship' were easy enough to find. I boldly used white azalea to symbolize 'first romance' and forget-me-nots for 'true love.'"

"How did you know what the meaning of each flower was?" I asked.

"Oh, I looked them up in a book. Everyone had them. I had *Kate Greenaway's Language of Flowers*. It said that a variegated tulip would let him know I 'admired his eyes,' so I added that as well. Still, I was desperate for the twines of purple flowers—like the one I'd made into a crown the day we met—so I walked all over town, but there were none to be found."

Grandma reached next to her, into the shadows, and suddenly her diary appeared in her hand. "Purple marker, this time, with the flower bouquet milagro." She passed it to me.

I scratched my head, trying to figure out where the diary had come from, but then went ahead and found the page.

May 1st, 1929

I have had another MIRACULOUS day! It started when I rested under the tree where I had seen the first fairy collect water. It's my favorite place to go—I'd been hoping for another sighting.

I was laying there today, thinking about the tussie-mussie I was about to make for Graham, right down to the doily wrap and the satin ribbon, and in no time at all, I fell into a deep sleep—a different kind of sleep, like a slumber over which I had no control. I've read about mortals being coerced to sleep by the faint singing of wood sprites, but I don't recall hearing any singing. And in what felt like a moment's time, the brush of something awakened me. It was another FAIRY!

I didn't see the fair one at first, but placed upon my shoulder was a lovely six-inch piece of a blooming trumpet vine! I looked around for a human who may have put it there, but I was alone. And besides, I haven't told anyone I was looking for a trumpet creeper, nor how I feel about Graham. Word might get around to him—maybe he doesn't like me back.

Then, I felt something land upon me, and in my waking daze, I saw a winged, iridescent creature flying overhead. This one had short filaments for hair, with anthers on the ends. Instead of wearing a dress, he had a little organic short suit made of green sepals and lavender petals—a fairy boy—and then he vanished into thin air!

Oh, how I wish Anna was around, so I could tell her all about it! Luckily, I have you, dear diary.

I lowered the book. "You're sure it was a fairy? I'm still having a hard time accepting the magic nymph thing. Sounds like dream-induced illusions to me. You were *sleeping* right before it appeared." I couldn't hold back my doubt. As much as I wanted to believe in something so remarkable, I just . . . couldn't.

"There are many phenomena in the world that just . . . *exist*. Sure, you can explain them through science, or write them off as a dream, but somehow that amazing occurrence shows itself to you—therefore, *it is real to you*. There are so many things in life that are simply miraculous. Like fire. We know it's real and scientists have proven how it transpires, but it's difficult not to get completely captivated by its mysterious beauty. Nature made it that way long before any scientists explained it. Can you imagine what early humans thought of flames the first time they saw them? Magical! And even today, the wonder of it never goes away."

"OK, I'll give you that," I said. "It's like how one of my favorite things to watch are the bubbles that pop up in a beautiful gush after I pour cream soda over ice. Science proves that it's a simple reaction between gases, air, and liquid, but it's still wonderful when it happens. The bubbles are kind of beautiful."

"Atta girl! You're catching on. Open yourself to the intricacies of life every day and you'll be given an abundance of gifts.

"The difference between dreams and reality was clear to me because I had something physical to prove it—a fully blooming piece of a plant that didn't exist anywhere else at that time. There was not another bloom like it anywhere in the county, I was sure of it! The fairies had listened to the longing in my heart and helped me," she said, tears welling up in her tired eyes.

I frowned to see her sadness.

"Now, don't mind those who cry, Claire," my grandmother added. "We're simply moved emotionally by nature and its gifts. It's so much better to *feel* life than to just go through the motions of living it. How sad to only believe in what you can see."

Uncomfortable, I tried to move on by asking, "So, how do fairies come into existence anyway? In *Peter Pan* it says fairies are born from the first laugh of a baby, which seems pretty silly. That's an elaborate fictional description, not an explanation."

"I have formed a theory, after all of these years, about that very question. Of course, being my scientific girl, you already know that a body decomposes upon death."

"Of course. Plants and animals go from life to death, then disintegrate back to the earth, nourishing life again."

"I've always wondered, though, where their *energy* of spirit goes after death. Our bodies are merely shells of protection for the spirit that lives inside. The soul goes to heaven, but what if that energy is separate? Wouldn't it seem plausible that it gets renewed back into nature, perhaps to spring forth the growth of flowers, cause the tremble of earthquakes, spark the electricity in lightning, and maybe even to create more fairies? Maybe this energy is another link in the circle of life, which encompasses the power of the fairies to make nature flourish on earth."

"Hmmm . . ."

A theory deserving further thought, I decided.

"Anyway, I was so dumbfounded that I didn't remember the journey across the fields between the creek and my front porch. My mother's friend, Miss Willie, abruptly ended my trance. She was visiting to discuss the latest gossip, as usual. Miss Willie would go on to open the tearoom your aunt owns now. It was a very popular place even back then, and she knew everyone's business because of it."

Grandma placed her hands on her hips, mimicking Miss Willie, and said, "My goodness, child, where on God's green earth did y'all find trumpet flowers? Why, that vine doesn't bloom 'til at least June 'round here!"

She'd purposely said it with a strong Texas accent and I couldn't help but laugh. But Grandma didn't laugh. Instead, she grew silent—her breathing more deliberate.

"Are you feeling okay?" I asked, feeling my forehead bunch up with worry.

"I'm just weary. Time's ticking away for me." She settled further against the couch back. "But I have so much more to tell."

"Maybe you should go back to your room to rest . . ."

"No, no. I'm going to finish my story first," she said with determination. Clearing her throat, she began again, "Delivering the tussie-mussie to Graham became secondary after seeing the second fairy. Had it not been for the beautiful basket my mother had shown me on her way to deliver it to our neighbors, I may have forgotten about my tussie altogether."

"You forgot about Grandpa?"

"Just for a little while, dear. And once I remembered, I completed it quickly and snuck it over to Graham's. Afterward, I was back to replaying my fairy encounters again and again in my head. As 'fairy infatuated' as I'd become, nothing else got much of my attention, not even new love."

"So, why do you think the fairies showed themselves to you those two times? What had you done by yourself that you and Anna hadn't?"

"I asked myself that very thing. At first, I thought perhaps all of the offerings I brought to the fairies with Anna over the years had made them happy, and they were thanking me.

"But I realized the two encounters had something in common: I had been brimming with strong emotion. First, sorrow over the departure of my most beloved friend, and second, bursting with the excitation of my first love interest. My feelings had become strongly tangible to the fair ones. Seeing into my heart, and empathizing, they assisted me with magic in my times of need. Healing me, they resolved my desperation and aided me back into happiness, with love."

"How can you believe that so fearlessly?"

Grandma looked at me a long moment. "Don't be afraid to believe in them, Clairy. Allow yourself to listen with your intuition. Let your imagination act freely. Young children talk of seeing fairies much more than adults for this simple reason: they trust their intuitive vision. They have neither inhibitions nor preconceived notions about numinous beings, and therefore, can readily see them. Children and fairies innately understand the importance of play and laughter, so they have a natural connection. Plus, children are pure of heart, so the fairies trust them.

"I believe you can ask the wee folk for anything, but you have to release your *fear*. Fear of accepting their existence. Fear of not being worthy enough to accept your wishes being granted."

Fear that your brother may never return from the war.

"Life is like breathing. A person spends a small amount of time consciously doing it, allowing it just to happen most of the time. Clairy, don't be like most people. Stop to feel the breath of life . . . hear its rhythm, its sound . . . and take the time to notice the little things with an open mind and heart. You might be surprised at what you've been missing." She waved a finger at me. "Also—and this is very important—trust in love."

Just then, Grandma became very serious, opening her eyes wide like an owl in the dark. "Oh! And one more thing . . ."

The pause was a long one, and Grandma used her knuckles to *knock-knock-knock* against the tea tray, then she used one finger and *crisscrossed*.

"Yes, Grandma?" I was nervous, though I didn't know why.

"Please, Clairy, don't come to see me when . . . when things get bad. I want you to remember us now."

"I'm not sure what you're talking about—the doctors say you're healthy."

She didn't seem to hear me. "When your grandfather died ten years ago, I was heartbroken. He was the love of my life. In fact, I fell in love with him over and over again throughout our sixty years together. From the first time I saw him, he was embedded in my heart.

"He was sick for awhile before he passed. That was a difficult time, but I forced myself to smile whenever at his bedside, in case it was the last time he saw me. Even when he could hardly speak, I knew he loved me back, just as much as ever. He knew I felt the pain of losing him, and understood why I was only happy around him—we wanted to joyously relish every second in each other's presence."

I gulped, bowing my head to hide my sadness.

"You know, as he was . . . *leaving me*, I felt angels all around us. I knew he wanted me to continue living a full life and to not be sad. I knew he would wait for me in heaven."

"So far, you've lived more than a decade longer," I pointed out.

"Yes, and I always felt there was purpose to my longer life. At first, I thought it was so I could gain knowledge of the fairies' lessons, but then I realized knowing their message wasn't enough. I needed to *tell* someone. I needed to pass on the knowledge to someone special. Someone who would listen. I think that someone is *you, Claire*."

I didn't know what to say.

Then, Grandma, obviously fatigued, reached next to her again, and in her hand this time was a single white carnation with pink stripes, like a candy cane.

"Where did that come from?"

My grandmother silently handed it to me, smiling. I held it to my nose, taking in its sweet, musky scent.

"I think I'll go and rest now—we'll talk more tomorrow. So much more to tell . . ."

Grandma stood up, grabbed her diary, and slowly picked her way across the room. Before I could get up to help her, Mom appeared, taking her by the arm. Together, they went upstairs.

I looked at the carnation in my hand. I should have freaked out—the flower seemed to just *appear!*

But I felt a peaceful acceptance instead, because it hadn't occurred to me until today how much Grandma needed me. She needed me to listen. She needed me to believe her. This was her singular wish in her twilight years. I was her only granddaughter, and I was open to learning. Who else could she pass these stories on to besides me?

17

The Jewelry Box

"Everybody needs beauty as well as bread, places to play in and pray in,
where nature may heal and give strength to body and soul alike."
—❧ *John Muir* ❧—

The next morning, I woke up slowly. My desk beckoned to me to continue sketching the flowers and seedpods waiting there for me. It was so nice to work while wearing pajamas! A true sign of summer. After about half an hour, I smelled breakfast cooking, which reminded me how hungry I was.

"Hey, Mom! Pancakes? They smell delicious," I said, pulling two plates from the cupboard to set the table.

"Well, Grandma's resting, so I had the time. What do the two of you do together? Run laps?" Mom teased.

"Well, she does remember her past in a marathon kind of way. Her stories go on and on, but I think I get tired before she does."

"I think it's nice you two are spending time together. You were a little reluctant at first."

"Well, it's important to know all of this old family stuff, for future generations." The truth was, I looked forward to four o'clock every day, but I saw no reason to announce it. Mom liked to make an emotional fuss over the silliest things.

"Well, even if you are the official family historian," my mom said discerningly, "you need to go easy on her. She's getting weaker fairly rapidly. Her vitals are fluctuating quite a bit lately."

"I thought you said the doctors gave her a clean bill of health."

"They did. I'm not sure what's going on with her."

"Will she be okay for tea later this afternoon?" Mom was so serious it worried me. "If not, I've got plenty of other things to do," I lied.

"We'll just have to see how the day goes. Now eat your pancakes before they get cold."

Four o'clock came about slowly. I usually felt time was never enough when it came to working on my sketches, but all I cared about was finding out how Grandma won Grandpa's heart away from that other girl. I hoped Grandma would feel well enough to tell the story.

Finally, at four sharp, I slipped downstairs to see if Mom was preparing the tea, but she wasn't in the kitchen. I held my hand over the teakettle and it was cold. I looked in every downstairs room, then out in the backyard. Neither Mom nor Grandma was there.

I came back through the kitchen door just as a *thump* came from the ceiling above. Then I heard someone raise her voice up there, unsure if it was happy or sad.

Was Mom in Grandma's room without tea?

I froze in my tracks.

What if Grandma was really sick and couldn't talk anymore? What if she fell out of bed again and got hurt this time?

Panicking, I took the stairs two at a time, stopping outside of Grandma's door. Finally taking a breath, I stuck my head in to see what was going on, my heart beating fast.

"There you are, Clairy! Come in, it's past four o'clock and I was getting worried about you," came Grandma's voice.

"We wanted to keep this a secret," Mom chimed in.

"I went downstairs to help with tea, and when I couldn't find any-one, I . . ." I was so relieved that I was babbling. "What's going on?"

Then, I saw two ice cream sundaes on the tea tray, with whipped cream and maraschino cherries on top.

"Am I interrupting something?" I asked.

"No, no, deary! That's the surprise—it's my birthday! Today I'm eighty-eight years old and your mother wanted us to celebrate."

"No one told me. Grandma, you could've told me."

"If I told you it wouldn't be a surprise, and after as many birthdays as I've had, they sort of lose their novelty," she said with a crooked smile.

"I'll just go and come back later then." There were only two sun-daes, so obviously they wanted to celebrate with just the two of them.

"Claire, those sundaes are for you and Grandma," Mom laughed. "I'm going downstairs to do some paperwork. Have fun, but don't stay too long. Grandma needs her rest."

"Oh, pish-posh," Grandma crumpled her brow. "Clairy-time is better for me than any old nap."

Mom raised her eyebrows at me before walking out the door.

I sat down on the bed. The sundaes oozed chocolate sauce, which dripped down the outside of the dish as the vanilla ice cream began to melt. Grandma and I picked up our spoons simultaneously, paus-ing to laugh at the fact that we'd, once again, done something at the same time without meaning to.

"Happy birthday, Grandma." I grinned.

"Cheers!" She clanked her spoon against mine.

If I were ever asked to describe one of my happiest moments, I thought, right now would certainly be at the top.

Grandma's hand shook as she dipped her spoon into the frothy cream, slowly bringing it to her mouth. After only two bites, she jumped right into her storytelling.

"I spent as much time as possible by the spring, after seeing fairies by the creek twice. All I did was sketch, draw, and dream about fluttering creatures with gossamer wings. My fixation was fueled when, a few weeks after my second sighting, I received my first letter from Anna."

"No way! How exciting!"

"Indeed. She was living in California. Mail traveled very slowly back in the 1920s, and she wrote as soon as she was able. Part of me was worried she'd forgotten all about our time together, or replaced me with someone else. It even crossed my mind that maybe she was living with a mean family that didn't allow her paper, pens, or postage—you know how one's imagination can run away sometimes. Turns out I had worried needlessly."

"So, what was her new home like?"

"Her letter, and the many that followed, described how hard she worked in the orange orchards, now her home. She lived in a farmhouse, isolated from any other dwellings."

"Did she tell you about the people she lived with there? Hmm. I'll bet that was so strange, to suddenly be part of a new family," I mused.

"Well, her new guardians were kind enough, but she had clearly been adopted to help sew, wash, cook, and clean so that the lady of the house could spend most of her day riding horseback across an enormous bridge, traveling to a distant city to sell their oranges." Grandma sighed. "I could tell how much she missed me."

"I wish I could see that letter for myself."

"All right, then. Please go over and look in that box on the dresser." Grandma pointed towards an ivory leather jewelry case.

I put my sundae spoon down and walked to the dresser. Shoebox-sized and a bit worn, with much of the imprinted gold decoration rubbed off of the outside, the jewelry box had a gold latch with a keyhole.

"Now open the small drawer on the left of the vanity. There should be a key in there."

Sure enough, inside was a tiny key with a faded red silk tassel on it.

I rubbed my hands together, like I'd been given a treasure chest. Twisting the key in the lock, I opened the lid with flourish. The inner lining was pale pink satin with hand-painted periwinkle, flowering quince, and orange blossoms. Among the flowers were fairies flying, hiding, and peeking out from behind petals and stems. The fairies fit Grandma's description exactly, with organic shapes and shimmering wings. There was depth and shadow, muted and bright colors; painting techniques I'd only dreamed of knowing how to do one day. The delicateness in which they were painted literally took my breath away.

Two stacks of letters, each tied with a different brightly colored ribbon, sat at the bottom of the box.

"The stack tied with the salmon-colored ribbon are letters from Grandpa," Grandma said, beaming. "Quince-colored, like my favorite flower. I wanted to paint the flowering quince because its orange-pink color is like nothing else. They symbolize 'the cheering of one's soul.'" She almost seemed to blush. "That's what your grandfather did for me."

"Wait a minute. *You* painted the inside of this box?" I said in awe, still taking in the remarkable beauty of the paintings.

"Yes I did . . . a long time ago. Like I told you, I drew and painted like there was no tomorrow. Now, below that stack are the ones with the periwinkle satin ribbon. Periwinkles were Anna's favorite flower, representing 'young friendship,' so I painted those, and then of course, to keep with the 'happy outcome' of her life's path in California, I painted orange blossoms."

"Where are the other fairy paintings and sketches you did?" I asked, dying to see more of Grandma's work.

"I will tell you about those, with patience, after I finish *this* story."

Yeah, yeah, yeah. With patience.

"Let's look at Anna's letters. Read the one on top to me, please." She touched a hand to her neck. "Goodness, I haven't read her letters in years."

The edges of the envelope were brown with age and worn with handling. I gingerly opened it. The writing was done in quill pen, black and grey lettering that was thicker in some parts and thinner in others.

Dearest Faye: July 12, 1929

This is my first letter to you since that terrible day at the train station. I traveled so long and far, stopping at town after town to be adopted by a new family. There were hundreds of us, and like me, many of the children cried a lot; others played games and made friends, but I wanted nothing of that—I missed you and my family too much! I couldn't eat and just laid on the sweaty leather seats wherever I could, not talking to anyone. By the time we hit the end of the line, I was shaky and weak, sure no one would want a scrawny, pale, weeping girl.

Finally, after days of travel, there were only fifteen of us children remaining who'd been rejected by families along the way, for one reason or another, like Jimmy, who had a lame foot. But we'd come to the last stop and the conductor refused to take any of us back eastward, so he told the farmers that gathered on the platform that they had to take all of us. The train pulled away and we just stood there while men and women argued over who would get which child.

A woman, Ellie, who was noticeably pregnant, walked up to me. "Well, I guess you'll do. I really need a girl to take over the household and to help take care of this here baby while I drive the team over the bridge to sell oranges. Can you do that?"

"Yes, ma'am," I said. I knew I couldn't risk being left there alone, now that the train was gone.

After a silent ride in their rickety horse-drawn buggy, we arrived at their little red farmhouse, tucked into acre after acre of beautiful orange trees that smelled so sweet, like air-honey. Their two older boys came out onto the front porch. They leaned against the river rock pillars and stared at me. Their job is working with their father in the orchard all day long.

Then a girl close to my age appeared. Her name is Aster and she's a year younger than I. She walked up to me and said, "It's nice to meet you, but let me make it real clear—I am their blood-related daughter. You'd best remember that." We're supposed to share the many household chores, but Aster picks her favorite ones first, leaving the drudgery to me.

I have chores from sunup to sundown, but I'm treated fairly—and so happy to live near a beautiful wildflower field. I go there every day, leaving offerings to try and attract fairies. They just have to be tending the magnicent wildowers, aromatic orange blossoms, and abundant wildlife in that stunning field filled with bright orange poppies and pink wild sweet pea. I sing the songs we always sang together, and read my poems aloud. So far, I've seen nothing.

I miss you more than I can put into words on this page. Please write back!
Your Forever Kindred Spirit,
Glorianna

"Wow. Letters really can tell a story, can't they?" I said, gazing at the yellowed page.

"Yes," Grandma nodded. "But the best is yet to come. Pull out the next letter from the top of the stack and read it now."

I eased it from the ivory envelope to see that this letter was neatly scribbled in pencil.

July 13, 1929

Dearest Faye:

I just mailed my first letter to you yesterday because Mama Ellie rode into town, but something incredible happened this afternoon and I have to tell you about it immediately!

Two days ago, my new father brought home sticks of crystallized sugar for all of the children. I pretended to eat mine, gently licking its rough sweetness with my tongue, but slipped it in my sock when no one was looking, saving it to entice the wee ones. When I went to the field that afternoon, I used the diamond-like encrusted wand in my dance, and left it as an offering on a tree branch next to a bunch of perfumed orange blossoms.

Yesterday, I received a note from my old aunt. She wrote to see how I was faring, but her letter made me feel angry that she didn't allow me to stay with you. I felt extremely homesick and couldn't concentrate on my chores—I got reprimanded by my new mother for not focusing. And Aster jumped in, adding that I never did anything right. I fought back tears the rest of the day.

When I'd finally been dismissed from my work, I ran to the center of the wildflower field to sit and cry. In that meadow, with eyes growing more swollen as each tear fell, I felt utterly desperate.

That was when I heard a hissing sound. A kind of a "ssss!" A rattlesnake? They certainly have them around here. Or was it the wind? I heard it again and listened more carefully, realizing it sounded more like a person trying to get me to hush: "sshhhh!" I looked around but not a soul was near.

It was then that a tiny woman appeared upon a large rock next to me. With a filmy dress and wings to match, she was covered in dewdrops that sparkled like diamonds in the fading sunlight. Her dress was made of fine white petals, with yellow threads of hair, green twigs for arms and legs, and a bright orange glowing aura.

Her wings began to flap, lifting her overhead, and as I tilted my face back to watch her, a single drop of dew landed upon my forehead, running down my nose. It tickled, and smelled of orange blossoms. I stuck my finger in the liquid, tasting thick, sweet orange-flavored sugar.

Then, as a second dewdrop landed on my chest, the raw feelings that had been tearing at my insides immediately subsided. I thought I heard her whisper "home," and she swooped her arm from left to right, showing me the field. Suddenly, I no longer felt rootless and knew, intuitively, I'd be all right living in this new place.

Can you believe it? I wish you could have seen it! It was so amazing! So wonderful! I can't wait until you get both of my letters and write back!

Adieu For Now—
Your Glorianna

"So, you wrote her back and told her all about your two sightings, right? She must have been so excited that you saw fairies too," I said, gently folding up the letter and slipping it back into the envelope.

"Oh, yes, she was very excited. And because we each saw them separately, without the other knowing what we saw, but nearly identically described how they looked and made us feel, we knew they were real."

"So, the fairy came when she was brimming with emotion, and it was the same for you during your two sightings, almost like your feel-ings gave you special glasses with which to see things differently . . ."

It sounded silly now that I'd said it aloud.

"Yes, something just like that. Ah, you clever girl, Clairy!

The fairies want us to enjoy the happiness of life and the world around us. Emotions are an important part of living, and fairies are afraid that if humans shut them out, replacing them with too many jaded or negative feelings, the world will never be healed in terms of pollution, abuses, or war."

Hearing the word "war" made me think of my brother—and fear gave my stomach a twist.

Grandma looked at me carefully. "Caring for others can be pain-ful because we get attached and then sometimes relationships end. Instead of risking the hurt, we tend to shut out the caring. Love is considered a leap of faith instead of what it should be—uncon-ditional. We fight the inevitable instead of finding the blessings in every precious moment."

She set her spoon on the tray. "Don't be afraid of believing in things you cannot see. We talked about being prescient, but do you know what the word 'clairsentient' means?"

"No, but it has my name in it. I thought you were referring to me at first," I joked, trying to lighten the subject.

Grandma chuckled. "Yes, so it does! How wonderful that is. Look it up and see if it's in you as much as you are in it."

"All right, I will. Did Anna mention anything else about her fairy sighting in other letters?"

"Yes, actually. She mentioned that the lovely glittery fairy was waving a large sprig of orange blossoms in one tiny hand. At first, Anna just thought she was trying to let her know that she was an orange tree blossom fairy, but the way she kept showing it to Anna made her think there was more to it than that.

"So, Anna looked in one of her 'meanings of flowers' books and found that orange blossoms represent 'a happy outcome,' which is why brides so often carry them in their bouquets. That's all I wished for Anna. Happiness."

A few tears raced down her cheek as she reached out to her headboard and knocked with her lanky, bent finger three times, then brush, brush.

Then she just sat there, gazing out the window in a strange way.

"Grandma, are you okay?"

"Yes, I'm all right. Tired . . . so very tired . . ." her voice faded as she spoke.

"Well then, it's time I go and let you sleep." I got up to leave, but then turned around. "But before I go, do you think you could answer one more question?"

"Sure, my dear."

"Why do you bang on furniture with your knuckles and then do a small sign of the cross?"

She laughed wearily. "That? I've done it for years—so often that I do it without thinking. I knock on wood three times for luck and the continued health of those I care about. The first knock is for my family, the second is for my friends, and the third for my acquaintances. All three groups affect a person's life, and their safety gives my own life happiness."

"And then you do the sign of the cross?"

"No, it's not necessarily the sign of the cross, but the creation of imaginary crossroads. Crossroads are thought to be especially magical since they essentially connect four important roads: the human road, the road of plants and animals, the road of Mother Earth, and the road of spirituality. Where they meet is the *point of enchantment.* I try to conjure a momentary pinnacle of magic to aid my well-wishes of others."

"Wow," I said, stunned by the incredible compassion my grandmother showed the Earth and all people in her life. "I am going to have to let that idea sink in, but it sounds really . . . nice."

I carefully returned the letters to the fantastic box, closing the lid, locking the latch, and returning the key to the drawer. Walking slowly toward the door with the tray filled with what was left of our melted sundaes, I turned and smiled. "See you tomorrow, Grandma."

"Yes, darling," she replied, blowing me a kiss before closing her eyes to sleep.

Even with all of my grandmother's information, I still had questions.

Was it really possible to see a fairy in today's modern world? Nature is just as beautiful as in 1929, so the caretakers of the flowers have to still be around, right? Perhaps they just needed a little more coaxing these days.

And who knows, if humans were to return to a more intuitive way of living—more in tune with nature—maybe the world *would* be a better place. If nature could truly heal us, humans were missing out on a very important resource right in front of their eyes. Besides, there were a lot of things that I already believed in that I couldn't see, like sounds, tastes, and feelings.

Maybe someday I'd be famous for discovering scientific proof that fairies exist. Maybe they'd be the answer to healing the sick, famines, and global warming. I'd help save the world! Dr. Claire Collins: Fairy Scientist and World-Renowned Expert!

Well, perhaps I was getting a little carried away. But the one thing I had on my side was perseverance. I planned to try even harder to see the little creatures—so hard that the only way I wouldn't be able to see them would be if they didn't exist.

18

Glossolalia

"Family faces are magic mirrors. Looking at people who belong to us,
we see the past, present, and future."
—✦ *Gail Lumet Buckley* ✦—

Grandma Faye slept for nearly two days straight again, and Mom was beginning to worry. I was too. I sat on my window seat and re-read my journal entries—everything my grandmother had told me so far.

She had asked me to look up the word *clairsentient,* so I did, and it was what happens when someone "perceives information as a feeling within the body." Was it in me as much as I was in it? I wasn't sure.

I thought about the fairies on the front of the cosmetic compact Grandma slipped into Anna's hand on the train platform. She had never told me what the note said.

Curious, I went on eBay to see if there was such an item as a fairy-decorated Djer Cosmetics powder container, and sure enough, there it was! "1920s Djer Cosmetics sterling compact, bids starting at eighty dollars."

Eighty bucks! That was way out of my league, but I couldn't help but wonder if it might be the same one my grandmother had given Anna. I zoomed in on the photo. The pattern on the front was just as she'd described: floral border and two willowy fairies, one obviously male and one female. It was their svelte bodies that made them so lovely.

I got up and looked at myself in my full-length mirror. I always hated mirrors because they never told the truth. Sure, they could tell me if my hair was messy or if I had spinach stuck between my teeth, but they never really told me whether I was attractive. It was easy to look at others and have an opinion on their beauty, but so much harder to get an overall impression of myself.

My parents always said I was pretty or cute, but one day, my mother told me, "beauty is in the eye of the beholder and is based more on strength of character than what's on the outside." Was she trying to tell me not to rely on my looks?

My best friend, Lacey, was the obvious kind of pretty. Everyone said so. And she had boys who talked to her in the hall and walked her home from school. I tried to study what she did to attract them so I could learn to do the same, and one of the main things was that she didn't completely freeze up around boys the way I did. I'd never have a boyfriend. Sure, I wanted a cute guy in my life who cared about me in a romantic way, calling me pretty and longing to be near me—but they'd never like such a nerdy girl.

So there I stood, gazing into the mirror as usual. Not long ago, I'd stood in this very place thinking how plain I looked—so tall, thin, and with metal braces. And my pupils were always dilated. Did I always have the eyes of a threatened cat? Tonight, however, I felt different. I expected to feel the anger I was accustomed to feeling about my plain looks, but instead, I saw my straight, newly braces-free teeth and my body's newly developing curves. But even more so, I saw my grandmother's cheekbones, and how my eyes were set the same way, below long, thick lashes. There was family history in my face! I couldn't help but smile at the discovery, and hey—today my pupils were actually a nice, normal size.

Startled by my cell, I picked it up to hear Lacey on the line. "Hey, you!"

"What's up, Lacey?"

"Nothin'. I just got the urge to check in. How's your grandmother?"

The question made my tummy twist a little.

"She's okay, I think. Just tired all the time lately. Why do you ask?"

Lacey's voice got softer, "I just had a feelin' somethin' was . . . wrong."

Hmm. Maybe *Lacey* was the clairsentient one. "She keeps telling me that our time together is . . . limited. And that she has so much to share before . . ." My stomach was in a knot now.

"Sounds like you two have become friends."

"Yeah, we have," was all I could muster.

"Well, Claire, sometimes you get pretty analytical and forget about feelin'." She paused. "You know you can talk to me about anythin', right?"

Plopping sideways onto my bed, I smiled. "I know."

"You also should know that denial is 'the inevitable's' best friend." Her tone was serious.

"I'm not in denial. I'm fine—and I'm not getting too attached. I'm strictly collecting information about my family history and that's all." But even as I said those words, I knew she was right. I was in denial, and I hated the thought of having to say goodbye to Grandma one day.

After we hung up, I noticed that a mockingbird had landed on my windowsill and was looking at me with one eye, its head tilted sideways. I yelled, "Boo!" and jumped off my bed, lurching toward the window, but it didn't scare. I sat on my window seat, just on the other side of the glass, and it still ignored me. I tapped on the windowpane; the bird just hopped back and forth, fluffing and bobbing, so I stayed there, studying it.

That silly bird made me think about my mom. It was her nature to nurture everyone and everything that needed care. I called her tendency "the needy bird syndrome" due to Mom's history of rescuing fallen birds. She was a magnet for attracting feathered friends in need, putting them back in the nest, or, if she couldn't locate it, bringing them to our house. Then, she dedicated herself to feeding them chicken baby food (yuck! and was that a sort of cannibalism?) and water, from the end of a straw, until they were strong enough to fly away.

I had to admit, it was truly wonderful to witness the day a recuperated bird flew away, and so many actually circled in the air above, as if to say, "Thanks for everything!" before leaving to embark on their second chance at life. But on the flipside, there were birds that didn't live. Mom would bury each stiff lump of feathers in the corner of the yard, near the bed of lilies, while silent tears dripped down her cheeks. How could she cry over a wild bird she'd only known for a few days? How could she have grown attached to it so quickly? I started to dislike those unreliable birds.

In the beginning, I helped my mom by feeding them when they squawked—baby birds need around-the-clock care—and cleaning their messy cages caked in feathery gray poop, but that all stopped after my experience with a baby mockingbird I'd found by the creek without a nest in sight.

Wait! No! I didn't want to think about this. I had suppressed this memory every time it surfaced, especially now that Val faced his own death in Iraq. Death was so final, and it often came due to some horrible mistake.

But the mockingbird on my windowsill didn't budge, and the longer it stood there preening its feathers, the more deeply I ventured into remembering . . .

It had been one of those sparkling days of blue skies, right after a rainstorm. The pitiful grey naked baby was nestled in a pile of wet leaves, squawking away. I'd carefully scooped it up, wrapped it in my jacket, and gently carried the wrestling bundle home. I'd put it in the cage we used for such orphans, and in a couple of weeks, with my continuous care, the bird became strong. It had grown such lovely black iridescent feathers that I had named it "Regal."

On the very day I had planned to let him go, I found him rolling and writhing around on the bottom of his cage, suffering as he died. It was terrible! I panicked and didn't know what to do or why it was happening. I just stood there and bawled, helplessly.

Mom found me crying and staring into the cage.

"Why did he die, Mom? All I did was love him," I sobbed.

She scooped me up and held me in her lap as she explained: "The lifespan of wild birds is very mysterious, darling one. You shouldn't feel badly—you gave him a longer, more comfortable life than if you'd never found him."

Her words made me feel better at the time, but soon after, I'd discover that she was wrong. There was a specific reason for his death, and I knew what it was, but never told anyone . . .

Stop—don't remember any more! And just then, the mockingbird on my windowsill spread his wings and flew away. I realized that I was shaking, so I went and laid on my bed, and began thinking about my grandmother and how weak she was getting. I was glad Grandma's physical needs were completely my Mom's responsibility right now. She truly did have a green thumb with living things, while mine was all brown.

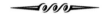

It was eight o'clock in the evening, way past tea time, when Mom finally summoned me to Grandma's room.

"Are you up to one of our talks tonight?" I asked, taking a moment to really look at my grandma before sitting beside her. She looked fragile, but that undeniable spark of life still glimmered in her true-blue eyes.

"Yes, of course I am. Please sit down, Clairy. I haven't told you about how I finally got my Graham. It was a fairytale romance, really." The mention of Grandpa lit her up. "Well, let's see, it would help you to know that my family became fed-up with my talk of fairies. Since I saw two real ones, I figured I didn't need to keep them a secret any longer. They were all I talked about and it drove my family crazy. So one day, my parents told me they had put up with it long enough, and they were done listening to my tall tales, forbidding the mention of the wee ones ever again."

"How old were you then?"

I had brought my journal and a pen, to take notes. Grandma looked at them and grinned. I opened the book up to a blank page and nodded.

Grandma nodded back before answering, "Almost fourteen, and back then, I was considered a young lady, so it meant leaving foolish fairy anecdotes behind me. In my household, my quest for little people was then referred to as 'that nonsense.'"

"Did you stop believing?"

"Oh, no, I could never do that after my encounters! But my mother was worried that I might not be able to decipher fact from fiction any longer, so I secretly carried on with my infatuation, but never spoke of it. Obeying my parents was absolutely expected. I was a good girl and didn't want them to be cross with me, so I minded their rules and didn't talk about fairies anymore . . ." she gave me a wink before adding, ". . . around my parents."

"So, you delivered the tussie-mussie to Grandpa Graham that May," I said, checking my notes. "How soon after that did this discussion with your parents take place?"

"Well, I received Anna's wonderful fairy-sighting letter in July, which made me even more fairy *crazy*, as you can imagine, so it was August."

"Did Grandpa reply to your tussie? If that's what people do, I don't know."

"If someone figured out who the tussie was from, he or she would usually write a little thank you note, but you had to be really sure you got the right secret admirer or there could be a problem." Grandma lifted her eyebrows. "I hadn't heard from Graham after delivering the tussie-mussie, and what happened next was a month before the annual back-to-school dance. Unfortunately, he seemed to be paying even more attention to a new girl at that time, so I figured he wasn't interested in me. The girl was Victoria Jones, my nemesis. She went by Tori. She hung on him, batted her eyelashes, and laughed way too loudly at his jokes. Bleh! She was pretty enough, with her jet black hair and dark brown eyes, but she was too showy around boys."

Grandma used one hand to flip the ends of her hair, mimicking Tori's flirtations.

"Then," Grandma leaned forward and lowered her voice, "a rumor went around the school that the reason Tori was with Graham was because she had made him a beautiful May Day tussie-mussie—with the same exact flowers I had used, including the lavender trumpet vine! She had taken credit for *my* tussie-mussie!"

"Didn't it bother you that he didn't automatically know that tussie-mussie, with the trumpet vine flowers, was from you? That should have been obvious," I said.

"You're right, but you know how boys can be," she said, as if she were a young girl talking to her best friend.

No, I really didn't know much of anything about boys, but I was willing to learn.

"They're oblivious," she confidently stated. "And I tried to tell myself he was just another boy, for goodness' sake—that it really didn't matter—but when I looked inside my heart, it did matter. I found myself going out of my way to see him at school, hoping that if he saw me enough, he'd finally remember the day we met and then connect the trumpet vines with that.

"From afar, I watched the way he smiled when he spoke to people, how he held the door for his teachers when their arms were full of books, the way he'd let a girl go first when in line for the drinking fountain . . . little things like that made me think he appreciated the small details in life, just like I did."

"Boys today aren't quite that chivalrous," I ventured.

"Well, your grandfather was. And when I told my girlfriends what Tori had done, they were appalled. We spent time brainstorming my perfect revenge."

"Revenge, Grandma? I didn't know you had it in you," I giggled.

"Well, an injustice had been done! Most of the schemes we came up with were silly or outrageous, like putting frogs in Tori's book bag—she hated frogs. I even wrote to Anna to see if she had any ideas. She wrote back telling me that if I put the dainty purple cup-shaped flower *harebell* on Tori somehow, while asking the fairies to help tame her spirit, she wouldn't be able to lie anymore. This gave me an idea.

"About a week before the dance, I made a couple dozen harebell boutonnieres and put them in a basket, asking my friend Betsy to pass them out to people, since she was the boldest of our group. She wandered the halls, chatting up our classmates, pinning flowers upon each girl's lapel with a smile.

"When Betsy approached Tori, she said, 'We're giving these out to girls who haven't been asked to the dance yet, so the boys know who's available.' Betsy held up the tiny flowers and a pearl-tipped pin.

"'I already know who I'm going to the dance with,' Tori told her abruptly.

"'Oh, so Graham *officially* asked you? You know it's only *official* if he actually asked you. Did he?' The word on the street was that Graham hadn't asked Tori directly and she was pretty miffed. She figured that if she just acted like they were going together, he'd have to oblige, being the kind-hearted boy he was.

"'Well, not *officially*.' Tori's forehead furrowed in frustration. 'I see you're wearing one too, so you must not have an official date yet, either.'

"Betsy smiled slyly. 'Well, give him a gentle reminder by wearing this today. All of the boys know the flowers are the signal,' Betsy lied. 'Here, let me pin it on you.'

"As she pinned it on, Betsy whispered to herself: 'Oh, fairest keepers of the harebell; make the truth all that she can tell!'

"'*Harebell? Tell?* What did you just say to me?' Tori said haughtily, jumping backward, her black hair bouncing.

"'I said, did you just hear the bell?' Boy, Betsy was quick on her feet!

"During this whole scene, the rest of us were hiding behind a large pillar, listening and watching. We all had said the fairy incantation along with Betsy to make sure the wee ones knew it was serious. Of course, the three of us hiding almost busted our britches with laughter.

"Betsy continued on, talking several of the others in the mean girl group at school into wearing some harebells too, so Tori wouldn't suspect anything. They all walked side by side, wearing their flowers proudly, flaunting them in front of any boy they encountered all day long. We were in stitches every time we saw them."

"You were in *stitches?*"

"Oh, an old-fashioned term for laughing hard . . . *Stitches* refers to the sharp pain one can get in one's side during a fit of laughter."

"I guess that makes sense."

"Well then, later that day, Rebecca, the tall, freckled redhead in my group, overheard Graham talking to Tori behind a forsythia bush in our school quad. They were discussing the tussie-mussie!

"Apparently, Tori flaunted the harebells pinned to her sweater. 'Remind you of anything?' she asked.

"Clueless, Graham remarked, 'Actually, those purple flowers remind me of what you gave me last May Day.'

"'Tell me again how much you loved that tussie-mussie I made for you,' Tori had said in her sweetest voice.

"'I loved it so much that it's hanging in my garage to dry and remind me of you,' he said. 'I even asked my sister to look up all the flowers' meanings—she had to look in three different books to find them all.'

"'Show me that you remember what each one meant.' Tori batted her eyelashes. The truth was that *she* needed the reminder since she didn't put the tussie together for him!

"'A peach rose, white azaleas, hostas, and periwinkle, all for friendship and romance,' he said. 'Which is very sweet of you. The trickiest one was the trumpet flower, though. I couldn't figure out what you meant by it. The books said it symbolized fame or separation.'

"'And what did I tell you it meant for *us?*' Tori asked.

"'The trumpets announce your feelings for me,' Graham replied. Makes you want to . . . what do kids in your generation say . . . barf, right?"

I laughed and nodded.

"Rebecca leaned closer to hear more, and there was a pause before Tori stammered, 'I have a confession. I didn't make ...' and then she stopped herself by abruptly slamming both hands over her own mouth, a look of shock on her face. She'd almost told the truth because of the harebells!

"'You didn't make what?' asked Graham.

"'I meant, if we don't go now, we won't *make it to class on time.*' That Tori knew how to cover her tracks.

"After Tori and Graham left the quad, it was time for my friends to intervene. During their art period, Rebecca got Agatha to help make a wreath out of green pipe cleaners and lavender tissue paper. It had to be done immediately, while the thought of trumpet flowers was fresh in Graham's mind!

"Knowing that I would never agree to wear such a thing and parade around in it in front of Graham, they gently placed the wreath upon my head between the last two periods of the day, when I bent down to pick up a pencil Agatha pretended to drop. It was so light, I never knew it was there. They even talked me into walking the long way to class, so that I would pass by Graham on his way to football practice."

"Oh, how sneaky of your friends! What happened when Grandpa saw you?"

"Well, I nearly bumped right into him as he came around the corner. He looked at me so funny, but kept strolling by ... but then, he did a double take and ran after me.

"'Faye! Hold on, now! I need to talk to you!' he called.

"As if magically disappearing, my friends left me to face him alone. 'Yes, Graham?' I thought it strange that he would want to talk to me all of a sudden!

"'I have made a big mistake. Forgive me! It was *you* who left the nice tussie-mussie for me on May Day, wasn't it?' he said, his eyes twinkling like a thousand tiny stars.

"I could only nod.

"'I was foolish not to realize the connection between you and the trumpet vines—and even more foolish to believe someone else who took the credit.' He grinned, then promptly looked down at his shoes as he said, 'I never dared to dream the beautiful Fairy Faye I found in my yard that day had feelings for me.'

"Had he just called me *beautiful?* I was stunned.

"'Would you like to go to the dance with me?' he said.

"'Yes,' was all I could manage while gazing into those amazing eyes of his. We just stood there, oblivious of life whirling around us. Then I had to ask, 'What made you suddenly realize the tussie was from me?'

"He pointed to my head.

"I reached up, feeling the crafted floral headpiece. My face was hotter than a chili pepper as I quickly pulled it off of my head. 'I didn't know I was wearing this.' Then I realized it was there due to my friends' sneaky plan. 'Wait until I get my hands on them!'

"But Graham just smiled effervescently at me, and it didn't matter how this moment had come about. I was going to the dance with him! I felt so giddy that I carefully put the paper wreath back on and wore it proudly all the way to chemistry class."

"Were you angry at your friends for tricking you?" I asked. "That was really embarrassing."

"How could I be anything but grateful to my clever friends? My friends, and the fairies, had helped me, and most importantly, the truth was out."

"Well, Grandpa Graham must have been angry with Tori for lying."

"Yes, he was pretty upset with Tori, and made it clear to her that she shouldn't have misled him. Sometimes things can change quite quickly in life, and oh, how my outlook changed."

I had to admit that after hearing that story, I was a little jealous of thirteen-year-old Faye meeting her Prince Charming in such romantic way. Even seventy years later, her girlish happiness shone like stars from within her. My grandparents had been married more than sixty years before Grandpa passed away—it was obvious that Grandma still overflowed with love for him. At that moment, more than ever, I wanted a love story for myself, and the bar was now set pretty high. I wished I could find a guy who would feel the same way about me, and me for him, as my grandparents felt about each other.

"So, how did the dance go?" I asked, longing to hear more.

"Oh," Grandma was far off in her memory now, "he picked me up from my house and . . . well, why don't you read about it in my diary. The orange ribbon."

I got the book from the drawer. "What is this shape?" I asked, holding up the milagro attached to the bookmark. "It looks like a pumpkin with a handle."

"Oh, that's a paper lantern. Now go ahead."

September 18th, 1929

Tonight, Graham picked me up from my house and gave me a corsage of all lavender flowers: lilacs, harebell, pansies, and of course, trumpet vine. The scent of the lilacs wafted around us as we walked to the dance with some other couples. Graham offered me his arm, which I took, and my yellow chiffon wrap, draped across the sleeve of his dark suit jacket, shimmered in the moonlight. The air was warm and comforting. Walking by his side was such a fabulous feeling. He was the one meant for me; I knew it at that instant. I don't think my feet touched the floor the rest of the night.

As we approached the dance hall, lines of lighted paper lanterns stretched over the front lawn—a wonderful scene of multicolored glowing spheres above us.

Tori was at the dance, throwing darts at us with her eyes from across the dance floor. Her mother had set her up with a young man from Fort Worth, a son of a friend. He seemed like a nice fellow, but she wasn't paying much attention to him at all. She made him dance every time Graham and I did, and demanded punch whenever Graham chivalrously filled my cup. Nonetheless, I felt badly. It was never my intention to hurt her. I only wanted the truth to come out.

I told Graham how uncomfortable I was feeling and I saw those green eyes of his register an idea. He took my hand and led me to the stretch of lawn outside. On the grassy dance floor, we still could hear the band, loud and clear, "I'll See You in My Dreams."

We laughed at first, but then stood face-to-face in silent ease. Holding each other, we slowly danced, and soon, I promise, we were levitating just above the fringe of grass. The cottonwood trees let go of extra cloud-like seedlings, giving the moonlit puffs the look of illuminated drifting snow, silently floating all around us. Colored paper lanterns bounced above our heads, while fireflies lit the dark bushes lining the edges of our private dance floor. The magic of love, mingled with the enchantment of nature, is the most incredible combination!

With my head on his shoulder, I closed my eyes for a bit, soaking up the wonderful way I was feeling. Then, I felt his head turn towards mine, hot breath upon my cheek. Lifting my face, I opened my eyes and saw him delighting in me.

Ah, the feeling of mutual admiration! Overwhelming for a young girl new to love, it felt like the most amazing magic I'd ever known. Still swaying to the music, he bent closer, gently pressing his lips to mine in a sweet, warm kiss that will linger on my lips for days afterwards.

Oh my gosh. Did I really just read about their first kiss?

Grandma and I sat in silence. I couldn't sort out my mind, which was floating on clouds, well enough to speak.

Luckily, Grandma spoke first. "I never forgot that night. We didn't say it out loud, but we knew in that instant that we'd become promised to each other forever in our hearts." She put her hand on her heart and looked towards heaven, dropping it as she said, "And then—*glossolalia!*"

"*Glosso*-what?" I asked.

"Glossolalia. When *unmeaningful speech, as if one were in a state of trance* occurs. Anna and I discovered that word—it's wonderful, isn't it? Especially the way it wiggles on your tongue!"

"You sound like a textbook, Grandma." I smiled, remembering Lacey often said the same to me.

"Glossolalia perfectly describes that moment after a first kiss, when your head is in the clouds, your feet are far above the ground, and the gut-fluttering feeling of love makes it difficult to utter a sentence that makes any sense."

"Glossolalia—I like it!" It did tickle my tongue. "So then, did you give up on fairies once you had Grandpa in your life?"

"Oh, no. I'd found true love due to the intervention of the fairy boy. Had he not brought that sprig of trumpet vine, there was no way I'd have been with Graham. I wanted nothing more than to communicate my fairy vision with him. Besides, when you discover something wonderful, you want to share it with those who are dearest to you."

"So what did Grandpa think about your belief in fairies?"

"I worried about that, believe me! Would he think I was foolish, like my family members did when I had tried to share my fairy experiences with them?"

"So did you tell him?"

"I did, eventually. I dislike regret. It can wear a person out, always wishing they had answered the door when opportunity was knocking. And I would have regretted not at least *trying* to let him know about the power of the fairies. They had the ability to help him in all of his endeavors, providing a life of happiness and fulfillment. He needed to know that they are always around, like love. And these, my dear, are the reasons why I have told *you* about them as well."

I was so moved that my words just wouldn't come out right when I tried to speak, "I . . . you told . . . Grandpa . . . believe . . . thank . . ." Then, I turned red.

Grandma smiled and simply said, "Glossolalia at its finest!"

We both laughed until our eyes were brimming with tears.

19

Regal

"And the day came when risk to remain tight in a bud was more painful
than the risk it took to blossom."
— Anais Nin —

My head danced with romance after Grandma's last story.
Who knew the feelings of love could be so contagious?
I pictured my grandparents' romantic night—the small
clouds of cottonwood fluff, the intimate dancing, the glowing moonlight—and I began to long for that feeling. How wonderful to be near
someone who you adored so much—but the tricky part was finding
someone who adored you back.

I was twisting my fork among my scrambled eggs when Mom
entered the kitchen.

I took one look at her face and froze.

"She's not doing well today." Her voice, which even in the most
stressful times sounded reassuring, was tinged with worry.

"Grandma? But she was fine yesterday."

"She was up all night with a fever. I think it's pneumonia."

I immediately remembered Mom and her nurse friends calling pneumonia "The Old Person's Angel" because it was a very euphoric way to die. No pain involved, just a slow eternal sleep.

"No! Wake her up! It's not her time!" I realized that I was shouting. More quietly, I added, "There's so much more for her to tell me. She was just beginning to make me understand . . ." I wanted to say *love*, but stopped myself.

How could I have allowed myself to become so vulnerable?

Mom must have seen the annoyance blaring through my eyes. She walked over and gently held my face between her hands. "Grandma needs you to be strong. You've always been so courageous, and I admire that so much about you. There's a quote on the wall of the nurses' station at the hospital that says, 'Courage is the only magic worth having.'" She dropped her hands. "Think about that, my darling. It's very true, especially right now. We've got to believe she can pull out of this."

The mention of magic made me grow even more agitated. Mom knew nothing about magic—not *real* magic.

"When do you think I can see her again?" I wondered. My head felt all cobwebby inside, my thoughts sticking to entangling strands.

"She's sleeping right now. Let's see how she is this afternoon, but she may be too weak from the fever." Mom paused before adding, "I'm sorry, honey, I know you two have become close . . ."

I felt the anger boil over inside of me. "She told us she was going to die, but we didn't listen." I took a deep breath before adding, "But it's a fact—every living being dies."

I got up and left the kitchen, arms crossed against my chest.

I locked myself in my room for the rest of the morning. I had important things to do, like finishing the drawings I'd neglected these past weeks. But as I got out my art supplies, my journal caught my eye, reminding me of all I had still longed to hear about. There were so many questions.

Where was all the beautiful fairy art my grandmother had created? What did the note in the compact say that she gave Anna as she boarded the orphan train? And what about the third fairy sighting?

My head ached as these thoughts flip-flopped around.

That's when I called Lacey, but when her voicemail picked up, I remembered she had a horse show today. So I went to see Delta.

When I slipped into the Tea Room kitchen, she was chopping celery and singing a gospel tune about a passing storm.

She was so enthralled with her song that when I caught her eye, she jumped. "Child, you done give me a heart attack." Delta clutched her chest. "Whatcha doin' up in here?"

"Got a minute?" I asked.

"I got 'bout three, but that's all. Honey-Claire, we're real busy today."

I sat on a tall stool, the words caught in my throat.

Delta stood with a hand on each hip—*akimbo*—and stared. "Well, that's one minute up. Now ya got two. Got somethin' to say, or not?"

Again, I couldn't speak. My thoughts were all jumbled in my head.

"I'm sorry, child, but customers are waitin'."

"I should just leave anyway."

Delta put one hand on my shoulder. "Yes, ya *should* go, but I know there's somethin' on your mind."

"Well, something is bugging me a little." I saw intensity in Delta's eyes. "My mom says my grandmother has taken a turn for the worse."

"Oh, I'm sorry to hear that. Of course you're upset. You're startin' to love that grammy of yours, I can see," Delta said compassionately.

"I wouldn't use the word *love*." I rolled my eyes. "But she's been sharing interesting family history with me."

"I think those stories mean much more to ya. I think *she* do, too."

Afraid I might cry, out spewed, "What if I never get to hear any more? What if my grandmother takes the rest of her stories to her grave? What will it be like around my house without her?"

"Your grammy's lived a long and happy life. It's nice that ya got to know her. And maybe someone else in your family can tell ya what she ain't gettin' to say."

I wanted to yell these words, but I said them through my teeth instead, "You don't understand. She knows things nobody else does."

"Like what?"

"Nothing . . . you wouldn't get it." I shook my head. "Real fairies" wasn't a subject you could discuss with just anyone. I took a deep breath and let it out slowly. "You're right. I'll be fine. Thanks for talking with me, Delta."

"Are ya sure?" Delta didn't sound convinced.

"Yes, I'm sure. Now I'll let you get back to your work."

She turned and started to walk back to her celery, but then stopped me, "Claire, your grammy is gonna be with ya, no matter if she's in heaven or on the Earth. She'll always be right here." Delta put her hand over my heart.

My stomach flipped like I was riding a large dip on a rollercoaster.

"You okay, child? Your face is ghost-white."

I nodded. "See you later, okay?"

"Okay . . ." she replied hesitantly.

I rushed out, needing fresh air.

Why did I care about the fairy sightings so much? I needed to stop thinking about them. I'd been wasting my time—sucked into silly beliefs by a crazy old lady. How could I have lost myself like this? Most of my day had been wasted thinking about Grandma, and fairies, and crazy grandmother stuff like that.

At about two in the afternoon, Mom knocked on my door.

"Grandma is asking for you. She's awake and seems a little better, considering she still has a low fever." Mom's voice still had that tone of concern, making me anxious.

I said nothing and didn't move, unsure of myself.

"Aren't you going to go see her?" Mom asked.

"I don't know."

"Well, I don't know how long she'll be awake, Claire." She sighed and left the room.

I sat on my bed until Mom was really gone, her footsteps clunking down the wooden stairs. I jumped to my feet and grabbed my journal and a pencil, but then stopped in my tracks.

Wouldn't it be easier to never visit again?

Putting the journal back on my desk, I set the pencil down on top of it, and left my room, bypassed the guest room, headed downstairs to the family room, and flipped on the television. The TV was on the news channel, which I liked to avoid—there was always a bad report about the war—but just as I aimed the remote to change it, a reporter came on.

"Two dozen soldiers arrived at the Dallas–Fort Worth airport today, happy to be back on American soil," the man in the navy blazer announced. "I am here at the scene."

Ambling through the terminal behind the reporter were young men, and a few women, in camouflage. Hundreds of civilians were lined up, waving at them, applauding, and cheering. The support was amazing, much like the salutes I'd seen along the road to soldier Joseph's burial.

Then, an elderly man was interviewed, wearing a plaid button-down shirt and a cap that had the letters "U.S. ARMY" on the front.

"I'm a Vietnam vet and an active member of 'Welcome Heroes Home,' a program that does just that. When I finished my duty 40 years ago, I'd walked away from dead friends and unthinkable conditions the day before returning safely back to America, as a young lieutenant. When I arrived at the U.S. airport, I was so excited to be home—but no one was there to welcome me."

"How did that make you feel?" The reporter asked.

Silly question!

"It left me feeling empty and lonely. Me and my war buddies had put up with horrendous situations in 'Nam—the horror of death, being in constant fear—all in order to maintain the freedom of our wonderful country. Greeting the soldiers today is the least I can do to show my deep gratitude and respect. I can't heal their wounds inside and out, but maybe I can make the soldiers feel less isolated and lonely. Now that I'm retired, I go at least once a week to local airports and welcome them home."

It dawned on me just how selfish I was being. Grandma asked for me. She wanted my company. She too had returned home and needed support.

I turned off the television and went outside to grab a surprise for Grandma. Then I headed quietly back upstairs for my journaling supplies.

When I entered Grandma's room, she was propped up on about five pillows, weaker than ever, barely able to hold up her own head.

"I was hoping you'd come," she said feebly.

"Mom said you're not well." Seeing her there, anger sprung up in me—anger at her age, her illness, her being there in my house. It flared in my tone, looming like smoke in the air long after.

She tapped her blue-veined fingers on the bed ever so slightly and I moved to sit on the edge. I revealed a vase filled with the flowers I'd just picked for her and held it near her face.

"Flowering quince, my favorite—thank you, Clairy. They feed my soul." She closed her eyes and inhaled deeply. "Why don't you set them down on the dresser where I can see them."

I set the vase of salmon-colored blooms on the edge of the dresser top, directly in front of her, so she could see them as she spoke.

Grandma watched me out of the corner of her left eye, barely able to turn her head, as I returned to her.

"When we first met, you were untrusting of anything but the facts," she began. "Those feelings of leeriness have returned, haven't they? And we were making such good progress too." I heard her exhale roughly. "You know, anger is only a secondary emotion. Something tells me there's more to it; it's not just because you're cooped up with someone who is . . . dying."

Her words rang in my ears. "You're sick, but that doesn't mean . . ."

"I'm dying, my dear Clairy. The fair ones forewarned me. It's almost time to stop, or so my body says. My mind is having a bit of a harder time accepting it."

"It's a fact of life, but . . ."

"You're a most sensible girl, and you've spoken to me many times about the importance of logic. I agree it has its place in the world, but even Albert Einstein believed in fanciful things. He said, 'Logic will get you from A to B; imagination will take you everywhere.'"

"Einstein said that?"

I'd never heard that quote before, but it made sense. It was creative thinking that assisted scientists in figuring out what to research in the first place.

"Yes," said Grandma. "So, on the factual side of things, you're right. Dying is a fact of life. But I believe there's more to life than the facts, and I've noticed something. It's *not* me who is having trouble with death." She turned her head toward me an inch more. "What happened that makes you hate it so much? Why is getting attached to others so scary for you? You can talk about anything to me, and besides," she got a funny grin on her face as she said, "I'll be gone soon, so I'll have no one on earth to tell." She chuckled a bit.

I didn't appreciate the joke at all.

Then a very strange thing happened—a soft mist came from the small gap between Grandma's unmoving lips, whirling around my head like a vapor trail leading to my ears.

Tell! The haze hissed as gently as a cool mist of rain on a hot scorching day.

"Grandma, how did you . . . ?"

Tell, it's okay; just speak from your heart! the mist whooshed.

As the words penetrated my mind, it softened the tightness that had grown in my throat, and I found myself speaking easily. "Tell what? Nothing happened." The wavering of truth showed in my voice. The verbal ear spray hissed louder and made me relax even more. I took a deep breath. "It's just that, I never think of death without remembering . . ."

Could I really say it out loud? I'd never told a soul before.

As if reading my mind, Grandma said, "Sometimes it helps lift the weight to tell someone your secrets."

Involuntary tears began to trickle down my face and I wiped each eye with the back of my hand.

I could do this . . .

I sniffled, then spoke. "There was this beautiful mockingbird I had found once, a long time ago. I named him Regal because he had the most amazing black iridescent feathers, like you'd see on fancy couture hats." I choked on the words more than I expected. "Mom used to raise baby birds that fell out of their nests all the time. We'd feed them, talk to them, and take care of them. They almost always got strong, flying away after a few weeks."

"So, what happened to Regal?" Grandma's voice was soft.

"Well, Regal was the first mockingbird I took care of all by myself. He was my bird. I woke up so excited to see him every day. In his tiny black eyes, I saw happiness to see me too. I wanted him to become healthy and strong, so every day I found him lots of worms to eat, once he graduated from the baby food. He'd let me feed him by hand. I wanted so badly to see him fly free again instead of being locked up in that small cage."

I took a deep breath. Grandma stayed silent, letting me continue when I was ready.

"Then one day, I . . ."

Could I really say this out loud?

"It was like any other day. I wet the ground early that morning and took my trowel out to the base of the trees in the backyard, turning over dirt to look for anything that squirmed. I found this plump, bumpy worm—the biggest I'd ever seen! I ran to the birdcage and held it wriggling between my fingers, and then Regal took it in his beak and gobbled it up. I swear he smiled at me to say, 'thank you.'"

Grandma grinned.

"I decided Regal was ready to be set free later that afternoon, once the sun had warmed the air." The tears dripped quickly from my eyes now, and I couldn't stop myself. "I went back to check on him about a half hour later," I was sobbing now, "and found him rolling around on the bottom of the cage, dying!" My breath sputtered. "It was all my fault! I stupidly gave him a *poisonous* worm! I researched it after he died—but I should have looked it up *before* I gave it to him! I should have looked up *every* worm I found—with the right information, if I had known the facts, he would have never died!"

"Darling girl, it's not your fault. Nature is mysterious," Grandma murmured.

"That's what Mom said too, but he *trusted* me and I *killed* him. I killed him with ignorance." Strange noises of inner pain came from my chest as I cried harder. The cork that had tightly sealed my emotions for so long had popped and they all came gushing out.

"There, there, sweetheart, crying is good for you. You'll feel better in the end," Grandma said, patting my hand. Her tilted face smiled lovingly at me. "And now you've made room to care about something or someone that needs you. Keep an open heart."

"And now Val." I couldn't stop spewing my feelings. "He's so far away and he could die too. He could be dead right now."

"There, there," said Grandma again, pulling me in by the arm for a hug. Surprisingly, her cool fingers calmed me.

I pulled away enough to look up at her. "Grandma, I don't want you to die either."

"I know, my dear. But I didn't come here to make you sad. I came to this house to see you, meet you, know you. And when you listened to my life stories, you gave me such a gift. Keeping these stories to myself has been burning a hole into my soul, just like how the story about the mockingbird has burdened you. It feels so wonderful to tell someone—someone who cares enough to listen and at least try to understand."

She was right. I did feel like a huge load had been lifted.

"In future years, when you think of me," Grandma continued, "I want you to know that I was very happy with my life, will be happy with Grandpa Graham in heaven, and that I love you. And know that none of it's your fault, not my death, not Regal's. All things happen for a reason, and if you don't gain something positive out of the experience, then it's all been a waste. What a shame that would be!" She put a finger beneath my chin and lifted my face to hers. "I know that when bad things happen, it can be extremely difficult to see the good in it, but that's where the wee ones can aid you. The fairies will heal your soul and give you clarity, if you let them."

"I tried one day, to see some . . . *fairies*," I confessed, still with choppy breath. "But I couldn't find any."

"Well, don't give up. Many people turn to angels for curative measures, and they offer wonderful help too, but people overlook the more closely accessible healers—the fairies. Unlike angels who dwell in the heavens, fairies live on the earth, and therefore, are very in tune with earthly things."

I sat up. "So the fairies can heal people?"

"Yes, and they can heal nature too. For example, a neighbor of mine in England had a beautiful birch tree. It got struck by lightning, causing half of it to splinter and turn white. After tree surgeons and arborists told him his tree was a goner, he didn't give up hope. He came to me and I helped him."

"What did you do?" I pictured Grandma, in her ripe old age, dancing beneath the tree and reciting poetry. I almost laughed aloud.

"I gave him some beautiful crystals to hang from the existing branches, and we met beneath the tree every day for a week, bringing chocolate and sugar cakes as offerings. And guess what . . . the tree lived. So, promise me you'll keep trying."

"I promise," I said. Grandma was so kind—I had to hug her again. During the embrace, the old woman's thin, fragile hands stroked my back gently.

Then, I got comfortable on the bed beside her, my back on the pillows and my cheeks stiff with salt. "But, Grandma, it seems so hard to see them. It took you years."

"Seek them with a pure, accepting heart and they will reveal themselves to you. Plans made, big or small, which come from good intentions and pursued with hard work, will find their greatness."

"Who said that?"

"I did!" We broke into laughter for a minute.

The sweetness of love in the air could have been scooped with a spreading knife and used to frost a cake.

"Grandma, will you tell me more? Or are you too tired?" I braced myself for her answer.

"Clairy, I will tell you as much as I possibly can."

I wriggled deeper into the fluffy pillows behind me.

Infinite Dewberries

"The most precious gift we can offer others is our presence.
When mindfulness embraces those we love, they will bloom like flowers."
— ❧ *Thich Nhat* ❧—

"Grandma, I'm curious about something. When was the last time you heard from Anna?"

"Well, she came to see me during dewberry season one year. We were both married and in our early twenties. She had received a train ticket for her birthday from her husband and he told her to go anywhere she wanted. She chose Highland Park, to come and see me.

It was a wonderful four days. We laughed and talked, like young girls again. We took hayrides, went boating on the lake in the park, and rode the trolley to watch a vaudeville show. Of course, any discussion of fairies between us was done secretly, and mostly while sipping lemonade on the front porch of this very house. My mother would have flipped if she heard us!"

"Had you both kept trying to see fairies, even though you were living separate lives?"

"No, at that time, neither of us were seeking the wee ones. We were adults and thought we had outgrown the ability to communicate with them. It wasn't until I was retired and living in England that I realized I could have been doing it all along."

"Wait, go back a minute. *Dew*berries?"

They sounded fictional, like never-dissolving Everlasting Gobstoppers.

"Well, in April, when the bluebonnets are popping and the redbud trees are in full show, dewberries can be found in east Texas. Quite delicate, they could never be shipped to grocery stores. Instead, they grow in the most random places like vacant lots, roadside ditches, or upon old barbed wire fences. We'd hunt them, buckets in hand, climbing through bushes, over fences—and often there were fire ants and snakes to contend with as well!"

"I want to hunt for dewberries sometime."

"You should. Dewberries are definitely a gift from the fairies since they are almost as difficult to find as they are, but the rewards are almost as amazing. There's nothing like dewberry cobbler. It's like magic in your mouth."

"And after that visit, did you and Anna keep in touch?"

"You know, we both had babies to raise and households to run— she moved a couple of times—and we were just too busy to write very much or visit. Apart in our lives, but never in our hearts." Grandma grew melancholy. "But we did make a pact to meet up the year we both celebrated our fortieth birthdays. A girls' trip, just the two of us. That would take a whole other afternoon to explain."

I wanted her to explain it now, but Grandma went on to a new subject, "Did you ever look up the story about The Bower of Bliss?"

"The Bower of what?"

"Bliss. It's in *The Faerie Queen*, the story where I got Glorianna's fairy name. Remember?"

"Oh! Yes, I looked it up. A very elaborate story."

"You're right, and the Bower of Bliss is a garden in it representing 'life in abundance.' As young girls we'd fantasize about opening a hidden garden gate and discovering the real one."

"Kind of like in *The Secret Garden?*"

"Exactly. And coincidentally, your grandfather always said, 'follow your bliss' instead of 'goodbye,' for as long as I'd known him—his unique way of wishing others well."

"I like that."

Then, Grandma got serious. "I want us to say that too, Clairy. Not goodbye."

The hollow ache in my heart returned. "Never goodbye, Grandma. We'll say 'follow your bliss' instead."

I hoped I wouldn't be saying that too soon.

Grandma Faye frowned as she looked at my tear-streaked face. "I cried harder than ever once, the day Graham left for the army. But I'm getting ahead of myself . . . allow me to backtrack a bit. Let's see . . . we left off with . . ."

"What you told Grandpa about fairies," I chimed in. Still sniffling, I got up, grabbed a Kleenex, and climbed back to my spot on the bed.

"Once Graham and I connected, whenever I went to the creek to sketch, I often brought him. And when I told him about the fairies I saw, he didn't make me feel silly at all. He said he wanted to believe in fairies too, but like most folks, he'd have to see them to believe in them.

He'd have sat by caves waiting for dragons, had I said they existed."

"*Do* dragons exist?" I had to ask.

"Of course not! Fairies are real, but dragons are not," she retorted.

"Just had to check," I chuckled.

"Now where was I?" She rubbed her right palm back and forth on the comforter.

"Grandpa, and the fairies—did he see any?"

"I showed him how to try to attract them. He was a good sport. He'd sit with me, completely still, for up to a half an hour at a time. I always knew the real motivation, though. He just liked to sit near me. Many times I'd catch him staring at me as I sketched, and when asked what he was looking at, he'd say he was busy catching the scent of my freshly washed hair in the breeze or imagining me with a necklace of sweet honeysuckle. Such a romantic."

"Boys today wouldn't say those things," I said. Or maybe they did? How would I know, never having a boyfriend before? "How old was he when he joined the army?"

"He was eighteen, and as the day neared for him to leave, we'd sit more often by the creek." Grandma tapped my leg with her stiff hand. "His braveness was inherited by your brother."

"I wish you could meet Val right now, Grandma," I said. "He is such a smart, kind person, even for a brother."

She laughed. "He's a fine young man with a good head on his shoulders. I don't think you should worry about him. In fact, the fairies tell me he's going to be all right. He'll be home soon."

"I wish I could be that sure," I said doubtfully. "I try to be supportive of the reasons why he chose to go and fight in the war. Some days I understand it, and some days I don't."

"Well, your grandfather came from a military family and there was no question he'd join the army after high school, draft or no draft. In 1930, he was sent to help U.S. forces occupy China where there were conflicts with Japan.

"We tried hard to prepare ourselves for being separated for a while, so one warm summer night, while stargazing, I told him any time we were apart, all he had to do was look up and find the last star on the tail of the Big Dipper. We could send thoughts of love to that star, no matter where either of us was in the world, and then our thoughts would connect at that common point in the universe." She sighed. "I still look up at that star. I still feel like I can talk to him directly that way."

"Why didn't you just wish on the North Star, like most people?"

"We didn't want our messages to get mixed up with others." She smiled. "We also had a favorite tree I could visit while he was away. It had a single root that amazingly formed the perfect sideways figure eight, *infinity,* symbolizing our infinite love for each other. Every letter and birthday card we ever gave each other had that symbol on it." Grandma looked weary, but spoke on. "Would you do your old grandmother a favor and look for it? Tell me, the next time you come, if you can find it. It was near the Cornell Bridge."

"I will look for it tomorrow," I promised. "And I'll take a picture to show you."

"Thank you, darling. So to answer your earlier question, while I was with Graham, not one fairy even glimmered."

"Why not, do you think?"

"Well, at first I thought they mistrusted me for bringing a stranger into their surroundings, but after reflecting on my experiences, I realized why. They saw into my heart and knew I didn't need their healing since I was enormously happy when Graham was around."

"But you had another encounter with a fairy, right?" I was hoping to help keep the story going in that direction.

"Yes and no."

What kind of an answer was that? "Did you write about it in your diary?" I asked.

"I did."

I grabbed the book.

Waving her hand in the air, she commanded, "The pink ribbon this time, with the . . ."

". . . butterfly milagro." I dangled it in front of her and she grinned.

February 16th, 1930

Today, my dear Graham left for the army on a train similar to the one that Anna had taken, from the same station. We kissed goodbye and I whispered in his ear, "May the fairies watch and keep you." He'll be so far away! China, for goodness sake! I pray he'll make it safely back home. How cruel life is to have taken away my best friend and now my sweetheart!

His last words to me were, "I love you, Fairy Faye. Follow your bliss," and then he climbed aboard, immediately sticking his head out the window to wave. I waved back to him from the train platform, watching until I could no longer see his gorgeous sandy hair blowing in the wind, and then I got that familiar feeling of overwhelming sadness.

Once again, I ran to the creek. I cried gutturally all of the way there, thinking about him being gone. I couldn't understand how life could continue on as it did—phonographs playing happy music on the porches, children splashing in the public pool. Again, my heart severed from pain, but the creek is my haven where I can safely cry. There, I sought peace within me once more.

This time, I was drawn to the gnarly roots of the "infinity" oak on the edge of the ravine, so I sat and looked at it. My emotions felt as tangled as the roots were, and through my tears, I felt hatred for that figure eight! It symbolized how deeply a person could love another, and that love was the cause of my pain.

This time, I felt stupid for allowing myself to feel that vulnerable, so instead of allowing the ache to rule me, I faced it head on. Taking out my sketchpad, I drew that figure eight— every shadow and splinter in the wood. My drawing would be clearly recognizable as our infinity root. Then, I'd planned to send it to Graham, without a word or a letter accompanying it and no name or return address. This time, he'd better not mistake whom this piece was from!

Now comes the AMAZING part . . . while I was deeply studying each contour, groove, and shadow, guess what I saw!

I heard the buzzing of wings, and out of the corner of my eye, I saw a promenade of color: a streak of glistening hues, a miracle of organic mediums—I was captivated by a phenomenal rainbow! Butterflies were streaming from inside a dark gap between the roots.

I turned my head, taking the risk of looking directly at the spectacle. Focusing even more, I realized there were tiny people with iridescent wings of their own tucked down along their posteriors, riding on the backs of each butterfly! It was a magnificent fairy parade! A fritillary stampede!

The butterflies were mixed in kind: cabbage whites, golden monarchs, painted ladies, patchy brush foots, and swallowtails! Then, looking down into the creek, I saw about twenty turtles in a queue, each also with a tiny fair folk upon its back. The sights, on land and in air, were more amazing than my brain could take in! I had to get closer to get a good look at it all! I stood up, slowly stepping closer—then I tripped and fell right into the creek!

> _The rude shock of cold water jolted me from my focus moments before. I looked around the creek bed floor, but the pageant marchers had disappeared, along with their miraculous riders. I struggled to quickly climb up the bank and relocate the magical procession above, but it was too late. I couldn't see them any longer._
>
> _And again, diary, the fairies made me feel much better. Although I still miss Graham terribly, I feel as if the fair ones gave me a message. They were letting me know that there would be a victorious parade welcoming home our military, and Graham would be a participant._

Grandma let out a sigh. "And that was my grand finale, my final clear vision into the fairy realm."

Visions of wings fluttered in my mind. "Fritillary for the military—now that's a tongue twister!" I laughed.

"It was a fabulous thing to see!" The frail woman looked strong in her excitement. Her cheeks were rosy, there were twinkles in her eyes, and she looked . . . beautiful.

This is the way I want to remember you.

"So, after having three glorious sightings, I learned to believe in fairies as much as I believed in the air that I breathe. Now, I told you that fairies receive additional energy when a human believes in them, right?"

I nodded, pen poised to take down her next piece of important information.

"Well, they were there to get energy from _me_ just as much as I was there to get healing from _them_. Humans and fairies are partners in the quest to take care of the earth. They want us to live intuitively together to keep nature thriving. Just think about the abundance in the world if humans and fairies joined together!

"Fairies hide from people with selfish agendas and harsh thoughts, though. Slow, peaceful moments bring them to you, or if you are in such emotional pain, they will come to mend. Just learning to be aware of your own feelings, as well as those of others, takes practice, but the result of paying closer attention is that you become more intuitive."

"So, I guess since you and Anna were so happy together during your fairy enticing rituals that the fairies didn't show themselves because you didn't need healing. And maybe they were around, taking in the energy from your believing," I said.

"Exactly right, dear!"

"So, let's go back to when you fell into the creek. What happened after that?"

"Well, my mother was truly worried about me the day Graham left. My parents and siblings had seen me flee from the train station sobbing, and had spent a couple of hours searching for me. My mother stayed behind at the house, just in case I returned while the others were out looking. Boy, was she surprised to see me standing in the doorway of the kitchen, muddy and soaking wet from head to toe!

"'What happened to you?' my mother asked, seeming relieved that I had finally shown up, but still sounding firm. She studied the smile on my face with such surprise. 'How can you last be seen in such despair, and then show up here drenched and grinning? What's going on?' She asked.

"I didn't hold back, as I would have normally done. 'It was my deep love for Graham that brought me the most extraordinary fairy sighting of my life! How can I be sad? Life is miraculous!'

"'*What* kind of sighting . . . ?'

"My father entered just then. He'd heard what I said and looked at my mother with a worried expression. 'Perhaps she hit her head.'

"Mother just shook hers, and said, 'No more of this nonsense, young lady. Let me draw you a bath.'

"While I bathed, she gave me the lecture of a lifetime. 'Fairies aren't real, and what is real are your responsibilities, especially to your family. Part of those responsibilities are to act sane and virtuous. You're going to be someone's bride one day soon, and then a mother. There's no room for imaginary nonsense. I thought you'd given up the whole childish notion of fairies. I'm very disappointed to hear you speak of them again.'

"She also took my father's suggestion to heart and was concerned my delirium was from hitting my head when I fell into that old creek, so she kept on checking my cranium for bumps!

"'I assure you, I didn't hit my head,' I said over and over again.

"'Well, I can't find any lumps.' She sighed, brushing wisps of hair from her face with the back of her hand. 'I'm sure a hot bath and sleep will cure you.'

"I remember sitting in the warm, steamy water that filled the claw-foot tub thinking, 'I don't want to be cured. Love is what ails me. Love for nature and Graham, all wrapped into one. And it's *wonderful!*'"

Grandma stopped for a moment and did her "tap-tap-tap, cross-roads" on the bedside table, then continued. "I did miss Graham, and I worried about him immensely. It was exciting for him to see the world, and in his letters he described such exotic places. He was stationed in China through 1932 when the Japanese invaded Manchuria. Scary times, but he made it through all right."

"Had you mailed the infinity root drawing to him, as you had planned?" I asked.

"I did. I also gave it a caption that read, *Though my insides feel so twisted without you, I have faith in the magic of our eternity together!*" Grandma grinned slyly. "But I still didn't sign my name, as originally planned."

"So, another question, whatever happened to all of the fairy paintings you . . ."

"*Shhh!* One minute, Clairy." Grandma tilted her head to the side, listening. She nodded and smiled, as if someone were whispering in her ear. "We need to stop now. Someone is coming here, to see you."

"But we were just about to . . ." I nearly whined.

"I promise we'll continue soon." She sighed dramatically. "Besides, this old body needs to rest again."

"Can we be more specific about when we'll meet again? Tomorrow morning, or at tea time?" My muscles tensed.

"How about tonight, after dinner, you come back to see me. Deal?"

My shoulders relaxed. "Deal." I skipped to the door. "By the way, who's coming?"

"Just go out on the front porch and you'll see."

I shrugged, then did as she asked.

21

The Paintings

"… if I could paint that flower in a huge scale, you could not ignore its beauty."
—❧ *Georgia O'Keefe* ❧—

I planted myself on the top step of the front porch. Warm, sticky air swirling around me as I thought about Grandma's story. So, the fairies protected Grandpa Graham in the war? I wondered, would they protect Val, too?

The cicadas chirped, counting down the seconds that passed. How long was I supposed to wait here for this mysterious visitor to arrive? Could it be G?

Then I saw Aunt Az walking up the sidewalk toward me.

"Hey there, little darlin'! Whatcha doin' out here on the porch all by your lonesome?" Her sparkly earrings glittered as she moved.

"Nothing."

"Delta told me you came and talked with her about your grandmother not doin' so well." She pointed to the space next to me; I nodded, and she sat. "Well, sugar, we are born fragile and get that way again at the end of our lives. Either the body or the mind can start to fade, or both. There's no tellin' when it'll happen."

"Aunt Az, can I ask you something?"

"Sure, darlin'. Anything."

"Did Grandma ever talk to you about . . . fairies?"

"You know, I've been thinkin' about that and I do recall a story *my* grandmother told me once." She scooted her bottom closer to mine. "After they were married, your grandfather was still servin' in the army when your grandmother was pregnant with me, and when she was six months along, she was put on bed rest."

"So she must have been on bed rest in this house, right?"

"Right. In fact, she mentioned to me the other day that her room was what y'all use as the guest room now." Aunt Az crossed her ankles. "Grandma Faye was on bed rest right when our cousin was gettin' married in Austin, so the family left her with a caretaker for a couple of weeks while they attended all the wedding events. Now, my grandmother said, at that time, your Grandma Faye was obsessed with fairies."

"What did Grandma's mother . . . my great-grandmother . . . say about that?"

"Well, she thought it was utterly ridiculous. And apparently, Mother had created a bunch of elaborate drawings while they were away, all of fairies." Aunt Az sounded shocked, but I wasn't. "Your grandma's mother was quite angry to see them when she returned home. Apparently, she'd given Grandma Faye quite a tongue lashin', tellin' her to stop all the fairy nonsense now that she was goin' to be a mother herself. Your great-grandmother wanted her Faye to have a good life, based in reality, so she got rid of all the fairy drawings."

"You mean she *destroyed* them?" My hope of seeing more of Grandma's work was dashed.

"She was doin' what she thought was in the best interest of your grandmother."

"Grandma must have been upset."

"Apparently she was, at first. But then she realized that she <u>did</u> have an obligation to be a more grounded person for her child, and children to come."

"So she promised to keep her fairy beliefs to herself, forever . . . that makes sense now," I mumbled to myself.

"Yes, and Grandma Faye never wanted to break her mother's trust again." Aunt Az rested her hand on my knee and said, "And she turned out to been a wonderful mother, and now grandmother, as well."

"Aunt Az, why didn't you have any kids? You'd be a great mother too."

"I wanted to, but it just didn't work out for me. But I do have you and your brother, whom I'm very grateful for."

I saw her eyes welling up, so I gave her a hug. When she left me on the porch, she was smiling.

And before I had the chance to think about what Aunt Az had just said, another person came toward me. This time it *was* G!

I could hear my heartbeat, which seemed as loud as the cicadas chirped.

"Hey there!" He sauntered over to me. "Funny meeting you here, again."

Inside, I was shaking, but I knew this was my moment. I needed to calm down and just act as normally as I could. What would Grandma do if a cute boy walked up her front walk? She wouldn't be all spazzy, that's for sure. I took a deep breath before saying, "I'm curious about something."

"Why I'm here, I suppose?"

"Well, yes, that and . . . what's your name?"

He walked right up to me and held out his hand. "I'm Grant."

I grabbed his hand and shook it quickly, knowing my palms were beginning to sweat. "Nice to meet you. I'm . . ."

"Claire. I know." I cocked my head as we let go. How did he know my name?

Be cool, Claire. Act normal. "So now, the other question."

"Why I'm here? Well . . ." Was he blushing a little? "I wanted to see if you would like to go with a bunch of us to the movies tomorrow night. You can bring a friend."

"Sure," I answered, barely containing my excitement.

"Great." His lips parted and I heard a gush of relief come from them. "I'll come over at about 7 and we can walk to the 7:30 show." He shoved his hands in his short pockets and turned to leave, but then spun back around on his heels. "See you tomorrow." Then, he flashed me an incredible smile. I almost melted right there on steps!

"Tomorrow." I gave him a serene grin, but inside I was jumping, yelling, and dancing.

I watched as he walked away, and just before he turned the corner, he pumped the air with his fist in victory. I laughed. He was as nervous as I was, but he likes me. He really does!

I entered the house with a spring in my step, barely noticing the dark—*somber*—mood that had taken over. I was too happy that G—ah, Grant—asked me out. I heard Aunt Az in the other room, saying goodbye as she left out the back door, so I went to find Mom in the kitchen.

"How's Grandma?"

"Not any better, I'm afraid. Your dinner is ready." She set a bowl of buttered pasta on the table. "Sorry, I didn't feel much like cooking today."

"It's great. Thanks, Mom." I sat down and picked up my fork. "Did Aunt Az get to talk to Grandma?"

"Yes, she's awake right now."

Excitement flared in me again. "Can I go up and talk to her?"

"I don't know. You need to eat and I don't want you exhausting her."

"Just for a couple of minutes, I promise." I gave her a pleading look.

"All right, but only for a few minutes."

I grinned, set down my fork, and dashed to Grandma's room. "You up?"

"Yes, Clairy, dear," she replied, in bed, snuggled beneath a blanket.

I pulled up the vanity chair so I could sit beside her. "Aunt Az told me all about what happened when you were on bed rest with her. Was it all true?"

"Yes, it was."

"So that's why you promised to keep your fairy beliefs to yourself, forever?"

"Exactly. But I never stopped believing in fairies—I just kept my beliefs inside. Someday you'll eventually understand why you're the one who needs to know about them. I'm entrusting you with the truth because you are a special girl."

"I am?" I asked, almost breathless. "You never told my mom about fairies, right?"

"Your mother was my second child, and kind of a surprise, since I was forty-five years old when she came into the world. I felt too old to believe in the fair ones then—seems silly now, since I believe in them more than ever at age eighty-eight!"

"Why did you go back to believing in fairies in England?"

"Honestly, through all of those years, I had this continued feeling of regret for not sharing with others their ability to heal the soul.

Later, living in an isolated cottage with a wild English garden growing all around, I could wallow in my passions for fairies and nature
once again, in a private way."

"Mom said you moved there to draw English gardens."

"Yes, illustrations for books—that's one of the things that drew
me there. I believe it was also the fairies' intuitive guidance that led
me there, to my own personal 'garden of bliss.' I wish I could take you
there right now and show you around. You would love it!"

I could almost see the tall foxgloves and hollyhocks in her eyes.

Grandma thought for a minute. "Perhaps I raised your mother too
much like a grown-up, since she was around them all of the time. She
really never used her imagination as much as most children, although
she has always been very kind and compassionate." Grandma turned
her head away as she said, "She would have never understood my life
there in England."

Then, turning back towards me, she motioned to come closer. I
gently scooted until I was directly in front of her face.

"I think your mother has raised you in the same way," she said.
"And your head's been filled with even more scientific facts because
of the world you live in today. The great advancements existing in the
twenty-first century have been the reason for a gross loss of human
intuition. But I dare say, your generation also seems more open-
minded. If I'm right about that, then the world is ripe for the miracles
of the fairies to get out."

"What makes you think my generation is more open to things like
fairies?" I wondered.

"Freedom of religion, rights for women and minorities—but it's
even more than that. America is actually hearing a lot of what the
fairies are saying about the environment."

"We are?" I was intrigued.

"Earth Day is an example. It was the fairies' idea to create a day where humans are more in tune with nature. And you know the catch phrase 'recycle, reduce, and reuse?'"

"Yeah."

"Well, that came from the fairies too. They all chanted it regularly until millions of humans heard it. Now it's a human mantra."

"And what are they asking humans to do now?"

"They want humans to join in *visualization*. What we visualize is what we draw towards ourselves, and then experience. We need to see an earth with fresh air, clean land and water. If we hold that ideal in our minds, we begin to take steps to make it a reality."

"And you heard all of this?"

She chuckled. "You can too, if you listen closely enough. I told you all of this because I want to give you the gift I never gave your mother or anyone else . . . before it's too late."

"I really want to try to hear the fairies, Grandma," I admitted.

"Believe in them, Claire, and even if they can't change the entire world right away, they will at the very least take care of you. Trust and believe—their love is everywhere!" Grandma waved her finger across the air, as if she were casting a magical spell.

The room went quiet. All that could be heard was the calling of the birds outside. Late afternoon shadows were stretched out across the old hardwood floor. I had the feeling Grandma was going over the things she had just said, one more time in her mind.

Weariness was etched on her face, but still she broke the silence by continuing. "I painted the biggest and most glorious paintings of fairies ever, if I do say so myself! They were the most colorful and accurate pictures of my fairy encounters . . ." She let out a great sigh.

"They are close by . . . but gone forever."

"Close by? Where?" She wasn't making any sense!

"Yes, they're around . . ." she trailed off, faintly smiling, then closed her eyes.

Oh please don't fall asleep, Grandma! "Oh, how I'd love to see them!" I tried to energize her with my voice.

But Grandma was drifting off, her eyelids fluttering as if she was fighting the sleepiness.

Slowly and shakily, she reached over her head and knocked three times on the bed frame, made the crossroads with her knuckle, but this time, she then pointed at me and patted her spindly hand upon her heart. Struggling to get the words out, she said, "Use your human magic and you'll manifest miracles."

"What do you mean?" I asked.

But instead of explaining it to me, she closed her eyes completely. I waited a few minutes, hoping she'd speak once more, but she slumbered away. Only her delicate vein-lined hand moved up and down with her ragged inhales and exhales.

"Grandma . . . you're sleepy now. I'll go," I whispered reluctantly.

Leaning over, I kissed the thin opaque skin of her cool forehead. Love can change one's whole perspective, can't it? The power of that thought overwhelmed me for a minute, so much so that I couldn't move.

"That's enough excitement," Mom whispered as she entered the room, giving me a loving look.

I smiled as I walked out of the room, warmth filling my whole body. This must be what an epiphany feels like. I grabbed my journal, writing every detail down.

. . . Grandma grew tired before telling me where the paintings are, leaving me on the edge of my seat once more, but she always comes through. She said they were close by. I'll take the shreds and use as much tape as needed to put them back together!

Writing this, I'm reminded of how I forgot to ask about the note in the fairy powder compact, and to ask about the fortieth birthday trip . . . where did she and Anna go and what did they see? And what does "use your human magic and you'll manifest miracles" even mean?

But such exciting stories! Many of the pieces are coming together now. I'll do my best to wait while she rests, but a day or two is about as long as I can stand to wait! I know that, as she says, with patience, she will tell me . . .

22

To Stray

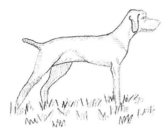

"Let the rain kiss you. Let the rain beat upon your head with liquid silver drops. Let the rain sing you a lullaby."
—⁓ *Langston Hughes* ⁓—

Bright rays of sun shone through the old warped glass of the large picture window at the top of the stairs. A clear, sunny morning—the weatherman predicted a storm late tonight— but it didn't look cloudy or anything.

I had slept in, so it was 11 o'clock by the time I was dressed and ready to start my day. Before going downstairs, I checked in on Grandma. Her door was ajar, so quietly I pushed it open a crack more, enough to see through. Inside, the tiny woman lay on the bed with her eyes closed, taking quick breaths.

I noticed that the vase of quince had been moved onto the bed-side table, but it had already begun to wilt. That was odd. I had just picked the flowering quince yesterday and it usually does well for days at a time in a vase.

Then I noticed Mom sitting in the nearby armchair at Grandma's bedside, reading. Did Mom always do that? Well, it didn't really matter, since Grandma seemed fine—just sleeping. I wasn't going to do her any good just by hanging around here. The urge to visit the creek tugged at me, unrelenting. If nothing else, it promised to lift me away from the solemnity that loomed between the corners of each room in that house.

I leisurely ate some cereal, got hooked on a cool documentary about beehives on television, and when I looked at the time, it was already past 1. Creek time!

Leaving with sketchbook in hand, I noticed that the "Welcome" doormat was laid backward, facing me as I left instead of outward to greet a visitor. That was odd—the gardener must have put it back the wrong way after cleaning the porch. I turned it around and continued on my way.

I ran across the front lawn and down the road to the place of comfort—*of solace*—that Grandma and I shared: the creek. Running in the humidity made my vision wobble, but soon I found a cool, shady spot, and was glad to feel a small breeze blow on my neck beneath my ponytail. Everything felt normal here, at least for the time being.

I spent the day alone, watching, drawing, and trying not to think. Inspired by a clump of red rain lilies growing between two smooth, brown rocks, I looked deeply into the shadows, shading and blending. I concentrated on the subtle curves of every edge, trying to get my drawing as perfect as I could.

Several hours passed before my mind began to wander back to reality. I kept wondering when Grandma would be rested enough to tell me where the torn pieces of her artwork were. I also wondered how the group movie date with Grant would go tonight. My tummy got all fluttery again just thinking about it. A boy had really asked me out? I still could hardly believe it! Thank goodness Lacey had agreed to go too . . .

Shoot! What time was it? 5:00! She was on her way to my house to help me get dressed! I packed up my supplies and ran, arriving at home just as Lacey was knocking on the side door. She was wearing a navy polka dot dress with capped sleeves and red flats.

"You're looking cute, Miss Lacey May," I said.

She twirled around, her skirt billowing out, and then stopped to pose like she was in a fashion ad. "Thank you, dah-ling!" She flicked both wrists down in emphasis.

We giggled all the way to my room.

"I was thinking about wearing this outfit." I pointed to the clothes I'd laid out on my bed earlier that day.

"I like the peach eyelet peasant blouse—the color goes well with your complexion—and those cuffed tan shorts are adorbs." Lacey abruptly put her hands on her hips. "But you are not wearin' your *creek* shoes."

I grabbed them. "But these are comfortable."

"They look like somethin' the creature from the Black Lagoon would wear on a date." She took the shoes from me. "Look, they have dried-up green stuff . . ."

". . . algae."

"*Algae* on them." She let out an exasperated huff, tossed the shoes aside, and walked to my closet. Digging around for a minute, she finally turned, holding a pair of silver sandals that I had worn only once. "Wear these instead." She handed them to me and I slipped them on, wiggling my toes. "Much better!"

I got dressed and then Lacey braided a small section of hair on each side of my face, pulling them back with a shiny silver clip. I slid my brown leather purse strap over my shoulder and checked myself out in the mirror. I looked kind of . . . pretty. I smiled, turning from side to side.

The doorbell rang.

"Grant's gonna like what he sees," Lacey commented before heading out the door.

I froze. Was I really about to go out with Grant? Could I even do this without turning into Super Geek? My hands started trembling.

Lacey walked back in. "You comin' or not?"

I nodded and followed her down the stairs. Halfway down, I saw my mom and Grant chatting in the front hall. He was wearing khaki pants and a blue plaid hoodie.

The second I came into view, Grant's eyes were fixed on me. "You look nice, Claire." He grinned.

"Thanks." I felt heat rush to my face.

"Now, don't be out too late. A big storm is coming tonight," Mom warned.

"Not until 11 o'clock, and the movie ends at 9, so no worries, Mom. Besides, Lacey's parents are driving us back. We'll easily be home before it hits." I turned to Grant. "This is my friend, Lacey." I flicked my head in her direction.

"Hi, Lacey. I saw you at the tearoom the other day."

"Right. You're the egg delivery guy," Lacey remarked.

"Eggs, *ladyfingers*," he said, looking right at me, "we carry them all."

I squinted my eyes at him, then smiled.

"My other friends are waiting outside. Ready to go?" Grant slipped his hands into the pockets of his jacket.

"Yeah. Bye, Mom." I gave her a half-smile.

"Bye. Have fun." She opened the door. "And be careful."

I gave Mom a quick nod and we left her standing in the hallway, closing the door behind us.

On the front walkway were two boys and a girl, laughing.

"Claire and Lacey, meet Eddie, Allie, and John," Grant announced, bobbing his hand towards each one. Eddie was tall, with longish dark hair and olive skin, and he held the petite redhead Allie's hand. John was blond, medium in height, and he immediately gave off pleasant vibes. "Now let's get going."

The fifteen-minute walk to the Village Movie Theater was full of small-talk and laughter. Lacey and John talked to each other most of the time, apparently in the same biology class. Eddie and Allie never let go of each other's hands, so I got Grant all to myself. His blue eyes flashed as we discussed our favorite bands, making me giddy.

All six of us sat in a row inside the theater—I was between Lacey and Grant. It was hard to concentrate on what I was watching with him so close.

Once the movie ended, we stood in the lobby, watching rain pour down onto the street outside.

"I guess the storm came early," Lacey remarked. "My parents just texted me and they're waitin' out front in their car."

I turned my cell phone back on. There was a voice message from Dad: "Hi, honey. I don't want to alarm you or anything, but something's happened and you need to get home right after the movie. Okay? Bye."

My heart began to palpitate and I felt the blood drain from my body. Grant noticed. "What is it?"

"It's my grandmother, I think. Something's wrong." I pulled the wadded up rain slicker out of my purse and put it on.

"Well, we'll make sure you get dropped off first . . ."

"Oh no!" My eyes widened. "The infinity root! I promised!" I turned and started walking away.

"The infinity *what?*" Grant looked puzzled. "Wait, Claire, where are you going?"

"I have to go to Cornell Bridge right away," I yelled, running into the torrential downpour.

"What? Are you crazy?" he called after me.

"I'll be okay!" My silver sandals filled with water immediately.

Suddenly, Grant was running alongside. "I'm going with you."

As much as I wanted him beside me, all that mattered right then was keeping my promise to Grandma. We sloshed through mud puddles, the wind racing against us, all the way to the creek. There was more water than I'd ever seen rushing by. Lightning crackled and thunder crashed, but I kept running.

Finally reaching Cornell Bridge, I took out the penlight on my keychain and searched the roots of the trees.

"What are you doing?" Grant's hair was drenched and water drizzled off his nose.

"Looking for a root in the shape of a sideways figure eight . . . there it is!" I pointed to the large tree on the other side of the bridge. "I've got to cross over and get a picture of it."

"Hurry up. Don't want you to get struck by lightning. Wouldn't make a very good first impression, especially with your parents."

I laughed. "I'm just going to climb down onto that rock over there on the edge of the creek bed, snap a picture with my phone, and then we're out of here."

"Be careful."

"I'm down here all the time." I crossed the bridge and climbed halfway down the bank, balancing on the rock. The water in the creek below whooshed by. My sandal sole was smooth and my foot slipped, but I caught my balance. I knew I should have worn my creek shoes!

"I'm going a little closer!" I yelled, stepping onto a boulder covered with green moss, and suddenly, I knew that the feeling of falling wasn't just a feeling.

That was the last thing I remembered.

I woke up in my bed, Dad and Grant at my side.

"What happened?" I tried to focus my eyes. "I was taking a picture of the infinity root and . . ."

"And then you slipped into the creek and hit your head," Grant said.

Dad reached for my hand. "It's a only mild concussion, but you had us worried."

"So I guess my phone is toast."

"Probably floated to San Antonio by now," Grant joked.

I looked at him. "You saved me?"

"Well, actually, she did." He pointed to the floor near the foot of my bed. There on a towel stood a wet, muddy, lanky dog.

"It looks pretty darn mangy. You sure it doesn't have rabies?" I asked.

"Well, this lost pup is a hero—ah, a heroine, it's a girl. According to Grant, she dragged you out of the rushing creek water by your jacket hood and onto the shore," Dad said, walking over and patting the dog's pointy head. The dog wagged her tail.

"She got you before I even had a chance." Grant looked at his feet, then turned up his eyes, sheepishly. "But I carried you home." A spark of pride.

The thought of being carried in Grant's arms gave me a warm, tingly sensation.

"Her owners need to be found, but they won't recognize her looking like this." Dad announced. "What do you say to a bath, girl? I'll get the water ready and come back. Staaaay . . ." The dog obeyed.

"Wait a minute, Dad. How's Grandma?"

Deafening silence filled the room. My heart started doing back flips.

"Well . . ."

"Tell me, Dad," I demanded, sitting straight up.

"Mom's at the hospital. Grandma's . . . in a coma. Dr. Hammond said there's really nothing they can do. I'm sorry, honey."

My voice caught in my throat. "Thanks for telling me, Dad," I managed, wanting him to hear a steadiness in my voice so he wouldn't worry.

Dad grinned sadly and left the room.

"Sure you're all right?" Grant asked.

"Yeah. Well, maybe. I don't know." I just sat there, as the reality of the situation began to sink in.

People could come out of comas . . . couldn't they? But really, I knew it was pretty rare for someone who was eighty-eight years old to recover from one.

"You probably want to be alone. I'll come back tomorrow, okay?" Grant walked to the door, then turned around. "I'm really sorry about your grandmother. But I'm glad you're okay."

"Thanks," I said, sinking back down into my bed.

When he was gone, I closed my eyes, feeling desperate, lost, and numb.

My dad whistled for the dog, and she left too.

Then, I had a vision—I'd read something like this was called a "wake-initiated lucid dream," which occurs when the dreamer goes from being awake directly into a dream state.

In the one I was having, I had tucked myself on the edge of the creek, beneath a thicket of oak trees that grew so low, no one could see me. Their timeworn branches reached downward, seemingly to sip the water with their bottommost leaves. I followed an unexpected urge to crawl on my knees among the blooming periwinkle that covered the ground like a creeping fog. Once the purple-blue flowers surrounded me, their tendril-like stems grabbing from all sides, I remembered what Grandma had said, that periwinkles symbolized friendship.

Then, in this dream, it overcame me that over the past few weeks, Grandma had somehow become my closest friend. Throwing my face into my hands, tears dripped through my fingers while disappointment and disbelief spun around in my head. Taking a deep breath, I stopped and looked around—searching the trees, the creek, the bushes that lined the bank . . . and then I caught myself.

How stupidly silly was I! There were no such thing as fairies! I'd been so foolish.

"Where are the fairies now, Grandma?" I screamed. "I need their healing! I need their magic! The stories you told me were tales and myths!"

And though the word *myths* echoed in my head, I still looked again for a glint of a fairy—someone or something to help me through my pain—but saw nothing. I had let love into my heart and it had crept inside crevices I didn't know were there, taking hold, like ivy that creeps from a neighbor's yard between the slats of the fence, into your own.

I cried until no more tears were left to cry, and the next thing I knew, I woke from this dream to morning light. My eyes felt swollen and I had a headache. I went to find my parents.

As I entered the kitchen, I noticed the dog. It was laying by the stove on a bed of old towels.

"Food's ready," was Mom's lackluster announcement. Her movements were slow, her hair and clothes slightly disheveled. "Oh Claire, you're up. How's the head?"

"Achy."

"I'll get you some Tylenol," she said, reaching into the cupboard by the sink and pulling out a bottle. "And a glass of water to wash them down."

"Thanks, Mom." I swallowed the pills. "So, what's the little cretin still doing here?"

"Now, is that any way to talk about your rescuer?" Dad scolded, entering the kitchen. "It turns out that she's a very valuable hunting dog—a Hungarian vizsla, see?"

He held out a sheet printed off the Internet. I glanced at it, curious.

"I gave her a bath and she cleaned up as pretty as a penny! She's certainly got the same coppery coat as one."

Huh. It seemed that this dog was making Dad more chipper than usual.

"We'll have to put an ad in the newspaper and some signs around town, but we'll watch over her until she gets back to her owners," Mom added.

"And what if no one claims it . . . ah . . . her?"

"Well, honey, why don't we just keep her, then? It would be nice to have a new friend around here . . . and if she does find her home, I'm not opposed to a puppy . . ." her voice trailed off.

"Great. First I'm forced to accept Grandma, now a dog?" I exploded. "Everyone just needs to leave me alone!" My head started throbbing. I pushed my chair away from the table and ran upstairs, slamming the door to my room.

It's funny how weather can match the way a person is feeling.

For me, it seemed right that the storm carried on for three long days. Clouds masked the sky and my heart. Grandma remained in a coma and the doctors told us all we could do was wait. So, I drew like crazy to keep my mind off my despair, refusing to leave my room except for meals.

Grant had stopped by to check on me the first day, but since he wouldn't exactly be seeing me at my best, I told Mom to tell him I'd call when I felt better.

The feeling of sorrow seemed endless, especially when I walked by the door that ominously reminded me of death. I couldn't bear to see it, be near it, think about it. And throughout those three days of being holed up, the dog followed me everywhere—even into the bathroom.

"Out!" I commanded. She'd turn, head drooping, and wait for me outside. And the second I opened the door, she wagged her tail and ran in circles. "You act like I just got back from a trip to Timbuktu!"

The darkness of the stormy sky matched my feelings, and when the sun finally peeked out, my psyche became a bit brighter, too. No change with Grandma, so I took it as no news was good news. I actually ate half of my lunch on that third day, which was more than I had previously been stomaching, and I was longing to go back to the creek to see what damage the storm had done. Sketching after a storm was one of my favorite things because nature got mixed up in ways that only wind and water could cause.

Again, as I left, the welcome mat was upside down. What was going on? I fixed it and continued on.

But then I heard the prancing of four happy feet behind me. "No, dog, you need to stay." I went back and forced her to go back in the house, shutting the door between us.

Approaching the northernmost bank, I discovered a great tree had fallen and was now a rough bridge extending across the lower part of the creek. Part of it had cracked in half from crashing upon a boulder, so I was excited to sketch the event with detailed artistry.

. . . and then I heard a whining sound.

Jumping up, startled, I heard it again, coming from behind the fallen tree. Leaves rustled back and forth, and I poised myself to run if necessary. Then, a reddish-brown nose peeked from between the branches.

It was the dog!

"Really? You figured out a way to follow me? I'm not in the mood to take care of you right now," I told her.

The dog sat a few feet away and cocked her head.

"Lay down," I commanded, and she did it immediately, placing her head upon her front paws and letting out a big sigh.

"Sorry, but if you stay right there, I guess I'll let you hang."

The dog lifted and tilted her head, her long ears cocked, trying to understand. The way her floppy ears perked just where they were attached to her head was kind of cute.

I sketched for about an hour, and the dog slept in her spot the whole time. When I'd collected all of the visual data I needed, I gathered my stuff and started to go. The dog sat up, watching me, but she didn't move.

"You're staying here? Well, okay. Good luck, mutt!" I said, turning to walk home. Then I remembered what Grandma had said about having room in my heart to take care of something that needed me. I turned and looked at the dog. Maybe she needed me. Maybe the fairies even sent her to me. I couldn't take any chances.

"Come, dog!" I called, and she took off running. When she reached me, she began to jump all over me, giving me slurpy licks.

"Easy, girl."

She was so happy that she started to walk on her hind legs, dancing like a bear in a circus. She paraded around in the sunbeams that softly drifted between the tree branches, finally landing back down on all four paws.

"Maybe you are a special dog after all." I smiled and patted her head.

We walked home side by side. "I guess you need a name. How about Penny?" She wagged her tail vigorously.

It was then that I realized I had added another place in my heart. I prayed that no one would claim the dog.

23

Sorrow

"Oh heart, if one should say to you that the soul perishes like the body,
answer that the flower withers, but the seed remains."
—~ *Kahlil Gibran* ~—

I had spent the night at Lacey's to keep my mind off things. When I got home at about 10 the next morning, Penny greeted me by jumping up and licking my cheek, but it was way too quiet in the house and there was an odd chill in the air.

I plopped my overnight bag on my bedroom floor, deciding what to do on that warm summer day. Distraction was key. Maybe I'd go to the library and find some new books to read, or see if Lacey wanted to join me for a swim at the public pool. And maybe I'd call Grant, too.

I found Mom in the kitchen at the sink. On the counter next to her was the vase holding the now brown and drooping quince sprig I'd given Grandma. My heart sank.

Mom began washing the dishes so vigorously that her hands became covered in suds. She dropped a coffee mug, shattering it in the sink.

"My mind is just not with me today," she said, shaking her head. I watched as she cleaned up the shards, wiped her hands, walked to the large window in the living room, and just stood there, staring out.

I followed her, pretending to look for a sketching pencil under the couch cushions.

"Mom, what's up?" I asked.

She turned away from the window and looked at me for a moment. "I need to tell you something and I don't know how." Taking a deep breath, she turned back to the window.

"It's okay, Mom. I just want to know what's going on."

"Yes, my clinical girl, you are full of the need for the truth—but lately, I noticed a change in you—for awhile, you opened up to the things in life only tangible to the heart. But I'm afraid you have your walls up again."

"Just give me the facts, Mom."

"Well, one fact is certain—your grandmother has been a good mother to me. She taught me to be practical in life, and so I taught you to be logical because of that. I also tried to show you how important nurturing can be."

I walked up behind Mom. Sadness radiated from her. I reached out and touched her arm. She looked at me.

"What happened to cause the trust inside you to be so fragile, Claire?" Her eyes bore into mine, questioning.

"Well, Val being so far away in a war has definitely been a strain on the whole family," I said.

"Yes, but I saw how your protected heart opened once your grandmother arrived. It was so lovely to observe, while it lasted."

It's true—I'd felt so different the past few weeks. But now it was like something within me had died. I was surprised Mom noticed.

"I pray the distrust won't be what remains, that's all. But you're right, I do owe you the truth." Her face confirmed the bad news. "Things got bad for your grandmother in the hospital late last night, while you were sleeping over at Lacey's. The phone call . . ." Mom's voice quavered. She looked down at her fidgeting fingers, and took a deep breath, ". . . is coming at any time. I'm going back there to be by her side. I just needed to come home to freshen up—and talk to you in person."

My mouth opened but then closed again.

"Although she's only been a part of our family life for a little while," Mom continued, "it's strange not to have her here." Her breathing quivered. "It was a good thing, her being in this house for a while. We spent quality time with her, and she was so happy to return to her old childhood home to . . . meet you."

I continued to stand there, glued to the floor. Mom ran her hand down the side of my face. "No matter how prepared you think you are for the end of a life, well, it's still terribly sad." A tear ran down each of her cheeks. "Just want you to know what's going on." The tears began to stream from her eyes then, so Mom took a tissue from inside her sleeve and wiped them.

"Oh," was all I could whisper.

And then it dawned on me. I was losing my grandmother, but my mom was losing her mother. It was awful to see her that way. A fountain of compassion gushed in me, and I wrapped my arms tightly around her, feeling her body shudder with sorrow.

I just stood silently in that window, holding Mom close. But I needed to say something.

"You're right, Mom, my time with Grandma was too short." I hated that Mom was so sad and I searched for words, truthful ones, to make her feel better. "Sometimes I do hate that I allowed myself to care so much for her, but then I wonder, would it really have been better if Grandma and I never had this time together? And the answer is no. I wouldn't have learned so much about our heritage, this old house's history . . . about Grandpa. Our time spent together was . . . amazing."

Mom stepped back and smiled at me through her tears.

The shrill ringing of the phone shattered the moment.

We held our breath.

Mom barely managed to say, "Your father will get it . . ."

We waited, then heard the click of the phone being set back into its cradle.

Dad entered, sadness pulling at his face. "She's gone."

Mom's body sagged as she covered her face with her hands, then she wiped each eye and looked at me. "I've got to go. Your father and I need to make arrangements. Aunt Az will be meeting us." She grabbed both of my hands in each one of hers. "Would you like to see her one last time?"

"No, Mom. I promised Grandma I wouldn't."

She looked torn for a moment. "Will you be okay here alone?"

Dad left the room, hands in his pockets and head low.

"Yes, I'll be okay. And Mom . . . I'm . . . I'm sorry." I felt my own sadness rising up in me, like lava in a volcano.

"Me too." Mom let go of my hands, then tenderly slid the backs of her fingers down my cheeks, grabbed her purse, and left.

I stood there until I heard the car pull away. Penny sat at my feet, waiting with me.

My talks with Grandma were over . . . forever. *Forever* felt so infinite. Was Grandma, who was tangible flesh and blood, really nowhere to be found on this earth that she loved so much? Could that large, impressive energy, which existed so brightly in her, have just vanished?

24

Human Magic

"Where there is great love, there are always miracles."
—☙ Willa Cather ❧—

After my parents left, I stood in my silent living room for a while. I wanted to be angry for caring, and my mind tried to go there, but my feelings didn't match. I wanted to forget all about my grandmother, but my heart wouldn't oblige. Instead, all it wanted me to do was honor her.

I went out the front door, Penny at my side, and glancing down, saw that the welcome doormat was facing the wrong way *again*. I turned it around, shaking my head, and continued on to the creek.

It was a cooler day than we'd had in weeks, and for once the heat didn't hit me like entering a brick oven. I knew exactly where I needed to go—to Cornell Bridge, to visit the infinity root again.

In the daylight, I saw how grand the old tree was, with maze-like roots. How had I never noticed it before? And popping out at me like a 3-D *Magic Eye* image was the sideways figure eight.

I climbed halfway down the riverbed to get a good look at it, and Penny came with me. It was a strong, thick, single root, undeniably forming the symbol for infinity—and that's when I began to sob. The sound that came out of me actually scared away a flock of birds in the trees above. Mourning engulfed me, and I stumbled to my knees in the dirt. I sat there, on the rock that had sent me slipping into the creek before, near the edge of the trickling water, as tears poured out of my eyes. All my feelings came out: sorrow, longing, and joy.

After a while, I climbed back up the embankment, the dog following me again, to where the ground was drier. There, I laid down and rolled up into a ball, muddy knees and all, in the wild purple bluebonnets mixed with tall yellow-green grass. The sheer serenity and beauty of hiding among such beautiful flowers caused me to cry again silently, the tears tickling as they traveled.

I cried myself into a sorrow-induced world between consciousness and sleep. Time was a river and I was floating on it, no feeling or care for how much time had passed—it could have been hours or minutes, I honestly didn't know. Finally, I became aware of my surroundings again and there was the dog: curled up, warmly pressing herself against my back.

How had I allowed myself to cry for so long? My sadness felt endless and my insides as knotted as the twisted roots of the nearby oaks. I let the warm rays of sun and the tender wafts of fresh air do their best to soothe me.

The dog noticed that I had opened my eyes, and she wagged her tail, rhythmically drumming on the earth. Then Penny got up and stretched, sniffing the air with her long red-brown snout. In the glow of the waning sunlight of the day, her coat was shiny, very much like a copper coin.

I gazed into the opal-glass sky streaked with light, the position of the sun suggesting that it was late in the afternoon. It would begin its descent soon. I knew I needed to go home.

"Come, Penny." The dog moved closer, wagging her tail as I patted her velvety head. "Sit," I said, testing the dog's smarts. She sat immediately. "That's a good girl!"

Then, she crept closer and closer, until "plunk"—she sat bottom-first in my lap.

"You goofy dog!" I said, pushing her bony butt off me. "Give me a little space."

But she wouldn't leave, sitting an inch away and looking me square in the face.

"I can out-stare you, pup, any day," I said, leaning my face closer to hers. She raised one of the furry bumps above her eyes, which looked like silly eyebrows, and I smiled.

The dog suddenly licked my cheek with her long pink tongue.

"Yuck!" I wiped my face, laughing. She certainly knew how to cheer me up a little.

Then a slight cracking sound came from behind us, turning Penny into the hunter her instincts told her to be. Crouching low to the ground, she slowly walked toward the sound, which seemed to be coming from a low-jutting branch. The branch must have cracked in the storm, as it was wedged broken side down into a labyrinth of roots protruding from a neighboring oak.

Dad had explained that dogs like Penny had natural hunting instincts and "pointed" at prey. Well, that was just what Penny was doing when she aimed her nose at this "something," bending her front right leg and extending her tail. She froze in place, waiting for me to get up and see what it was.

I moved cautiously, searching the twisted branches and pointy leaves for a creature. What if it was a skunk or a nasty possum?

Tentatively I searched, seeing nothing but thick tufts of leaves. And just as I was about to turn away and give up, I saw something move oddly from side to side. It swayed peculiarly, but familiarly—with a closer look, I was eye-to-eye with a praying mantis. It turned its triangular face, definitely noticing me.

Was it the very same mantis I captured and drew a couple of weeks ago? It was identical in its green color, with brownish lines in the exact same places . . .

That's when Penny ran up close to sniff it, and then she made an unusual sound for a dog. It wasn't a bark, nor was it whining, but more like "*ar-rar-roo!*" as if she were . . . talking.

The mantis extended its papery wings and fluttered away.

"Bad dog!" I scolded, feeling like she'd just frightened a friend.

I wanted to catch it to see if it was the same mantis as before by comparing it to my sketches. I'd been keeping an eye open for another one for weeks, and the dumb animal had scared it away.

I expected Penny to skittishly run away from my reprimand, but instead, she oddly resumed her "pointing" stance.

"Why are you pointing again? The mantis is gone. What do you see?"

I walked closer to the spot where the mantis had been, and lying across a large twig in the same exact spot, the reflection of the fading sun caught something iridescent.

Wings? Yes, it was definitely wings that were poking out between crisp green leaves on the branch. An injured mantis or dragonfly?

I drew in my breath as I spotted tiny human-like arms and legs made of flower stems, dull pink petals that had nearly lost their color . . . wait . . . could it be?

It was a fairy! An honest-to-goodness *fairy!* The mantis had been protecting an injured wee one! I couldn't believe what I was seeing!

I literally pinched my arm to make sure I wasn't dreaming. I even closed my eyes, shook my head, and looked again.

Yes, it really is a lifeless fairy!

Penny wagged her tail and barked once. I felt guilty for scolding her earlier. "Good girl, Penny. Good girl." It was Penny's sharp instincts and senses that got me to notice the injured fair one, so I stroked the dog's soft, bony head.

Then, I tenderly freed the tiny body from the tangle of sticks, holding the delicate being in my left palm. With tiny feet and hands, she was definitely just as Grandma had described. Tiny—*infinitesimal*—face and fine, root-like strands for hair, her whole body was oddly plant-like and organic, with the wings of a shimmering dragonfly.

Mixed feelings flooded my heart.

On one hand, I was so amazed to be able to see and hold a real live fairy in my hands—well, "amazed" didn't cut it. I was *awestruck!* I had wished to see one in real life, and here one was, so close I could study every nuance.

However, as I held the tiny creature, I felt the tiniest of breaths coming from it. Holding the fairy up to my ear, I heard a distant flutter of life.

Great. How exactly did a person nurse a fairy back to health? Grandma never taught me that! And what if the fairy died? It would be all my fault and I didn't think I could bear it!

I stood there, not knowing what to do.

Sadly, I put the tiny pixie back where I'd found it. Perhaps the praying mantis would come back to take care of this fairy. Mother Nature had a natural way of taking care of her living beings, and I needed to leave it up to fate and not interfere.

But what if I was its only chance? I couldn't walk away and not at least try to help. Besides, there was something about the way the praying mantis had stood by the fairy so watchfully, as if the mini green guard was protecting the fair one . . . until I came closer. Then, the insect virtually nodded at me and left, revealing what it had been holding vigil over. Did it want me to help the fairy?

I reached over and gently picked up the fairy again.

If nothing else, she would surely expire in harsh weather. The crackling air indicated another storm was coming. Perhaps she had a better chance with me? Finally, mind made up, I promised myself that no other human could know about the wee one. I knew I couldn't ask any adults' help, remembering that Grandma said disbelievers would not only be unable to see it (and if I was the only one who could see it, everyone would think I'd gone crazy!), and that fairies gained energy from human belief.

I couldn't risk disbelief draining the fairy's energy.

I pictured what happened to Tinkerbell in *Peter Pan* when that famous pixie almost died. She didn't revive until the children in the audience had clapped to show their belief, which brought her back to life once more. It all made sense now, in a mad sort of way.

Just before getting to the house, I picked three azalea blooms from my backyard to use as a cushion inside of my sweater pocket, and then gingerly tucked her in as well. I had to conceal her, and my pocket seemed like the safest place.

Penny and I entered cautiously through the front door, as if I was a crook and Penny my accomplice. We passed over the upside down mat (hadn't I fixed that?) and started up the stairs.

"Are you okay, Claire?" Mom was sitting at the kitchen table with red, swollen eyes and a box of Kleenex beside her right elbow.

I entered the kitchen, realizing I probably had the same puffy eyes but that I had forgotten about my sorrow. I wanted to run over and hug Mom tightly, but couldn't until the fairy was safely upstairs in my room.

"Please sit down for a minute." Mom motioned to a chair and I obliged, but anxiously sat on the edge. The sadness in the room was as thick as maple syrup. "Where have you been?"

"I went to my usual place . . ." I answered, hoping this would be a short conversation.

"The creek, honey?"

I nodded.

"I thought so. I wasn't worried," Mom said, crumpling a tissue in her hand. "I knew you needed time . . . but I'm glad to see you back at home—another storm is due soon. You look exhausted, why don't you rest before dinner."

"Yeah, I'm tired, all right," I faked—*feigned*—yawning.

"I'm ordering pizza. I don't feel like making dinner tonight."

Enough small talk—I needed to get upstairs and take care of this fairy in my pocket!

"Sounds good," I said, getting up to leave.

"Wait. I almost forgot. Your grandmother shared something with me during her last coherent moments."

Dread washed over me. "Let's talk later. I need to go wash . . ." I said, pointing to the mud on my knees and turning to head upstairs.

"Here . . ." I heard a "thump" on the table and turned back around to see Mom sliding Grandma's jewelry box—the one full of letters and exquisite fairy paintings—across the table.

"For me?" I was awestruck. There was no other object in the world I would have cherished more! I picked it up.

"Yes, she wanted you to have it. It's locked, though. Maybe you can figure out how to get it open. You can keep this as a reminder of her and . . . spending time here, together."

I embraced the box in my arms. Mom had no clue what this plain-looking leather vessel had to offer. Happy warmth filled me.

"Thanks, Mom." I was finally free to go, but stopped in my tracks—the tea tray, still with the yogurt and napkin on it, was sitting on the counter near the sink. "Is that the tray I saw outside of Grandma's room?"

"Yes, I can't seem to bring myself to clean it up."

"Did you replace the flowers?" I was looking at the same vase, in the same position on the tray, except the flowers were fresh and bright with the beautiful coral color back in their petals.

"No, dear. They're still the ones you gave to your grandmother, which was very sweet. She told me you picked them for her and asked me to move them closer, so she could look at them from her bed."

"But, they were nearly . . ." I stopped since "dead" wasn't the best word to use right at that moment.

I couldn't believe it! The flowers had revived! Could that be a sign that the fairy could be revived too?

I gave Mom a quick smile, then scampered away to my room.

A minute later, I heard a scratch and a tiny whine at my door.

"Okay, you can come in," I told Penny, who immediately curled up on the rug next to my bed, half watching, half sleeping, and occasionally snoring.

25

The Periwinkle Patient

"...there is a subtle magnetism in nature
which if we unconsciously yield to it, will direct us aright."
—∽ *Henry David Thoreau* ∾—

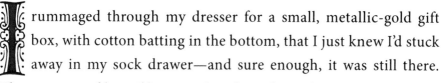

rummaged through my dresser for a small, metallic-gold gift box, with cotton batting in the bottom, that I just knew I'd stuck away in my sock drawer—and sure enough, it was still there. The memory of how I'd received a silver charm bracelet in it for my 10th birthday rushed back to me for a moment.

Now it would hold something even more precious!

I peeked into my sweater pocket to check on the hidden fairy, and I could have sworn I saw her move, ever so slightly. Gently lifting her out, I laid the delicate nymph on the cotton inside the gift box, which made the perfect gilded bed for such an amazing being.

Placing the box beneath the light of my desk lamp, I studied her more closely. Her long filament-hair and hourglass shape definitely meant she was a girl—and the fairy maiden's tiny chest did move up and down ever so slightly, although her minuscule eyes were tightly shut.

What should I do? Think, Claire, think!

I remembered the green book I'd found at the library. Making sure the fairy was safe and secure in her box on my desk, I looked on my shelf, but couldn't find the book anywhere. I even scanned the bookshelf systematically from left to right, but still, it wasn't there. I was certain that was where I'd put it.

Where could it have gone?

I crawled around on the floor, looking beneath my desk and bed. I even searched my book bag, but it wasn't there. That book was my only hope of finding helpful information on how to nurse a fairy back to health, but where was it? I needed it! The fairy would most certainly die if I didn't find it! I felt panicked, my breathing becoming more difficult.

After looking in the same places a second and third time, I finally gave up and returned to my desk in complete aggravation. The book seemed to have vanished into thin air. I just stared sadly at the amazing, ill-fated creature, trying to calm myself down. I needed a clear head since I'd have to come up with something on my own.

Let's see . . . Grandma's last words were to use my "human magic" to manifest miracles—and boy, did I need a miracle now—but I had no magic. What had she been talking about? I rested my chin on my hands, with bent elbows on the desktop, and thought for a minute. Suddenly, I sat up briskly.

Love! A while ago, Grandma had said that *love* is the only true magic humans possess. It seemed a little silly now, but I had actually looked up "love" in the dictionary on my computer, which was right behind my fairy. I slid out the shelf just below the desk, where my keyboard rested:

love |ləv|—*a strong affection for another arising out of kinship or personal ties*

It made perfect sense. I loved Grandma and I was tied to this tiny fairy due to her, so my actions needed to come from the affection I felt. I closed my eyes, smiling at the memory of sitting beside Grandma on her bed while she told her stories, to see if I could remember other hints that may have assisted me in caring for the fairy.

Now, what did she say about where fairies get their energy? Ah, yes—from believers! Boy, am I ever a believer now! I opened my eyes and repeated, "I do believe in fairies!" over and over again, while looking at the resting fairy before me, feeling the words coming from some deep, truthful place within me.

I searched my memory again. Perhaps the fairy needed to be surrounded with natural things, like flowers and water—and familiar things like . . . other fairies!

I quickly left the tiny one's side and grabbed the box Grandma had left for me, which was sitting on my dresser, and set it on my desk.

I crept down the hall to Grandma's room—how vacant and echoing it seemed without the full-spirited woman there. I knew I'd become very sad if I took the time to think about how the room matched the emptiness I felt without her. It helped to know I was on a mission Grandma would approve of. Walking over to the vanity and opening the little drawer, I took out the key.

Quietly, I hurried back to the box. Sticking the key into the lock, turning it sharply to the right, the latch snapped open and I lifted the lid, revealing the glorious paintings. If the fairy saw these pictures, she'd surely recognize her friends!

Pulling out the letters, I hid them inside my sweater drawer. In the bottom of the box were two more things: an old, well-worn Kate Greenaway book called *The Language of Flowers* and a postcard with a photo of the island of Maui, Hawaii on it. Turning over the postcard, I saw a handwritten note:

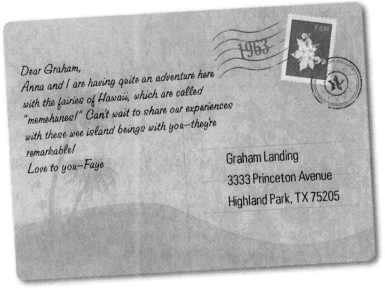

Dear Graham,
Anna and I are having quite an adventure here with the fairies of Hawaii, which are called "menehunes!" Can't wait to share our experiences with these wee island beings with you—they're remarkable!
Love to you—Faye

Graham Landing
3333 Princeton Avenue
Highland Park, TX 75205

It was postmarked 1963. Her and Anna's 40th birthday trip!

Slipping the postcard into the Kate Greenaway book to study later, I gently lifted the tiny creature in her cotton and gold bed and laid it tenderly on the bottom of Grandma's box. Around her, I tucked the azalea petals from my sweater pocket. Surely they'd give off a familiar scent of green—*verdant*—growth, if nothing else.

Filling the cap of a half-empty Dasani bottle until the water made a reflective dome, I set it near the golden makeshift divan. Still, the fairy didn't stir—only the scantest movement of her chest moving up and down could be seen.

Chocolate! Grandma definitely mentioned how much fairies love chocolate! I'd have to ride my bike to the store to get some—it could be the magic ingredient that rescued my little friend! But in the meantime, bread and sugar had a chance of helping her as well.

Downstairs in the kitchen I pulled a piece of bread out of the breadbox and got the sugar container out of the pantry. Now, I needed a serving dish.

I searched through the Hoosier cabinet for the right thing—a small saltcellar, a clear bowl with the diameter of a fifty-cent piece, was just right.

"Claire, have you gotten your appetite back?" Mom said, looking at what was in my hand. "Craving bread with . . . sugar?" She looked confused.

Shoot! How would I explain myself? Luckily, she let me off the hook.

"Well, whatever sounds good is okay by me—it's better than nothing. But sweetie, the sugar will never stick on its own. How about some butter on the bread first?"

"Butter! Of course! Thanks, Mom." To skirt any more discussion, I added, "Can I eat it up in my room?"

"Sure, sweetie." Mom looked a bit worried.

I buttered the bread and sprinkled some of the sparkly sweetness on top. I'd managed to secretly—*covertly*—slip the saltcellar in my pocket so there would be no questions about that. I was close to making a getaway when Mom stopped me again.

"Before you go, let me see you take a bite. It will make me feel better to actually see you eat."

"Ah, sure, Mom." I wasn't thrilled to eat such a mixture, but crucial seconds were ticking away, possibly toward the demise of a waking, hungry fairy.

"See?" I opened my mouth after reluctantly biting into the bread-butter-sugar creation. "Mmmm, good," I said with my mouth full.

It's not half-bad.

I slowly and mournfully walked up the stairs, quietly racing up two steps at a time once I was out of Mom's sight.

Peeking into the jewelry box, the fairy continued to sleep, so I carefully set the tiny crystal bowl next to the water, tearing about an eighth of the sugary buttered bread into tiny pieces and placing them in the bowl.

I still didn't feel satisfied.

"I'll be right back," I whispered to her. "Like Grandma taught me, I'm listening to my intuition and it tells me that you need chocolate. Please get better while I'm gone," I pleaded, hiding the jewelry box with its invaluable contents under my bed.

"Stay, Penny, stay," I commanded as she tried to follow me.

Grabbing my wallet, I tiptoed out the door, over the mat that was upside down (something crazy was going on!), to the backyard where my bike was waiting in the shed.

I rode to Tom Thumb and parked my bicycle out front, not bothering to lock it. Feeling time tick away, I ran along the ends of the aisles, searching for chocolate chips, since they were the smallest pieces of chocolate available.

Let's see . . . canned goods, cereal, and crackers . . . baking section!

I ran down the aisle. There, near the cake mixes, was a sign: "CHOCOLATE MORSELS, ½ OFF with your Tom Thumb Card."

Crud. That explained why the shelf was empty. Darn it!

With one more determined search, digging through the bags of nuts and coconut, butterscotch chips and white chocolate morsels, I spotted the last package of miniature semi-sweet chocolate chips shoved way in the back behind the neighboring row of one-pound sugar bags. I reached my arm into the depth of the shelf, farther and farther, until I was up to my armpit.

Just half an inch more . . .

"Ah, can I help you?" Just as I had the bag of chips in my grasp, a voice came from behind, startling me. I turned quickly, chocolate chips in hand, knocking down a bag of sugar. The sugar hit the ground and burst like a large water balloon.

"Oh my God! I'm so sorry, I . . ." I stammered, staring at the sugar dune by my feet, knowing my face had turned cherry-red.

Then I looked up—I was face to face with Grant.

"Oh, Grant, I made such a mess. It's just that I'm in such a hurry. I have a personal emergency and . . ."

Stop rambling, Claire!

"Well, I've heard of chocolate lovers, but never heard of a chocolate emergency before," he said in good humor, smiling at the big white glittery mess on the floor.

"It's hard to explain. I'm sorry, but I really have to go."

"I understand. No worries. I've got a big broom in the back that will have this cleaned up in a jiffy." He paused for a second. "How's your grandmother?"

I shook my head.

"Oh, I'm really sorry."

"Thanks." I smiled. He was really sweet to ask.

But I had to get back to my fairy!

"I've really gotta go, and I'm *really* sorry. Thank you, Grant. Thank you for cleaning up. I owe you one."

I ran to the checkout counter, paid, and quickly rode home. Concealing the bag of chocolate chips under my shirt, I managed to make my way back to my room unnoticed, to the side of my fairy patient.

I looked in the jewelry box. No change in the fairy's condition, she was still snoozing away.

"Please wake up!" I whispered over and over again, adding a few chocolate chips to the dish still full of sweetened bread.

Using the magnifying glass I kept in my desk drawer, I took the opportunity to get a closer look. The fairy's pale pink dress petals were actually a faded purple-blue. They exquisitely made up the bodice and skirt of her garment, which seemed to sprout from her twig-like body. Green tendrils and perfectly placed small shiny green leaves covered the top third of her arms and legs. Her hair was made of long, fine white flower filaments, with tiny poofs of yellow pollen-like powder on the end of each strand.

"You must be a periwinkle flower fairy!" I said softly. "Periwinkle grows like a weed by the creek, and your dress is a faded version of the periwinkles' color, with the same white edges. Tending so many, since it grows so wildly, must be a large job for such a minuscule one!"

Then, another thought dawned on me. What if food couldn't breathe life into a wee one as much as a growing plant might? Perhaps it's all about surrounding the fairy with the right kind of plant energy. If I left my bedroom window open, maybe the flower "vibes," or whatever signals the fairies received from plants, could call other fairies to her.

Finding an inconspicuous place for the box near the window, I left the lid open to keep any magical sources flowing. As I opened the window of my room, a gentle breeze moved the green leaves of the pecan tree branches just beyond.

Outside in the potting shed, I collected a trowel and a terra cotta pot, and jumping back on my bike, headed to the creek where the periwinkle grew the thickest. I rode with one hand, carrying my tools in the other. I don't recall ever riding that fast before, and this time, Penny followed my every move, running speedily alongside the bicycle.

Finally at the creek, I dug up a clump of abundantly blooming purple-blue flowers, shoving their dangling roots caked with dirt into the pot. Before I knew it, Penny and I were reentering the house, the brick colored pot with periwinkle vines pouring over the sides in my arm.

As I passed through the kitchen, the house was quiet and luckily Mom wasn't around. I saw the vase of quince I'd picked for Grandma on the windowsill near the sink, still blooming in all its glory, and, deciding it couldn't hurt either, I grabbed it with my other hand. Something was going on with those quince flowers, and whatever it was, it might have been the magic that needed to be near my tiny friend.

I set the pot upon my windowsill, hoping the periwinkle fairies would come tend these lovely flowers, and stumble upon their injured friend. Then, I set the vase of orange-pink quince flowers next to it.

Had I just been imagining their brown droopiness? But there were even petals falling off before! Could merely a change of water revive them back to vivid color again? Scientifically, there was no way that could happen. Once the color—*pigment*—changed to brown, it chemically couldn't return to vivid orange. No, that small vase held a true miracle. The problem was, no one else had noticed it but me.

Now there was nothing to do but wait as the last of the dappled daylight stroked the tiny fairy's body and slowly turned to mottled moonlight. Long shadows drifted across the purple-blue periwinkle and salmon-hued quince nearby, reminiscent of the flowers painted inside the box, and the ribbons that tied the letters, symbolizing the kindred connection between Anna, Grandpa, Grandma, and now, me.

A sweet serenity filled the room as I sat, looking out the window, feeling the warm summer evening air swirl around the contours of my face, reaching wispy fingers up into my hair. There was a friendly presence nearby, I could feel it. Maybe Grandma was watching and approving; maybe the tiny folk were doing the same. Nonetheless, I had the feeling I'd done something right today.

That tingling warmth that kept creeping over me lately came again, in a wave, and I didn't fight it. It felt too good.

Penny was curled up in her favorite spot on the rug again and I went over and sat by her, which caused some rapid tail wagging. I stroked her coat. Penny closed her eyes and groaned, settling down to sleep. This dog had trusted me, even when I was mean to her, and gave me the opportunity to meet a real fairy. I would always be grateful for that.

"Good girl, Penny," I said as I scratched behind her droopy velvet ears.

Again, all Penny did was moan, this time adding a sigh.

The call for dinner came echoing up the stairway—pizza. I tried to think of an excuse to stay in my room, but knew I'd be pushing my luck. I reluctantly decided to go on down for dinner; Penny woke up and followed me downstairs.

I tried to speed things along by getting out the plates from the cupboard, but as soon as I had the table set, Mom announced that she wanted us to use paper plates instead. "I just don't feel like dealing with dirty dishes tonight."

I re-set the table with paper plates, then sat in my chair, ready to eat.

"Not just yet. I sent Dad for some milk and the line at the store was really long. I told him we'd wait for him. The pizza's warming in the oven," Mom said.

When Dad finally arrived ten minutes later, and we sat down together, Mom said a long blessing before eating, and then announced that she had an apple pie in the oven for dessert. Again, more waiting while it baked and cast smells of apple-cinnamon about the kitchen. My knee vibrated and my heart thumped the whole time, anxious to get back upstairs. Finally, after eating my dessert like I was in a timed pie-eating contest at the County Fair, I was free to go.

I ran to the jewelry box to check on my fairy and saw something rather surprising. The areas where the fairy's wings connected to her body were glowing ever so slightly, very much like the glow stick I wore around my neck every Halloween for trick-or-treating.

Was it the waning daylight that was bringing out the radiance, or a sign of revival?

Then, I noticed something else—the fairy had definitely shifted her body into a new position. Perhaps she really was healing!

There was no way I could sleep that night and miss any more changes! I dragged my desk chair next to the box, since it was more comfortable than the bench seat under the window, and sat watching the fair one, getting up only once to brush my teeth and quickly say goodnight to my mom and dad. I then sketched for hours, study-ing—*scrutinizing*—the tiny fairy's features.

By three o'clock in the morning, however, I felt myself beginning to doze. I needed to get up and walk around to get my blood flow-ing so I could stay awake, but Grandma had said that fairies only showed themselves when one held very still. What if the wee ones were watching me, and just when they were about to come to the fairy's aid, I moved and scared them away?

Self-control was something I was good at, so surely I could stay seated and make myself stay awake.

I . . . must . . . stay . . . still . . . and . . . awake . . .

26

Pixie Dust

"Garden fairies come at dawn,
Bless the flowers, then they're gone."
— Anonymous

As light came streaming in from the window, I awoke with a start, only to find myself in the cozy comfort of my own bed. *MY OWN BED? NO!*

Sitting up quickly, I noticed the window was closed, and the pot and vase of flowers had been moved from the sill to the window seat.

Grandma's jewelry box! It was still there, next to the flowers, but the lid was shut.

I ran to the box, opened it, and saw that the cap of water was still full. The sugar-bread and chocolate in the saltcellar seemed as if a bit was missing, but most importantly, *the fairy was GONE!*

Tears welled up instantly. Had the fairies come and taken my tiny patient as theirs? Had she healed overnight and left to go home?

Then the dread crept in. What if she died and simply disappeared?

I picked up the bottle cap and threw it to the floor, water spattering on impact. Then, I dumped the saltcellar contents into the trashcan. I couldn't believe she was gone! How could I have fallen asleep? How could I have missed it? I'd listened to Grandma's words, I'd tried to use my human magic; I'd loved that little fairy!

I forced myself to take three deep breaths.

Maybe I couldn't see her anymore because a non-believer had come into my room and ruined the magic! Was the fairy invisible and still asleep in the box?

I took a moment and closed my eyes, digging down into the bottom of my soul to bring up the largest lump of total and complete fairy belief I could muster. Then, I looked back into the box, trying hard to see with my mind's eye, but still saw nothing. I had a strong feeling (perhaps my intuition was telling me) that the fairy was no longer here.

I held the painted box in my arms, cradling it like a baby. I failed my tiny friend . . . and Grandma.

After another minute or two, I blinked the water out of each eye. Crying wasn't helping, and as my tears dried and vision became clearer, I noticed something new in the bottom of the painted box. There was a hollowed-out half pecan shell teetering back and forth, with what seemed to be a clear liquid filling half of it.

Wait a minute. I didn't put that in there.

Looking even more closely, I saw a fine powder glittering around the shell's base. I set the box on my desk where I could shine the desk lamp's light to see even better, grabbing my magnifying glass.

The nutshell had a flattish bottom that kept it from wobbling too much. It had jagged edges as if a squirrel had chomped it open.

I recognized that squirrel-cracking technique since I'd cut my feet on, and raked up, hundreds of broken pecan shells just like this one, in my own backyard.

Beneath the pecan shell was the spattering of fine glitter. It looked similar to the sparkly kind scrapbookers use, but it was made of even finer chips of iridescent white, lavender, and green—the exact colors of the ill fairy's wings.

Was this . . . ? Could it be . . . ? Was I looking at pixie dust? I thought pixie dust was only found in fairytales. Why hadn't Grandma ever mentioned pixie dust in her stories?

Hearing footsteps downstairs, I set the box down beneath my bed and ran full speed until I found Mom in the living room, sitting with the newspaper.

"Oh, you're finally up, sleepy-head!" Mom's eyes looked drawn.

"What time is it?" I asked.

"Why, it's almost 11:00 in the morning. You were so tired when I found you asleep next to the window I—"

"You came in when I was asleep? Did you put me into my bed?" What was she doing in my room last night? What might she have seen?

"Of course, I did, darling. You must have been gazing out the window for a while, because that's where I found you." She set the neatly folded newspaper in her lap. "Your head was resting right next to Grandma's box . . ."

I gulped. "You didn't see anything . . . unusual . . . about the box?"

"Yes, I saw the fairy—"

I gasped. "The FAIRY?"

"Yes, the beautiful fairy paintings inside the lid. They're lovely. Did Grandma paint them?"

Fairy *paintings!* Whew! That was good news.

"Yes, they're all that's left of her fairy paintings . . . ah, she did a series, which was destroyed . . . and . . ." I rambled.

"I can see why she left that jewelry box to you. It's very special." Mom then turned her attention to reading the newspaper, adding, "There are some pancakes in the refrigerator. Just zap one in the microwave if you're hungry."

As I munched on a pancake with warm syrup I wondered what might have taken place in my room after I'd fallen asleep. Where had the fairy gone? If fairies died (could fairies die?), did they disintegrate? Did Mom's presence zap all of the wee one's energy away? And would I have to live without ever knowing the truth?

But, just being near a fairy, even an injured one, had felt like a blessing. I guessed all I could do was listen intuitively, like Grandma had said to do, and in my heart, I felt the fairy was okay, though I had no logical explanation of why. But even if the fairy was all right, I was still really sad that she was gone.

Bedtime found me sitting on the window seat again, Grandma's box at my side. The flowers returned to the sill and replayed my fairy adventure in my head.

Grandma would have known just what to do to help the little fairy, and she probably would know what had happened to her too. I missed my grandmother so much. I opened my window once again and returned the flowers to the sill, replaying my fairy adventure in my head.

The fresh air cleared my mind. The chirping of the cicadas soothed me, lulling me into a trance-like state. Suddenly and swiftly, from the corner of my eye, I glimpsed a few flashes of light near the branch of the tree closest to my window.

Fireflies? They usually didn't fly this high up, but I supposed it was possible. Then again, the light wasn't the yellow-green glow they usually emitted. In fact, there were three small flower-shaped lights in three distinct colors: a purple-blue, a pure white, and a vibrant yellow.

Looking deeper into the dark, I tried to make out the illuminations—they stretched about two inches tall—but just when my eyes started to focus better in the darkness, all three swooped down to the lawn below, stopping on the grass.

I rubbed my eyes. What was this? Had I fallen asleep at the window once again? Or was I experiencing another lucid dream? I slapped my own face to make sure. Ouch! Yep, I was awake.

I watched as the lights flew back up to the branch, and my eyes could now make out the faint outline of a tiny person's figure within each glowing shape. But when I tried to zero in on more details, the three lights fluttered to the ground and waited once again.

Fairies! And they were trying to tell me something! I felt as though they were beckoning me to come downstairs. I gently picked up Grandma's box to carry with me, feeling like I'd need it, but I didn't know why.

Sneaking down the creaky stairs, I slipped out the back door, reaching the place where I had seen the glowing figures on the grass. I couldn't spot them anywhere on the ground's grassy fringe, but when I looked up at my window, the three were back up in the tree!

They wanted me to come down, and now they want me to go up— were they playing with me? I wished they would make up their minds.

I concentrated hard and tried to send them my thoughts, just like Grandma had said to do. *Please come back down here and let me know what you want me to do. I won't hurt you. I believe in you more than anything!*

Not exactly a voice, but a clear message in my mind said, *Drink!*

Puzzled for a moment, I then envisioned the pecan shell in the bottom of the jewelry box. They wanted me to drink the water in the pecan shell? I lifted the tiny vessel to my lips, noticing how closely shaped it was to a heart. Each swallow brought happy energy that trickled down my throat, mending any sadness I felt. Grandma's words echoed in my head: "Fairies are made of love; love is the closest thing to magic humans have."

Love and fairy magic had been around me all along. I was so lucky to be able to tap into it now!

Once I swallowed the tasteless but healing liquid, I looked up at the fairy lights to "hear" what to do next, and that's when a twinkling cloud came floating down upon me. The lighted fairies were high on the branch, shaking from side to side, flitting their glowing wings as a fine glitter of fairy dust fell onto my head, face, and shoulders. I reached out to catch some in my palms, smiling at the wondrous sight!

Suddenly, it stopped. Now what?

I stood perfectly still, opening my mind to another message—and that's when a funny sensation began in my middle, as if someone was tickling the inside of my stomach with a feather. Before I knew what was happening, I felt light as air as I began to levitate toward the tree branches above me!

No freaking WAY! I was flying!

Up, up, up I went until I caught myself on the first tree branch I could grab. Taking a moment to trust this feeling of flight, I let go, floating up even higher to the next branch, and then the next, until I was eye-level with the limb supporting the three fairy lights. I found that I could keep myself from ascending any farther just by *willing* myself to stay where I was.

Inches away now, I could make out the details of each fabulous fair folk. One was most definitely the fairy I had rescued, and what a relief it was to see her! She was even more beautiful, now that she was fully illuminated, her purplish petals bursting with life. Two other females were at her side, one sitting, the other crouched, and all three of them were laughing.

I smiled, careful not to make any sort of sound or sudden movement to scare them off, taking in the beautiful detail of each one. All three of the fairies had long filament locks of hair that moved gently as if being blown by a breeze. Their tiny eyes glistened, like glowing drops of dew, outlined with minute green eyelashes. Each had a tiny human-like nose and a perfect, diminutive, bow-like mouth.

For sure, my own little patient was a periwinkle fairy, for now her green tendril-like arms and legs extended from beautiful purple-blue blooms. Her white flossy hair had yellow glowing pollen at the tip of each strand.

Another fairy wore a dress of white rose petals, which were faintly pink at the base, covering her minute body with large, oval-shaped organic scales. She wore a collar of jagged dark green leaves, and her limbs were smooth and green, with thorn-like fingers. Her pale yellow hair was held back on one side with the tiniest, most perfect white rose I had ever seen.

The third fairy, dressed in bright yellow, resembled a flower I recognized as a bellflower, with a flounced petal dress, fitted at the top and flaring out at the bottom, and dark slender leaves growing from her shoulders atop her woody green-stem arms. She reminded me of the hollyhock ladies I made with Grandma, only much fancier. Her full, wavy hair was bright yellow and curled at the ends.

Their sheer beauty caused me to forget how far above the ground

I was, and the accuracy of Grandma's jewelry box painting was remarkable! I could only hope to be able to create such faithful drawings later.

We all looked at each other for a while, the fairies smiling and laughing. I was certain I could smell the sweetness of their blossoms. But soon, I began to drift an inch or two back down to the ground. My magic was wearing off! So, the yellow fairy turned swiftly and sprinkled more glittery dust from her wings onto my face and shoulders, and I floated upwards again.

Quickly then, the fairies formed a huddle, conversing so quietly I couldn't hear a word, while they did something with their tiny hands that I couldn't quite make out. When they finally broke from their private circle, they came closer to the edge of the branch with outstretched arms, each holding a flower exactly matching their attire: a white rose, a yellow bellflower, and, of course, a series of blue periwinkle blossoms on a long vine-like stem.

For you, I heard in my head.

I took each perfect specimen, held all three offerings in one hand, creating a tiny tussie-mussie that reminded me of the one Grandma had given to Grandpa. I knew, however, that by giving me these wonderful gifts, the fairies were getting ready to leave.

Please, don't go yet!

But the rose fairy drifted off of the branch, flitted from side to side, and touched my left cheek with her hands. Her rose perfume wafted through the air and was more sweet and intoxicating than a hundred roses together. She circled my head once, and flew off into the sky.

Next, the yellow bellflower fairy hovered upward, landing on my right shoulder. She brushed me with a quick flutter of wings upon my ear, and I tried not to move, but it tickled quite a bit! Her scent was the sweet blend of honey and morning dew. She slowed her wings, and then circled me as well before flying away.

My patient, the periwinkle fairy, was the last wee one on the branch. She rose up and hovered right in front of my face, her radiant smile instantly making me happier than I'd been in a long time. I clearly heard, *Thank you,* and then the fair keeper of the periwinkles kissed my nose, circling me twice before joining her friends by vanishing into the atmosphere.

They were gone.

I came back to myself, realizing I was sitting high in the boughs alone. Now what? I guess I'd just wait until the pixie dust wears off, but shouldn't I be a little worried when it does? I'm a good twenty feet in the air!

But I remembered the tenderness of love, and the miracles it could create. I would be all right, as long as I believed in the fairies' kindness—they would never put me in harm's way. And after a minute or two, the weight of my own body pulled me slowly down to the earth, landing ever so gently upon the grassy ground.

I stood there for several minutes in disbelief. Had that really just happened to me?

But there, clutched in my right hand, were the flowers I'd been given. These were symbols of the perfection of nature, and living proof of the existence of their caretakers. Although the fairy dust magic wore off, I felt as though I was cushioned by clouds as I walked back into the house.

And as I crossed the threshold back inside, the "welcome" mat was, again, upside down. And as I bent to turn it back, I stopped, intuitively knowing that the *fairies* had turned around the mats. They were welcoming me! Welcoming me into their world! They had known I was coming. They had expected my discovery of their existence all along.

27

Rooted

"When you are sorrowful, look again in your heart, and you shall see that in truth you are weeping for that which has been your delight."
— *Kahlil Gibran*

When I woke up on the morning of the funeral, Penny was curled up on my bed.

"Mom would have a fit if she saw you up here," I told her. She rolled over, demanding tummy rubs, which I gave her. And while scratching her, I noticed something. The quince, but not the vase, had mysteriously disappeared.

"It was there when I went to bed last night. What are those fairies up to now?" I said to Penny. She just jumped off the bed, ready to start the day.

Today, I wanted to carry the old photo of Grandma and me when we were in her English garden together so long ago. I kept it in my nightstand, and as I pulled open the drawer to retrieve it, I was surprised to find not only the green library book about fairies I'd looked everywhere for, but Grandma's diary as well.

I picked both books up. My photo was sticking out between the pages of the green book where an artist's portrayal of a periwinkle fairy was, in all its watercolor glory. Below it was the caption: *They don't need a manual to tend living things; their hearts tell them how.*

I smiled, putting both books away for reading later.

Walking over to my closet, I pulled on my best dress, a navy shift with red piping, and stuck the photo in the pocket.

It was a double funeral. Apparently, Grandma had brought Grandpa's ashes with her from England—and in her hatbox, no less! That was so like Grandma! And since Mom and Aunt Az never really got to say goodbye to Grandpa, he was honored as well.

Mom didn't want to worry me, so she hadn't mentioned that Grandma had insisted on ordering her gravestone, secretly adding Grandpa's to the order, when she first arrived. She'd paid the funeral director in cash and had told him she'd come back for them soon enough.

It was a sad day, but I kept the promise I made to Grandma, that I would always remember her as the vivacious storyteller she was, with the two of us sharing special time together. Today wasn't goodbye. Today we'd say, *Follow your bliss!*

The ceremony was held in the chapel at the local church, and when I walked into the ornately gilded room, the sweetness of blooming flowers entered my nose—there were flowers everywhere! Roses, lilies, and gardenias dripped off the end of every pew, and an arrangement in a white basket, that was taller than I, sat on the altar. And beside the centerpiece was a linen-covered table with two Victorian urns and a photo of Grandma Faye and Grandpa Graham. They were embracing and smiling at each other. I could see their love.

It was a small gathering of only close family and friends. Lacey sat next to me. My aunt and mom took turns getting up to speak, sharing joyful memories of their childhood, the way Grandma and Grandpa would have wanted it. I watched the happy light dance in Mom's eyes when she told her story, and when she sat back down in the pew, I saw Dad's hand go immediately to her shoulder, where it remained for most of the day. Everyone agreed, Grandma was a wonderful, talented woman who had lots of love to give, and Grandpa was a courageous, caring man.

A policeman on a motorcycle led the procession of cars to the cemetery where a tent had been erected over Grandma and Grandpa's gravesite. I approached the tall, marble gravestones, set side by side, and stood in front of the one that read: "Faye Katherine Landing." Beautiful reliefs of fairies and flowers decorated the stone, and I recited, to myself, the famous quote engraved below her name:

"Two roads diverged in a wood and I—

I took the one less traveled by,

And that has made all the difference." —Robert Frost

That fit Grandma so well!

Grandpa's headstone had carvings of delicate tree branches, and an American flag, and below the engraving of the name "Graham Thomas Landing" was simply "Follow your bliss."

Buried next each other, there was no doubt in my mind that Grandma was happy to be reunited with her loving husband. I vowed to visit my grandparents' grave as often as possible, just so I could feel their happiness. I swore I could.

And as I stood there, something orange caught my eye down low. Did someone put the quince flowers upon Grandma's grave? I tugged them gently to see if someone had stuck fresh-cut flowers into the ground, but felt the earth below being grabbed by roots.

I asked the members of my family if they had planted it, and they all denied it. No one even knew that quince was Grandma's favorite flower.

Had the fairies taken the magical quince from the vase in my room and planted it on Grandma's grave, to honor her? And wasn't it just like Grandma and the fairies to know how to shine light into the grayness of such a sad day.

28

Clairsentience

"... thank you God for this most amazing day, for leaping greenly spirits of trees,
and for the blue dream of sky and for everything which is natural, which is infinite,
which is yes."
— E.E. Cummings —

 week after Grandma's funeral, I woke up on that sunny Saturday morning just knowing it was going to be a red-letter day. Dad always said that red-letter days were days when things came together in such a special way that you'd remember it all your life.

I looked over at Penny and she was sitting on my bed. "I guess no one claimed you, but I'm glad you're mine." Then I gave her a big hug.

Today, I vowed, I was going to make an effort to notice the fairies' work. Even if their stellar bodies weren't visible, their gifts to the earth surrounded me with every blooming flower and living creature—the fair folk were everywhere!

And I was definitely feeling clairsentient today. Something wonderful was going to happen, I just knew it.

I finally understood what epiphanies were, those small openings between the mundane minutes steadily ticking away, which swoop in and dazzle. The more in tune I was with nature and its celestial attendants, the more I realized how deliberate coincidental moments are, and several coincidences—more like wishes-come-true—were about to come my way, hand in hand.

I took out the pile of sketches I had done of my three special fairies. I'd used Grandma's book, *The Language of Flowers,* to look up the white rose and yellow bellflowers. Grandma had already told me that periwinkles meant *friendship,* but I learned that white roses symbolized *remembrance* and yellow bells, *joy.* All three were special gifts that I had received from knowing Grandma.

The flower bouquet I'd received from the fairies was in the vase, on my windowsill, where the mysterious quince once was. The petals were slowly turning brown on the edges, but they would always look beautiful to me. They may have been fading, but I had sketched them so much, they would live forever in my drawings.

Setting my drawings aside, I got dressed and went downstairs. A note on the kitchen table read,

Claire—
Went out on an errand.
Decided to let you sleep.
I will be home by noon.
Love, Mom

Lacey was coming over at 11 just to hang out, so I had the place to myself for a whole hour. I took my bowl of Cheerios and Grandma's diary outside on the back patio—it was too beautiful a day to sit inside.

Soaking up the rays of sun, I read about Grandma's life, and the feeling of true happiness enfolded me. I was so content that I needed no fairy healing today, but I couldn't shake the feeling that something extraordinary was on the verge of happening. I could feel it in my bones.

Just then, the front doorbell rang. Was Lacey here early?

I ran back in the house and swung open the front door with a broad smile on my face, expecting to see my best friend, *my* kindred spirit, and I froze in my tracks . . .

It was Grant at my door! We had texted a few times, but this was the first time I'd seen him in person since the sugar spill at the grocery store.

"Hi, Claire."

"Hi," I replied.

The pull of attraction, like magnets, tugged on me. Was it just my imagination or did he feel it too?

His dark hair swooped over one brow and his navy t-shirt brought out the color of his blue eyes. He was holding a small package stamped "first class."

"I delivered some more groceries to the lady next door," he said, nodding to his left. "Some mail got delivered to her house by mistake, and with her hip surgery and all, she asked me to drop it off to you." He held out the box with an envelope taped to the side, addressed to me.

"Thanks," I smiled.

"No problem." He smiled back, lingering.

"It's such a beautiful day, Grant, do you have time to sit on the front porch with me?"

"You don't have a chocolate emergency or anything?" he teased.

"No, not today." I laughed, instantly feeling at ease. "So, let's sit over here." I pointed to the two wicker chairs.

"The place where we first met."

I smiled and nodded.

I sat in one chair, and he sat in the other, dragging it nearer to mine. His close proximity made my heart skip a beat.

Grant leaned back in his chair. "I hope I didn't make you feel bad, startling you like I did, and causing that bag of sugar to fall. Like I said, I'm really sorry."

"That wasn't your fault. I'm the clumsy one." I felt myself blush.

"Your head giving you any trouble?"

I looked at him funny at first. "Oh, you mean after my concussion. I'm all better."

He paused a moment, then asked, "I've been wondering, the ladyfingers and the chocolate—who were they for?"

"Oh, well . . ." I looked down at my hands, my brain racing, trying to figure out how to answer. "It's a long story. I'll have to tell you another time."

I didn't want to blow it by talking about fairies too soon.

Luckily, he continued on.

"Another time? I hope that means you'd like to . . . hang out some more. I'd like to get to know you even better, and ah . . ." He bowed his head, looking at the ground to stop himself.

Was he blushing now? I was right, he was really sweet.

"You mind if I open my mail?" I asked.

"No, I don't mind." He gasped as if he'd been holding his breath, the change of subject had suddenly helped him to relax.

I pulled the envelope out of the tape that held it to the box, tearing it a bit. "It's addressed to me, but I don't know anyone by the name of Alani

Pua, or anyone who lives in California."

"Well, opening it is a good way to find out, unless you have x-ray vision," Grant joked.

I rolled my eyes at him playfully before pulling at the place where the envelope had torn. My fingers unfolded the letter and I could feel Grant's eyes on me as I read it silently.

> Aloha Claire!
>
> I just received an e-mail that you are requesting information about Anna Connelly Larkson from the Orphan Train Society. Well, she passed away about six years ago, and she was my grandmother.
>
> Noni, as I called her, often spoke about her dear childhood friend, Faye Landing, who I noticed had the same address as yours. I have a bunch of old letters from Faye that my Noni saved all of these years. How are you related to Faye Landing? I am hoping we can correspond and share what we know about those two special ladies.
>
> I am 14 years old and I live in California with my mom and dad in the old farmhouse where my Noni was raised, after she got off of the Orphan Train. We spend every summer in Maui at a family beach house there, and it was Noni's 40th birthday trip with Faye that caused our family's obsession with Hawaii. I am half Hawaiian, since my father was born and raised in Maui.
>
> Anyway, please write back! I have enclosed my contact information.
>
> Mahalo!
> Alani Pua

I lowered the letter. First Grant's visit and now the letter! I was right about it being a special day.

"Well, do you know who it's from after all?" Grant asked.

"I do. It's from the granddaughter of *my* grandmother's best friend," I said, still holding the letter in my hand. "I was trying to find her, to learn more about my Grandma."

"That's nice," he said, grinning.

"What are you smiling about?" I asked.

"Being here with you." His words made me happier than the rays of sun shining down so beautifully on us that day.

"I like being here with you—" and that's when a gust of wind swooped in, taking the letter right out of my hand.

I jumped up to get it, and the white light-reflecting paper danced and bobbed just above my head, remaining barely out of reach as if on an invisible string. Grant ran after it too, the white rectangle floating across the front lawn. Penny, who had been sleeping at my feet, went racing and barking alongside us as we laughed and scrambled for it. Almost teasingly, the letter flew towards Grant, and he jumped to try to grab it, but it flew up into the air even higher, spinning and hovering. And just as the breeze lifted the letter higher and higher into the air, while we exchanged glances of defeat, it dramatically plummeted down, landing in a patch of thickly blooming lilies.

We giggled like little children as I clambered into the plants, grasping the paper firmly, both of us plopping on the grass to catch our breath.

"Would you like something to drink? I think we have some lemonade," I said.

"Sure! That letter put me through quite a workout," Grant laughed.

We went into the kitchen, Penny following us, and I poured the tangy yellow liquid into two glasses, the ice crackling and snapping.

"Let's go out in the backyard. That's where I was sitting when you came. It's such a nice day."

"That it is!" He flashed me his stunning smile, inferring a double meaning from my statement.

We sat side by side on the deck steps that led to the back lawn. Penny snoozed at our feet, allowing the day's warmth to seep into her coppery coat. Grant's leg brushed mine, making my fingers and toes tingle.

"So, your grandmother was an interesting lady?" he asked.

"Yes, she was." I enjoyed the sureness of my answer. "Do you like poetry?"

"As a guitar player, I like to write lyrics, so I'm always inspired by poems."

"Well, there's one at the bottom of the letter I got." I reached into my back pocket where I'd slipped it before getting the lemonade.

I guess Alani likes poetry too; after all, it ran in her family, since Anna had been quite the poet.

"It's by Marcel Proust: 'Let us be grateful to people who make us happy; they are the charming gardeners who make our souls blossom.'"

I felt as if Grandma had a hand in everything that day, from the boy to the letter to the quote.

"That's nice," Grant said, gazing at me dreamily.

Just looking at him at that moment made my stomach do somersaults. His eyes were an amazing color, like the sky that morning, and they swept me up just as the wind had carried my letter. The stories of how Grandma met Grandpa had made me wish for love. Could it be here for me now? Had my wish been granted? *Grant-ed?*

I grinned.

"What are you smiling about?"

"You," I said.

He beamed and leaned his face closer to mine. "You . . . I'd like . . . well . . . if I . . . kiss . . ." Grant turned red and frowned in embarrassment.

I just smiled and said, "Seems you have a case of glossolalia."

He looked perplexed for a moment, and then grinned again, reaching out and touching my face with sweet tenderness in his fingertips.

He leaned even closer and gently kissed my lips, which revealed a new world of splendor to me, and we suddenly found ourselves under a downpour of bright pink flower petals falling from the sky! We both looked up—there wasn't a blooming tree anywhere near us!

Pulling away, we looked at each other in disbelief. While reaching out to catch the satiny confetti in our palms, the lingering perfumed scent of roses wafted and whooshed through our hair and clothes.

"Where are these petals coming from?" Grant asked.

I just shrugged my shoulders, looking up at the deluge.

After half a minute, it stopped, and I sat there looking at the fuchsia petals in Grant's hair, in our laps, and by our feet—it was a present from the fairies, no doubt.

"You know, I had this crazy great aunt who said that falling flower petals means someone is thinking about you. I guess that sounds sort of silly," Grant said, running his fingers through his thick hair, the mysterious silky bits fluttering down.

"No, that's not silly at all," I said.

"Hey there! Sorry I'm late," said Lacey, walking through the back gate.

"Oh, hi, Lacey," I said, feeling the heat of my now-red face.

"Hi," the other two said to each other in unison.

"What were you guys doin'?" Lacey asked.

Was she really being so bold, asking if we'd been kissing?

"What do you mean?" I stuttered.

"There are petals all over the place!" She laughed.

Phew!

"Well, we're not exactly sure where they came from, ourselves," Grant explained.

"And what's in your hand?" Lacey asked.

"Oh! It's a letter from the granddaughter of Grandma's friend Anna. She got my query about Anna leaving on the orphan train and wrote to me," I said excitedly. "Here, read it." I handed Lacey the paper, and she began reading it silently.

"Wasn't there a box that came with the letter?" Grant reminded me.

"Oh, gosh, I forgot all about it!" I said. "I'll be right back."

I ran to the front porch and found the package on the table between the two wicker chairs. I grabbed it and ran back to Grant and Lacey. Pulling at the cardboard tab that unzipped the side, there was a note stuck to a clear plastic bag with something hard inside, wrapped in white tissue.

The note said: *Noni wanted Faye's family to have this. –Alani*

Then I tore at the thin paper to reveal a silver compact with two beautiful fairies on the top! Anna's Djer sterling compact!

"This was the gift Grandma gave to her friend Anna as she boarded the Orphan Train," I said.

"I remember you telling me about that. Open up the compact and see if the note is still inside." Lacey looked just as excited as I was about the treasure.

I pushed the protruding metal tab on the edge and the top popped open. A slip of yellowed paper drifted to the ground.

Grant jumped to pick it up, handing it to me. "Don't want this to fly away too."

"Thanks." I read it out loud, *Follow your bliss and the universe will open doors for you where there were only walls.—Joseph Campbell.* "Where there were only walls" was underlined.

Where there were only walls . . . Oh my goodness!

"Follow me!" I said, running into the house. Grant, Lacey, and Penny followed.

We ran up the stairs and stopped once we reached Grandma's room.

"See if you can spot any peeling paint," I told them.

"Up there, in the corner," Grant said, pointing to some hanging plaster.

I dragged the vanity seat beneath it, stood on top, and carefully picked the loose paint away from the wall with my finger. Beneath I saw something colorful.

"Here's another chipping place, by the baseboard," said Lacey.

"Carefully peel back the paint and tell me what you see," I said.

"I see—leaves and flowers! What's under here?"

"Grandma's paintings! She'd said the fairy paintings were 'around,' but I didn't think she meant literally. Apparently, while on bed rest with her parents away, she hadn't used canvases or large pieces of paper to paint on, she used what she had . . . the walls!"

The three of us worked for over an hour, gently pulling on loose paint, revealing random sections of fairy wings, flowers, and faces, just as I had seen myself. Now they were peering at us from the walls.

"Claire, I'm home! Where are you?" Mom called from downstairs.

"Up in Grandma's room! Come see what we've found!" I shouted.

Footsteps on the stairs, then, "Wow!"

I turned around and saw Mom with a dropped jaw. I wasn't sure if her shock was from the paintings or the mess.

"What is going on here?" Mom said.

"It's a long story, but basically, Grandma painted fairies on these walls over sixty years ago, when she was on bed rest with Aunt Az, and *Great*-Grandma had painted over them."

"My goodness, they're beautiful." Mom studied the paintings that were revealed, then she studied my face, which I felt illuminating happiness. "We'll have to look into getting them restored."

"I was hoping you'd say that." I ran over and gave her a big hug.

"And the berries on the walls, I'll bet they're dewberries."

"Dew-*whats?*" Mom asked.

"Dewberries. Claire was telling us that people go on dewberry hunts every Easter in East Texas, ma'am."

"Oh, hello, Grant."

He walked over and shook Mom's hand. "Nice to see you, Mrs. Collins."

"Hi, Mrs. Collins," said Lacey, brushing plaster dust from her hands onto her t-shirt.

Mom smiled. "I guess I missed a lot during those couple of hours running errands."

More than you know, Mom. More than you know.

That night, snuggled in my bed with Penny and the lights out, I thought about the wonderful day I'd had. Grant, the letter, the compact with the note, the paintings! I just knew it was going to be an extraordinary day and, boy, was it! And none of it would have ever happened without Grandma being a part of my life.

"Thanks, Grandma!" I said out loud. "Thanks, fairies!"

There was only one more thing that I wished to happen—for Val to come back home from the war.

One arm wrapped around Penny, I reached up with the other and knocked on my headboard three times, then slid my pointer finger one way, and then the other way, hoping that where the invisible lines I made crossed had created a point—*a pinnacle* of magic, like Grandma often did.

I'd do this every night, until Val safely returned. Something told me he'd be home soon.

Flower Fairy Cakes

12 servings

CUPCAKES:
    1 c. heavy cream
    1/3 cup milk
    4 c. ladyfinger cookie crumbs (about 36)
    3 eggs and 1 egg white
    2 T. butter
    coarse sugar
    1/4 c. edible, unsprayed flower petals chopped into "confetti"
    (pink rose petals, orange marigolds, yellow violas, and purple pansies)

ICING:
    1/2 c. powdered sugar
    1 T. fruit lemon juice
    2 t. orange zest

DECORATION (Crystallized Flowers):
    fresh flowers for decorating
    superfine sugar

Break ladyfinger cookies into a food processor and pulse to make crumbs. Combine cookie crumbs with the cream, milk, eggs, and flower petal confetti until all ingredients are evenly incorporated.

Line 12 muffin tins with cupcake liners and spoon in the batter, filling to top. Bake at 350 degrees for 30 minutes or until a toothpick inserted into the center comes clean.

Allow cakes to cool a few minutes, then lightly butter the top of each one and immediately sprinkle a little coarse sugar over the tops. While the cakes cool completely, trim the stems off the decorating flowers. Beat 1 egg white in a bowl with a fork until frothy. Use a paintbrush to coat each flower with egg white, following with a generous sprinkling of superfine sugar. Let sugared flowers dry on wax paper.

Mix powdered sugar, lemon juice, and orange zest in a bowl to make icing. Drizzle each cake with icing and decorate with your crystallized flowers.

Texas Longhorn Apple Muffins

24 servings

INGREDIENTS:

½ c. butter, softened
1 ¾ c. packed brown sugar
2 eggs
1 1/3 c. buttermilk
1 t. vanilla extract
2 2/3 c. flour
1 t. baking soda
1 ¾ t. ground cinnamon
1/8 t. salt
1 c. chopped, peeled apples
1 c. shredded carrots
*3/4 c. chopped pecans optional
1 large apple cut into 48 thick slivers, skin on

TOPPING:

1/3 c. flour
¼ c. packed brown sugar
¼ t. ground cinnamon
2 T. cold butter

In a large bowl, beat butter and brown sugar until crumbly. Add eggs, one at a time, beating well. Stir in buttermilk and vanilla. In another bowl, combine flour, cinnamon, baking soda, and salt. Add dry mixture to wet mixture just until moistened. Fold in chopped apples, carrots, and pecans*.

Fill lined muffin tins three-fourths full. Stick two apple slivers halfway into the batter of each cup, close to the center (to create 'horns'). Combine flour, brown sugar, and cinnamon to create the topping and sprinkle over the tops.

Bake at 350 degrees for 20-25 minutes until a toothpick comes out clean. Cool 5 minutes before moving to wire racks.

❧28❧

Acknowledgements

The inspiration for *The Fairies of Turtle Creek* occurred while taking a family walk along beautiful Lakeside Drive in Highland Park, Texas. My children were young then, searching for fairies amongst the sprawling periwinkle and squiggly tree roots along the bank. A couple of years later, we moved away from that lovely creek for nearly a decade, but its magic stayed with me, relentlessly pushing this story from an idea to fruition. Many thanks go to my husband, John Sayre, for encouraging me to follow my dream and write, along with my three children: Alden, Cambria, and Kyla, who were understanding and supportive of my new venture, putting up with years of "fairy chasing".

Writing this book has been a blessed journey, and I have met so many wonderful people along the way, beginning with my critique partners Karen Jones and Rosalind Oliver, who are encouraging and intelligent fellow writers, each in possession of immense talent. I am grateful that they graced my work and life. My dearest friends and beta readers Jo-Lynn Battany, Danielle Gay, Marianne Williams, Nina Browning, and Shannon Gilliland, along with Annie Swanson, my "muse" who researched the sayings for chapter starts and helped name each chapter. She kept me inspired, as did her insightful daughter, Emily. I thank Jane Corbellini for illustrating the fantastic map at the front of this book that assists the reader in picturing this special town with a creek running through it. To Signe Pike, author of *Faery Tale*, for her edits and thoughtful suggestions that propelled my story to a higher level. To Cheryl Ammeter, author of *Ivey and the Airship*, for taking me under her wing and sharing her insight, knowledge, and kindness so openly. She introduced me to the talented Ted Rubyal and his amazing staff at Wisdom House Books, who helped me make this the book I had always dreamt about.

Finally, to my parents, Kay and Tom Bowers, for raising me in a home that encouraged creativity, as well as teaching me to see real-life, every day magic. To families and their loved ones who fight or have fought in wars to keep America safe. And to all grandparents, including our dear Grandpop, who touch their grandchildren's lives with stories from the past, words of wisdom, and unconditional love.

About the Author

Jill **K. Sayre** had lived all of her life in a small town in California, but suddenly moved to Texas, looking at it as an adventure. Little did she know she'd fall in love with her new town, especially with the beautiful creek that runs through it.

The Fairies of Turtle Creek is her first novel, set in Highland Park, Texas. Drawing on the history of the area, she sets the stage for her story, weaving in folklore and modern fairy beliefs. Magical realism is a favorite of Jill's, to read and write. She also loves nature, art, music, and seeking everyday beauty that is hidden in plain sight.

Jill holds a degree in art and elementary education, specializing in gifted students. She currently teaches children and teens at a local conservatory.

Jill lives in Dallas, Texas with her husband, three kids, two cats, and a vizsla.

CPSIA information can be obtained at www.ICGtesting.com
Printed in the USA
LVOW08*0845121214

418520LV00002B/4/P